KILLING PLACE

KILLING PLACE

BARNABY WILLIAMS

Mainstream Publishing
EDINBURGH AND LONDON

To my marvellous and unique agent,
Anne Dewe

Copyright © Barnaby Williams, 1995
All rights reserved
The moral right of the author has been asserted

First published in 1995 by
MAINSTREAM PUBLISHING COMPANY (EDINBURGH) LTD
7 Albany Street
Edinburgh EH1 3UG

ISBN 1 85158 735 7

No part of this book may be reproduced or transmitted in any form or by any means without written permission from the publisher, except by a reviewer who wishes to quote brief passages in connection with a review written for insertion in a newspaper, magazine or broadcast

A catalogue record for this book is available from the British Library

Typeset in Garamond by Bibliocraft, Dundee

Printed and bound in Great Britain by Butler and Tanner Ltd, Frome

Vegetarians stink.

They cannot help it. It does not matter that they have put on clean clothes that morning, or that they have washed with soap. Out it comes, this decayed aroma of decomposing cabbage, oozing from their very pores.

They stand too close to you when they address you, and it wafts towards you – somehow they are always upwind – and it wrinkles your nostrils. Over the years their bodies become steeped in half-digested by-products of vegetable-encrusted spaghetti and things, always brown in colour, formed from grated nut and carrot. The pores widen in a desperate attempt to rid themselves of it all, and it all washes over you. They open their mouths to speak and their teeth are bad from all the sweet things they keep stuffing down. They go a sort of yellowy dirt colour, like a rat's. More rot.

Something happens to their skin. It becomes simultaneously thick and flabby, the consistency of a loaf crust that has been left out in the rain. They move anxiously from one foot to the other under the frantic urgings of the enormous quantities of foul-smelling gas being generated within their intestines. They vanish suddenly under the effects of lentils and you have to open the windows when they are gone.

I have the windows of the house open now. The place airs easily. It is the old peasant kind of wooden dwelling, very rustic; it's *völkisch*, if you understand what that means – not that many do, these days – with the wooden tiles and gables. There is a covered porch where I sit sometimes in a rocking-chair and smoke a Meerschaum pipe. If anyone could see me they would say I looked the very image of a twinkling-eyed old peasant, with my long white beard. Not that anyone does, for I'm out on the mountainside on my own here, and nobody comes but my accountant Willi and, sometimes, his family.

But they won't be coming any more. That's what the young policeman came to tell me.

I don't know what to do about that. I have the windows open as much to try and blow away the memories that have suddenly come back to me as much as the smell. I wish the policeman had not been a vegetarian, for that does not help. The smell of the vegetarian is as much a part of the problem. I had managed to put it aside all these years and now it is back.

Perhaps the mountain air blowing down from the peaks will help. I have always loved it up here, high amongst the peaks; I may look out and feel that I am a bird. When I die, if there is a God, then perhaps He will send me back as a bird. I tried hard enough to be one all those years ago.

I fell in love with it up here in the mountains the first time I saw it. Speer designed it for me in a few spare moments. He dashed it off on the back of an envelope while he was coming to grips with the scale of one of the Führer's new buildings ... or possibly it was a new desk – they were all of a type; you could park a Panzer in or on either.

Göring was having some vast extension done to a hunting-lodge, a dining-hall to carouse in. He liked me, because we survived 1918 together and I could shoot. You didn't survive 1918 if you couldn't shoot rather well, and I could shoot very well. As could Hermann, of course. One tends to remember the Reichsmarschall as he was in his later days, a drugged-up fat kleptomaniac buffoon in comic-opera uniforms of his own design. But in 1918, when his life was worth something less than a bent Pfennig, as were all the lives of those who inhabited that cold killing air above the smoking battlefields, then he was as chill and ruthless a killer as there was, and a fine pilot.

I shot a charging boar with him in his own forest; it had tusks on it that could have opened up plate armour. I can see them now – I have its head up on a shield on my wall. It still has that frothing snarl on its face as it rushed towards me from the undergrowth and I shot it so close its bloody snout chewed my boots. How it wanted to gut me from crotch to throat! Göring liked balls.

It delighted him, that did; it was the principle of survival of the fittest in full operation. He had this builder there doing his dining-hall and he had him come over and put up my *völkisch* peasant dwelling for me out of the spare timber. Hermann wanted the hall like Valhalla. You could have entertained most of the *Das Reich* regiment there with their girlfriends – and he probably did – so I ended up with my house designed and built for nothing.

That's how it was in those days, of course. Göring stuffed away half the art treasures of Europe without paying for them. I got a free house.

I'm not an old peasant, as you have gathered. I'm an old Nazi.

The policeman who came, whose odour of decayed cabbage is finally leaving, he didn't say anything about that. It's all history to the young, of course. They probably can't believe that anyone from those days is still alive, but I am, and I was in the first great war we lost, along with Hermann and the Führer himself. I met *him* there too, when his life wasn't worth a bent pfennig either – in fact, I saved it. Imagine that: the whole world different if I hadn't been looking the right way.

But the policeman didn't mention that either. He just came to say that Willi and his family wouldn't be coming any more.

People died like insects in a firestorm, all those years ago. I ought to be used to people dying, but I'm not.

I don't understand why anyone would want to break into Willi's house at night and murder him, his wife and their children. To cut their throats and butcher them like hogs.

Why would anybody do that?

It's not a war.

It is the policeman who has brought it all back. The smell, that faint odour of corruption. The same pale blue eyes, rather protuberant, looking through you at some world of their own devising. I could tell the policeman was just doing his job, telling an old man about the death of his accountant. His mind was on something else, like the Führer's was.

He was an ordinary fellow, but then so was the Führer. The infantryman, Hauptmann Hoeppner, told me, as we sat gasping in the trench covered in mud and gore, watching the British

Tommy gargle to death and wondering if another wave was coming over, for they were low on ammunition. He told me that Corporal Hitler had reached his promotion ceiling, he was unfit for higher command.

Well, so he was, but he had to involve all the rest of us to prove it.

I wonder what it was the policeman was thinking about as he told me of Willi's death. A detective, he was, the policeman; he told me how he had seen the scene. All the bits. He came in his little car in his plain clothes and his badge. The Gestapo had plain clothes, only you knew them. Leather coats and green hats with the badger's brush they liked. The policeman, he had jeans and canvas shoes, and a shiny grey padded jacket. The Gestapo would never have taken him on looking like that. Arrested him maybe.

How times change.

The smell's gone, but the memories haven't. I think I must do what I haven't done, all this time. I must write it all down. I'm so old I may be dead this time next year. There are so few left who can remember it all. How it started. He consumed half the world by what he did, but he was a little fellow with a big moustache the first time I saw him, very muddy, yelling urgently to me from a slit trench half full of water.

I was even muddier than he was – it was in between my teeth even – but if you crash a Fokker biplane into no-man's-land you will at best be completely saturated with the stuff. At worst you get turned into it.

That's how it all started. I shouldn't have been there at all; I should have been on my way to give Hilde one, if not three or four. Now that I am so old and have four stiff limbs and one supple, it is strange to recollect how different it all was when I was young and crazy.

It was Walter's fault. He got drunk the previous night and they found him in a ditch with his car on top of him the next morning. That left the *Jagdgeschwader* even more under strength than usual, and Göring said Hilde would have to wait. That's how I flew Walter's Fokker and wrecked it for him, not that he cared.

Very good. Ink, pen and paper.

May 1918

The scent of apple blossom was seeping into my tent. I don't know why I should have smelled it even in the dark but I did, unless I was imagining Hilde's sweet perfume, which I probably was. The *Jagdgeschwader*, our fighting group, was quartered in an orchard. It was about three in the morning, not yet dawn, but I was up. And not for dawn patrol! Or so I thought. I was dressing with care, in my best uniform. I have a photograph of myself back in those days. I barely recognise the fine young man looking out at me in his high-necked Prussian cavalryman's uniform. I have the Iron Cross at my throat, my shiny-peaked officer's cap on my head; I am doing up my long pale-blue coat with the gold buttons and the dark, blood-red collar. Since I am so smart, I have my medals on my chest beneath. I am probably on my way to see Hilde – she liked to show me off. And – wonder of wonders – I came back every time, and she did not have to look for a new beau.

I have the feeling the photograph was taken about that time, for I have the look, the look we all got, those who survived for a while; our eyes appear to enlarge but our sockets are hollow; the flesh has fallen away from neck and hand and wrist, you see the bone that lies beneath. We stare, all of us, somewhere past the camera with unfocused eyes. What can it be we are looking at? Can it be Hilde, or Heidi or Hanna?

I always said that it was so. I am thinking of you, darling, I would say, and she would laugh in delight, for she was very vain. But of course it was not so. Like all the others, I was wondering if it would be *feucht oder getrocknet*, wet or dry.

I do not mean the weather. I mean, would my death be one in which I was burned or mutilated.

But that morning, with the apple blossom seeping in through my tent flap, I should have been happy. Three days' leave! Three wonderful days of Hilde's beautiful body! If someone had taken a photograph of me at that moment, I should have been whistling as I set my Iron Cross at its correct angle and rubbed cologne over my shaven skull.

A head poked itself through the flap and grinned in grim amusement. 'You smell like a fucking whore.'

It was Göring. He was not dressed in full fig but in thigh-high sheepskin boots, long black leather coat, scarf and helmet in his hand. 'Walter's stuffed his car. We're under strength as it is. They say we have some new men coming later. Fill in on the first patrol.'

'*Ja.*'

His head vanished. A few seconds later a servant brought biscuits and hot chocolate.

I decided to keep my best uniform on, having gone to such trouble to get ready. I took off my shining boots and pulled on my sheepskin ones, dragged my leather coat on as I munched and gulped. You have to, despite the inner *Schweinehund* eating away at your very insides. Then I went out to the lines where the other pilots were getting ready in the dark. My own Fokker was in the shop, so I took Walter's.

One after the other the engines started, that crisp bark of the 160 h.p. Mercedes engine, sharp flashes of exhaust like anti-aircraft fire in the darkness. I taxied out with the others. Göring opened the throttle and we all rolled forward, the wheels bouncing, the controls beginning to stiffen, to bite against the air, engines thrumming at full power. One last tap on the ground and we were flying, climbing up into the pale cinnamon of the sky above.

Now it was height, height, height, and we hung on our props to get to combat altitude. It wasn't safe to hang about down there; as the dawn brought vision, the anti-aircraft gunners were looking for you. Below, the ground was a black carpet in which tiny flashes of red and orange showed up the guns.

Then my nose snuffed up the damp cloud and the battlefield below became grey. My eyes tapped out a signal of morse, checking the airspeed indicator, lateral bubble, and the soggy air about me, for it was all too easy, while keeping a steady climb and your wings level inside this mass of cotton wool, to fly smack into one of your comrades and emerge from the bottom to the view of those below as so much illuminating fireworks.

Feucht oder getrocknet indeed.

Two thousand metres. A halo of the sun, the grey mist turning golden, a welcome sheen of colour. Wisps of white whipping past the cockpit, and suddenly palest cinnamon blue, below the cloud bank sparkling white like a pavement of pearl, radiant and clean. The ragged vic of our fighters gathering themselves together.

There were eleven of us. In the fresh light the razor-edged biplanes rocked in their line like boats on a gentle swell. The sun lit up our diagonal scarlet stripes (we had been all red when Richtofen was alive) against our royal-blue fuselages and our bold markings (lightning flashes, an arrow, the skull and crossbones, a branding iron). We belonged to an earlier time: we demanded that the enemy knew who we were, before we killed him.

The cloud had slid away; it was clear below now. We all scanned the sky anxiously through fur goggles, looking for the slow-moving black specks against the land or cloud that meant full throttle and the vertical plunge with screaming wires, our bodies as taut as bow-strings, breath still in our chests: sudden battle.

We threaded our way through rising cloud pillars, budding cumulus. The battlements, castles and cathedrals of the heavens, alive with light, radiant white; then, like a girl's satin slip, soft and smooth, gold and rose-tinted as we passed by, mysterious mauve shadows like a girl's eyes.

Sudden stink. Cordite. Black cordite.

All of us, heads searching vigorously, frantically. Black, stinking, toxic smoke in the crisp, clear air. Our own anti-aircraft shells. Not fired at us. Our wings banking this way and that as we searched. The Tommies and the French, they fired ones with white smoke.

What was that? Pin-point clusters of orange fire in the sky. Anti-aircraft shells. Below, the land like a survey map, a dim green and yellow, and across it a scrawl going any old way. But away into the distance, two dirty black lines like a child might have drawn with two pencils in its hand. The *lines*.

The lines, all the way from the sea to Switzerland. Barbed wire and dead men rotting in water-filled shell-holes while the survivors shoot at each other over the top.

And us, climbing ever higher in search of people to kill.

Below, images moving in the corners of my goggles like slides in a lantern show. The shattered streets of a village. The corner of a wood, some trees still standing. A supply column moving slowly up to the front, the horse teams pulling waggons of shells.

What's that, shining gold in the distance? The sea. Something dark beyond: England. The dawn is lighting up their towns and woods. Pretty girls in bed. The scent of tea coming up the stairs. What is it the English eat? Toast. Toast and sticky orange jam. Marmalade. Pretty girls thinking about getting up. Warm under the covers, not freezing cold in a hundred-and-sixty-kilometres-an-hour wind.

I snapped myself back to attention, checked the cocking levers, the twin dark guns in front of me, the whirling prop shimmering hypnotically. The altimeter showed between six and seven thousand metres. What's that for the Tommies? Twenty thousand feet. I was gasping like a landed trout. The air was thin, thin and cold. You try to drag as much into your lungs as you can but it's so thin, and so cold. The chill gets in from the outside, and from the inside too. You can feel your lungs like icy balloon bags.

Pretty girls in warm beds. How I could crawl in there and get warm. Poor girl, with my freezing blue-edged hands on her breasts, between her thighs. What a shock.

What's that? Sudden adrenaline, stabbing into my cold stomach. A red light, curling up from Göring's cockpit, and falling away. His Fokker altered direction and our patrol kept close, our gauntleted hands shifting throttle and stick, feet like lumps of ice squeezing the rudder pedals, but our eyes as bright as a pack of hounds on the scent, the razor-edged fighters suddenly moving together, noses sniffing, looking for the kill.

There! There they were, a thousand metres below us. Eight black crosses. Enemy scouts. They slid below. We waited, almost interminably, as they came within diving distance. Göring let them slide until we got to where the sun would be at our backs. Then his lead Fokker swayed sideways. The signal for each to take his man, and then he dropped, the sun flashing gold on scarlet.

I took one last great gasp of air. Stick and rudder over, the world below me rotating, all of us falling from our height like a hawk stoops from its wheeling glide, wings tucked, hurtling down upon its prey like a thunderbolt.

We were scattering in our headlong dive, the gale shrieking in the wires, the engines screaming, outstretched planes trembling. Three hundred kilometres. Controls stiffening. The enemy scouts like chocolate bullets below, the coloured rings on their wings like bullseyes. British scouts. SE5s of the RAF.

There! They saw us, wheeling suddenly like startled pigeons. As always, I felt the savage joy of it all. On the ground, the wriggling, worming inner *Schweinehund*, up in the air, *life*.

Into the swirling mêlée. A chocolate thunderbolt flashed across my path, the pilot crouching forward over the controls, machine-guns ripping. Smoke in my nostrils, pulling tight to keep a hold of his tail. Planes snapping left and right, the world whirling like a top. Crimson streaking from one of our Fokkers, the SE5 cutting into it from left and right, and I had him in the sights. One, two bursts, and the Britisher seemed to stagger, pulling up in a huge leap with me snapping behind him, leaping high in the sky like a trout hooked on the end of a line, then falling. I saw his belly, streaked with oil. He swooped and began to spin, the plane flashing as it caught the sun, and suddenly tracer streaking between my own struts.

I rammed on full rudder at full speed, skidding across the sky and the scarlet knives cutting into air. Stick hard back, my vision grey, pulling my head up against the forces. On the other side of a whirling arc, the dark form of a British scout, the pilot glaring through goggle eyes; both of us straining, our planes shuddering, engines screaming, gasping, dragging in breath as we whirled about trying to get our gun on to the other, bent only on killing or being killed, as cold-blooded as angels of death.

A thunderbolt flashed through the centre of our demented duel. Blue and scarlet, an axe. Göring. The British flyer rolled slackly on to his back, smoke pouring from his engine. The oil-tank lit and he fell in glory, lighting the cloud on his way down.

Suddenly nobody was there.

I was alone in the sky. A white cloud gleamed like fresh snow. I dived through it and it became grey. As I shot out of the other side something hit the aircraft like a sledgehammer. The Fokker was tumbling like a leaf in a gale, the ground and sky slapping past me, white and mud, blue and green. I had no control. The nose fell, and the plane began to whirl. The rudder pedals were slack under my feet.

I shut off the engine, and in the sudden hush heard just

the wind singing and moaning in the wires. The ailerons were working, and so were the elevators. I brought the aircraft out of its vertical dive, but we were still going down and round. Round and round, in slow, spiralling circles.

Smoke! The smell of fire in my nostrils. My hands scrabbled frantically at the wide leather belt that held me in my seat. I would not burn. No. Like all the others, I had made my own decision on that one. I would jump, spend some last few seconds flying in the clean air.

Air. Clean air. I had flown through somebody's smoke. A thick trail went all the way down. The man who had hit me as I came out of the cloud. Who was he? One of us or one of them? I would never know now. I saw him, tumbling down below me, and then suddenly the form was so much crumpled wreckage, a burst of light against the dull muddy ground below.

My turn next. The wires moaned a mournful song as I struggled to gain control. The lines. There they were, the straggling black lines. The sun flickered on yellow and green festering pools.

An engine, its exhaust crisp and powerful. A dark form swooped around me, its shadow whipping across my cockpit. British. An SE5 with its square front. I could see the big roundels on the wings. The pilot stared up at me in his tight turn, looking through the mounted gun on his top wing. Would he kill me? Even in 1918 we were still meant to be gentlemen: dead stick aircraft were left to their chances. But I knew even in our own Jastas of those who would not turn down the chance: the tallymen, the novices eager for an easy kill, the cold-blooded, the incendiaries. I had seen it done.

The Fokker tumbled slowly, round and round. The ground came closer.

The British pilot zoomed at me. He came past so close I could see his white scarf, the wave of his hand, tipping his hat to me: goodbye.

Then he was gone, and there was just the singing of the wires, and the singeing smell of his exhaust.

It was getting close. I could steer it a little. What to aim for? Mud and wire, reels of it. Pools. Shattered tree-stumps. *A hill.* A slope. Round. Round again, the landscape growing clearer and more hideous. A stench coming off it like some noisome marsh. A hundred metres, trying to steer for the slope. The ground whirling towards me, me seeming to be still, and it rising up to hit me. A shattered cart, a dead horse, shelled trees reaching up at me with jagged, poking fingers, the plane shuddering as I wobbled it and –

We hit with a ripping crunch. All the breath left me as the wide leather belt punched into my stomach. Something banged into my face – my instrument panel. Shattering glass and boiling liquid in my face. I screamed and jerked back. A fire hose of mud drenched me. One of the planes beat me on the shoulder as it tore free. The Fokker stood on its nose and I was suddenly flying again, hurtling over a pool and slamming like a landed fish into the lip on the other side.

It was still. Something was hissing and there was a terrible scent in the air. My hands, which knew what to do when I did not, were frantically scrabbling at the buckle of the belt. My legs and arms knew what it was when I could not remember. I could not see. I was blind. My gyrating body forced me from the wrecked cockpit, tearing at the shattered longerons to get free. I tumbled over the side into the mud, my legs shoving like pistons, and suddenly the whole world was hot.

The petrol-tank exploded like a bomb all around me. My legs ran until I fell over, and I was still blind. I lay in the cold mud. Hilde would not want to lead a blind soldier about.

I reached up to my face, and felt cold hard claws fumbling. My gauntlets! Yes, my gauntlets. I shook them free, and I had hands. My face was covered in gore, cold and slimy. But it was mud, not my lacerated flesh. But what of my eyes? Why could I not see, when metres away the Fokker blazed with incendiary heat? I felt for my eyes. What was this? What had happened? What hard excrescences were these?

Light. A smear of light in front of my eye. My finger. Why could I see my finger? My goggles. I pushed them up into the slime that covered my skull and glorious bright fire flooded into my head. I was not dead, I was not blind. I knelt in the mud a whole man.

The blazing Fokker lit up the battlefield. Nothing moved. It was a vile building-site of stinking mud. Rusting wrecked wire and rotting posts stuck up here and there. Putrescent yellow pools stood stagnant, covered with a diseased, pockmarked skin.

A soldier. I saw a soldier nearby. One of ours, in a coal-scuttle helmet, he kneeled by a pile of sandbags, his rifle resting before him, pointed at the enemy, wherever they were hiding in this dreadful landscape.

'Hulloa!'

He did not look round, keeping his vigil; I pushed myself to my feet, slipping and staggering over the ground like a man wading on the mudflats, waiting for duck at first light. The glutinous ground sucked at my boots, and I fell next to him, clapping him on the shoulder.

My hand went through his body.

The rotting corpse collapsed further into the sandbags, in a rush of vile gas. I pulled my hand from him, yellow and blue flies buzzing about my face. A rat emerged from a hole in his trousers and stared arrogantly at me, as big as a cat, to see who had disturbed its feeding. I scrambled backwards, away from the horror, and found myself on my feet. The corpse was on one side, the burning Fokker on the other. I staggered and slipped away from them both, my boots as heavy as lead.

Somebody was cracking a whip. I peered about me to see who it was. I could see no one, but this invisible whip cracked in my ears, whining like a bee as it did so. The ground was broken up somehow into holes and pits. Something came out of one like a demented badger and grabbed at me, pulling me down with it. I fell, and it scrambled backwards into the pit it had emerged from, yanking me with it by the boot. Unable to stop myself, I slid down into the ground, and landed on my back in half a metre of water.

It was a man. A man in a filthy, muddy uniform. One of ours. A coal-scuttle helmet on his head. His face divided by a wide black moustache. Pale-blue penetrating eyes stared at me.

'Hauptmann, Hauptmann,' he said reprovingly. 'It is not the place for a Sunday stroll, out there.'

'I suppose not,' I gasped.

'They are *shooting* at you. Now, *komm*.'

The man scuttled off along the pit, bending low like a baboon, more animal than human. Perceiving that he was my only guide in this place without maps or signposts, this wilderness, I heaved myself to hands and knees and splashed and scrambled after him, half-swimming and half like a dog.

He stopped at a crossroads of rotting sandbags, looking back impatiently. '*Komm*,' he insisted. 'Quickly now, Hauptmann, the Tommies, they are coming. I must tell the officer.'

I stopped for a moment by the little wall, breath gasping, leaning against a ledge with my hand. I was touching another's hand. Soggy leather claws stuck out from the soil, a uniformed cuff. I pushed myself away and lurched after my guide, who went along at a great pace, stopping at intervals. Then he would sense the very air like some feral beast, sniffing the noisome breeze itself, listening for sounds that only he understood. I knew that this was the kind of creature the battlefield bred. He was at home, this strange thing.

He smiled at me. 'Nearly home,' he said.

Home? What was home out here? We emerged into a trench where duck boards kept our feet from the sloshing water, where evenly sand-bagged walls stood up high to a parapet, and we went along the short zigs and zags, lumps of mud falling from my boots as I ran along.

Soldiers. People. Men on guard, and men resting in small bays cut into the walls. An officer wearing a steel coal-scuttle helmet was peering through a kind of periscope, looking over the wall, and my guide bounded up to him, saluting. He reached inside his grubby jacket and produced a dispatch.

'Here, sir. The Tommies are coming.' He looked to me, as pleased as a hunting dog that has successfully retrieved a kill for its master. 'I found him,' he said. 'A flyer. He crashed.'

The officer turned to look at me as well. Aristocratic eyebrows raised themselves. 'You are one of ours?' he enquired. 'Or one of theirs?'

I was outraged. 'You cannot recognise an officer of the Prince of Bavaria's Cavalry?' I demanded. 'A pilot of the *Deutsche Luftstreitkräfte*?'

He smiled. 'I should not recognise the Crown Prince, no, nor the Kaiser himself, if he looked as you do.'

I looked down at myself, as he was doing. I was standing in a small but growing pool of dirty yellow-brown mud, that was slowly sliding from my form.

'*Ja, ja . . .*' I said weakly. It occurred to me that underneath all this mud I was wearing my best uniform. 'I crash landed,' I explained, 'and did not know where I was. This soldier brought me in.'

'You are lucky. Corporal Hitler is our runner. He knows the lines better than any of us.'

'I must get back to my unit. Can you spare him to show me the way?'

The young officer shook his head. 'The British are coming. Can you shoot? A rifle?'

'At home, I am a hunter.'

'Corporal Hitler! Get a rifle for . . .'

'Wolff. Leutnant Wolff.'

'Hoeppner,' he said, introducing himself. 'Leutnant Hoeppner.' He broke off to issue a machine-gun burst of orders, and the soldiers in the trench began running about like ants. The runner scuttled off and came back with a military rifle and a box of ammunition. I had taken off my long leather coat and was attempting to scrape some of the clinging mud from my form. My Iron Cross swung at my throat and the Corporal smiled with a sudden bout of fellow feeling, opening his top button to show me that he, too, wore the award. Then he scurried off to some position.

'He's got the Iron Cross,' I commented. 'Unusual for a corporal.'

'He's a good soldier. One of the best runners. He gets through with the message,' Hoeppner replied, peering through his periscope. 'I hope they aren't using *verdammtes* gas . . . We didn't want to make him a sergeant, so we gave him the Cross instead. *Nein, nein.* The wind's from the wrong quarter, no gas. *Gottseidank*, how I hate gas.'

'What are you looking for? Can you see them coming?'

'You'll see in a minute,' he promised grimly. 'But I'm looking for Feldwebel Neubach. He went out before dawn and didn't come back.'

'So he's dead?'

'Perhaps not. But, you see, you can't move out there in the day. The snipers. Oh, *Scheisse. Scheisse. Scheisse*, here they come.' He left his periscope and pulled himself up the little ladder to peer over the top. There was one near me and so I did the same.

As my head poked over the top a roar of noise hit me. A hundred metres away the grim horizon had become a wall. A strange, hurling wall of mud and debris flying up high and raining down in a yellow-and-brown curtain. Things were flying in there, too, unidentifiable things that had lain buried.

'There he is!' Hoeppner yelled, 'There's Neubach!'

In front of the wall a figure was moving. Staggering, slipping, falling, scrambling towards us. The wall was pursuing him. I suddenly realised that the wall was advancing towards us in its terrible rumbling roar. Its height seemed to be climbing and it was coming at us, continuous red flashes shot up inside it, illuminating the flying mud from within.

The frantic, staggering man looked over his shoulder at the dreadful monster behind him. He slipped and fell, tripped by some piece of wreckage. He was on his feet again, redoubling his efforts, but the thing was at his heels. He screamed, the scream of the damned, and it caught him.

He was suddenly no more than a disintegrating scarecrow flying through the air in a cone of flame, falling in pieces and consumed by the wall. I stood mesmerised on the ladder, watching the vast monster coming. The day went dim, the sun was no more than a dim halo, and then nothing. I looked about me. The trench below was empty. Nobody.

A head poked out from a hole in the ground. It was my guide, the corporal. 'Get in!' he screamed, 'Get in, *Dummkopf*!'

Yes, yes. I was moving so slowly, it seemed like I was in honey. I dropped through the air so slowly, my feet echoing as I hit the trench bottom, and then I was tumbling down a flight of steps to fall through the gas curtain and land in a heap at the bottom. They were all there, the air thick, sweat-laden. Big eyes white in the light of the little storm lanterns on the walls. Guns and knives and bombs, the clank of metal and the rising boom from above, and then a whistle and a rising shriek and the whole floor lifting up under me, all the very air whooshing from my lungs, air rushing from the pit with incredible violence. I pushed myself up from the floor and a torrent of mud and sand and stones spewed down on top of me from above.

The monster had come. It threw its weight on top of me,

squashing me flat. Dirt was down my neck and in my mouth and eyes, my whole body in the clammy grasp of something so inert and hard I could barely thrash against it. Violent terror ripped into my soul. I was a creature of the air, not a badger of the dark – this was not how to die.

Hands. Hands grabbing and pulling, heaving at me and I emerged from the earth like a corpse on the day of the dead. They had pulled me out, four or five of them. They roared with laughter to see me come up from my sea of dirt, and I laughed with them like a man who was mad. One stuffed my rifle into my hand and I held it like a talisman.

The entrance to the tunnel was almost blocked. They attacked it like moles with their trenching tools, flinging the filth and debris to one side, and stinking, beautiful air gushed in. There was a spade going begging and I grabbed it, stuffing it inside my coat. Hoeppner was by the entrance to the steps, waiting, listening to the roaring avalanche of noise, his eyes wide and white. He was waiting for something he knew about, and they did too. He stuffed a whistle in his mouth; he was waiting.

'*Ja, ja!*' he yelled, and blew a savage blast on the whistle. Then he was up the stairs and running, his whistle shrieking like a train at speed, and the whole crew were running after him, with me in their midst, our feet pounding on the steps, slipping on the mud, scrambling up into the world of light.

The trench had half fallen in. The raised wooden floor had vanished into some kind of glue that seized our boots as we waded through it. The others were scattering, scrambling, seeming to know where to go in the ruined gash in the earth. A machine-gun began to chatter, two of them tending it. I scrambled up the side of the trench – it was easier now it had fallen down. They were firing all around me, and behind us was the roar of the barrage. I got to the top and threw myself down. The spade gashed my chin and I cursed it.

Soldiers were coming at us in the new sunlight, men in khaki wearing round tin helmets. Somehow I hated their helmets. The sun glittered on their bayonets, held high at the port. The Mauser in my hands was just like my hunting rifle at home. I took a bead on the soldier coming for me and it pumped in my hand. The bayonet flew, the rifle tumbling over as I blew him backwards.

He tumbled back like the first rabbit I shot with my little rifle as a boy, spinning round, and I suddenly felt the same intense satisfaction.

They weren't in a line, these men; they were moving in rushes from one bit of the ruined landscape to the other. I saw one crouch behind wreckage and I held my sight where I thought he would come out, just like I was waiting for a hare to move. They were shouting to one another as they came. I heard the strange voices shouting in English, not at all like the way Herr Jacobsen, the English master, spoke. My man bolted out in a rush. I squeezed the trigger and spun him around, a running shot that got him in the leg. He flew round in an arc and lay in a heap, clutching his thigh.

They were close now. Small black balls flew against the sun.

'*Share that among you!*' some Tommy yelled.

I stuffed my head down into the dirt as metal screamed above me. As I got up, one of the round-helmeted men was on me. He lunged at me with steel. I was on my hands and knees. I dropped down, the bayonet passing over my shoulder, and he tripped over me, knocking me backwards, falling down, sliding down the wall of the trench. We lost our weapons. He clawed at me and I at him, grunting and thrashing in the glue of the trench, our teeth gritting. A thumb in my eye, a hand grasping in my face for my throat, my teeth clamping into filthy callused leather, his scream, jabbing frantically into his eyes, suddenly free, the spade in my hand, almost unable to see through mud and tears, hacking at something that squealed and sobbed like the cutting of a pig; standing, panting, not knowing, something dying, wiping my eyes, men scrambling in the trench, dead and dying, fighting.

One of ours tumbling backwards, a round helmet above him, bayonet high, his back to me. I whirled my spade in an arc and the helmet flew across the trench. He fell forward over my comrade, and I hit him again in the head, blood and brains flying. I reached down and pulled my man clear. It was the corporal, my guide. He grinned savagely through gore and muck, his teeth red and white. He grabbed the Tommy's rifle and went scrambling back up the trench, bareheaded.

Suddenly it was quiet. A last shell went over, making a noise like a train. The soldiers were manning both sides of the trench. Their rifles cracked as they shot at the round-helmets. Men were groaning. My spade was covered in a nameless gory mess and the breath tore at my throat. I suddenly bent double, spewing biscuit and chocolate over the mud that enveloped my feet.

Something moved weakly in the slush, something like a log, face down, gargling to death in the mire. I reached down and turned it over. I couldn't tell whether it was one of us or one of them.

A water-bottle was sticking up. I reached down and got it. I drank wonderful clear water. The man at my feet was weakly wiping his face clear of mud with one hand and I gave the bottle to him. His sodden uniform was beginning to stain red, little rivulets of it ran out of his hair, plastered flat to his skull.

'Thanks, mate.'

I supposed he was speaking English.

My legs were like rubber; as I stood by the wall of the trench, they gave way, and I slid slowly down to sit in the glue, unable to stop myself. The Tommy gave me back the bottle with a bloody hand.

'*Ja*,' I said. '*Danke*.'

Hoeppner was shouting orders somewhere. Up in the sky I heard the sound of an engine. Then another. Fokkers, swooping low. A bomb fell from one, and I heard the rip of its machine-guns before the boom of the bomb going off. It climbed away, gleaming in the fresh sunlight.

My hand was stiff from so much writing, the fingers reluctant to release their grasp of the pen. I had put so much down in the blue notebook with its stiff cardboard covers. So many years later, it was as though it were yesterday.

I had the fat round bottle of black ink in the drawer of the desk where I sat. I eased out its cork and dipped in the nib of the pen, depressing the plunger to expel the air and suck up the ink. I wiped it dry with the rag I kept for that purpose, and put everything away ready, for the next day. That is something you learn when you have had a life like mine: if you wish to live to fight or to run away, then refuel and re-arm at the first opportunity. That, and you must have method. When you are a hunter you must study your prey, get to know him like a brother. Take long hours. Some rules, you will discover, are simple. A bird on the ground is like an aircraft: it will always take off into the wind. Your dog will want to hunt on the lee side of cover for maximum game scent for minimum effort. When it catches that scent and crashes into the far side of the cover, it will drive your bird out your side, where it will take off into the wind. At this point a fair offer is yours, and roast pheasant on the menu later in the week.

I am fond of rabbit – both because a bolting bunny in broken cover is a great test of your ability to shoot straight, and because when cooked with bacon and onions it is a delicious meal. I am also fond of ferrets because they like the hunt as much as I do, but I do not like them to eat. Which is why, when a bunny comes out of its hole like a rocket, it is best to wait a second before shooting to see if your ferret is attached to its scut. Rabbit and ferret pie is not a gourmet meal.

I closed my notebook. I had written enough for the day. Outside the sun was dipping towards the white peaks. The fire had died down low and I went and put a few logs on, and the embers took a grip of the dry bark. There was a spurt of flame, the scent of burning apple-wood.

A noise. A car engine. I get no visitors – everybody I know is dead, I am so old. Only my accountant Willi who came on a regular basis – to see if I was still alive, I should think; and I am alive and he is dead, which is not the way it should be.

I made my way across the wide polished wooden boards of my room, laid by Göring's builder so many years ago. I am stiff. I do not move like I used to. There was a knock at the door as I shuffled into the hall. It was him. Cabbage-Breath. The policeman.

'*Ja?*' I am not used to visitors. 'You have some more bad news for me?' I enquired.

He smiled apologetically. 'No, no, Herr Wolff. But after I drove away this morning it occurred to me that you said your accountant was your only regular visitor, and you are, if I may say, many kilometres from the nearest village or town.'

'That is why I live here,' I replied testily, 'so that I do not have to be bothered by people.'

'I understand that,' he said hastily, breathing half-digested nut-loaf over me. 'But what of supplies? How will you get food?' He glanced at the ancient bakelite telephone that lay in the hall. 'Perhaps you have somebody you can call, who will deliver?'

'The telephone does not work,' I said. 'Some years ago I asked them to disconnect it. People used it to interrupt my day, to try to sell me insurance and double-glazed windows, things I do not require.'

'But how did you know when your accountant would be coming?'

'He came when it suited him. It is some years since I went anywhere. I am, as you see, very old.'

'I have some groceries in my car if that would help. Here, let me get them —'

He bounded off in his rubber and canvas shoes. The young have this habit of moving quickly. He was back, carrying a box which he brought into the hall.

'I had to do some shopping,' he explained. 'I bought extra for you in case you needed it. Will you help yourself?'

I looked somewhat dismally into the box. It was as I had suspected. Rice. Root vegetables of various kinds. Brown bread. Enough lentils to keep you sentenced to the latrine for hours. Bottled water. A brown jar of what I certainly suspected was some kind of nostrum. It is always the same with the carrot-chewers: their religious bigotry cannot be confined simply to fruit and vegetables. Out it breaks, to include water gathered from some suitably remote and high spot where, they suppose, the animals have not shat in it – though what about the fish? – nor have the toxins of pollution got at it. This they use to wash down tablets of doubtful origin, efficacy and progeny. Hitler was always at it. His breath stank of old cabbages and half-digested spaghetti as well.

I have, it is true, become tetchy in my old age. But if I had to purchase food for one of these afflicted people I would be decent, and get them their root veg and bag of lentils. I would not include a nice thick steak. But what about me? This root-chewing cop had not bothered to think that *I* might like a steak. Or more likely, could not bring himself to sully his box with it.

'I thank you.' I selected some onions, some rice, some tomatoes. 'I will have these. I was intending to make a chicken stew. I am fond of chicken stew.'

'Chicken . . .' He looked slightly downcast. 'But I brought no chicken.'

'I have my own,' I said. I reached to the peg and put on my jacket. 'Perhaps you would like to accompany me,' I suggested.

At the back of my house I have my garden. I paused to take my knife from my pocket and harvested a cabbage, and then we made our way to the chicken run.

'Are you fond of eggs?' I enquired.

He looked shocked. 'No, I do not eat eggs.'

'I would have given you some. Willi and his wife liked my eggs. Your wife, she likes eggs, perhaps?'

'I am not married, Herr Wolff.'

'No, no . . .'

The chickens saw us coming, and the cabbage, and set up a great clucking.

'They are like you,' I said. 'They like cabbage.'

I undid the chicken-wire door and we went in. He stood uneasily on the guano in his canvas shoes. I used a needle to push string through the cabbage and hung it for them to peck at, which they did, clustering round with what passes for glee in a chicken. They are not intelligent birds.

'There was something I thought of when you had gone,' I said. 'Willi's wife, the little girls . . . they were not molested by this murderer?'

'No, no,' he assured me. He seemed slightly shocked by the idea. That seemed odd, to me.

'I was trying to think why anyone would want to kill them,' I said.

'We live in strange times,' he said.

'I know. That is why I live here. I wish to live out what is left of my allotment in my own manner.' I looked about the flock. 'We shall have to put you in the hen-house soon,' I told them. 'Herr Fox is about.'

There she was, the old speckled hen. I reached down and scooped her up, tucking her under my arm, where she clucked aggrievedly at being deprived of her portion of leaf. I led the policeman out again.

By the shed, out of sight of the run, there is the old bench, and I sat down there. I tucked the speckled hen between my legs and, taking her neck in one hand and her head in the other, I wrung it, quickly and cleanly with a snap. The eyes stayed open, not even surprised; she lay in my lap, simply warm and inert. I glanced up at the policeman and was in time to see a strange look of calculation and certainty on his face.

'Do you feel you have the right to do that?' he asked. 'To take life?'

'I do,' I assured him. 'Without me, the hens would not be alive at all. They have a good life here, out in the open, well fed, free from disease, warm at night and protected from those that would kill them in the wild.'

'Except you,' he pointed out, 'their executioner.'

'Except me,' I agreed. 'But I give them life to begin with, and in return, they enable me to live.'

'You could eat vegetables, like me.'

'You will excuse me if I say I would rather be dead. I have eaten meat since my mother weaned me from her bosom, which was, if I knew anything about her, something that happened to me at an early age. I have drunk alcohol since I was old enough to, and have done so every day of my life since. I am over ninety years old and may make one hundred yet. A shock course of beetroots and sauerkraut would see me off, I would imagine.'

'We shall see, won't we?' he said musingly.

'What?'

'Whether you make a hundred.'

I began to pluck the feathers from the chicken, putting them in the old sack. The sun was going down; it was getting cold.

'It is a clean end, this,' I told him. 'Not what happens to most. I have seen enough death in my time to know that when it comes, something quick that does not hurt is what is devoutly to be wished for. A fox does not wring the neck of a bird first. A crow eats baby birds alive. Disease, cold and lack of food all kill slowly. I have been ill, freezing and starving in my time, and I assure you, it hurts.'

He turned, and walked off towards his car. Then he waved, by the door, and smiled his strange smile. 'I'll see you next week,' he called. 'I'll bring you some more supplies.'

He drove off down the little lane that leads over the narrow bridge that crosses the ravine, with the tumbling white river below.

I appeared to have lost my accountant and acquired a swede-gulping lawman instead. It did not seem to me to be a fair exchange.

The sun dipped behind the far peak, sending golden fingers being chased by the dark up the hillside, above the old wooden outbuildings. I went inside, to clean the bird.

1918

Grass, sprinkled with flowers, all about half a metre or so high. A lane that we trudged down, me and the Tommy and the two corporals, happy enough to be out of the maze of dug-outs and trenches.

Over in the distance there were a few huts, some kind of staging area for troops coming up to the front, although there was none that we could see. A crossroads, where I could get a lift back to the Jasta. The lines were all cut. Hoeppner had sent the runner, Hitler, with a message. Another corporal, Eisenmann, the Jewish machine-gunner, was guarding the Tommy on his way to the rear. The air was fresh back here; I thought I heard a bird sing. It stopped, and I cocked my ear. The bird had heard what I heard then, the rushing whoosh of a big shell. The soldiers all seemed indifferent, so I curbed my natural impulse to fling myself into the ditch.

They were right. We heard it go over with a shout and a scream, right above our heads, and then there was a sudden belch of black smoke down among the huts and, a second later, the deep crump of the explosive going off.

'Coal box,' the Tommy said laconically. I saw what he meant. The smoke sprang up and hung in the air like the debris from a load of slack.

The runner, Hitler, broke into a trot. 'Someone may be hurt,' he said.

'Someone may be dead,' said Eisenmann, but we all speeded

up as much as our wounds, burden of mud and general exhaustion would let us.

The smoke was drifting away when we got down there. Part of a hut had been blown in. On the floor by a table was a quartermaster sergeant, stretched out flat. He still had a tumbler in his hand; a bottle of brandy had emptied itself next to him. He might have been drunk, but when Eisenmann turned him over with his boot, with the contempt of the fighting man for the man in the rear, he was quite dead. We all, I think, looked down on him with a measure of satisfaction. It was good to see justice visited upon those who tried to evade it.

Eisenmann saluted in mocking fashion, and began to chant like a bugle call:

'*Sixty-four, ninety-four!*
He'll never go sick no more:
The silly bugger's dead.'

We all grinned at that, including the Tommy, who began to sing himself:

'*If you want to find the sergeant-major,*
I know where he is, I know where he is.
If you want to find the sergeant-major,
I know where he is.
He's boozing up the private's rum.'

Hitler was scowling now that the Britisher was singing, and he stepped forward and slapped him. 'Quiet! You are a prisoner.'

'Don't be like that, mate,' the Tommy said, unconcerned.

'Let him sing,' said Eisenmann, setting the chair up and sitting down.

'Get up!' Hitler yelled. 'It is no time to rest. We have to be back with the unit.'

I looked at the walls. The quartermaster had some nice Kirchner posters of pretty, half-dressed girls in lacy lingerie, showing the best of themselves.

'We can have some of those,' said Eisenmann to me, 'he won't want them. Oh, piss off, Adolf, the war will still be there when we get back.'

Hitler went to the door. '*I* know my duty!' he yelled. 'You should do yours!'

'I'm doing it,' said Eisenmann wearily. 'I'm going to wait here for someone to take the Tommy away.'

Hitler went out, and we heard him marching away.

'Fucking white crow,' Eisenmann muttered derisively. 'Thinks we're going to win the war . . .'

The shell had blown open the rear of the store, and boxes lay tumbled about.

'Here, Herr Flieger,' the Jew said, brightening. 'You off on leave? Better take something with you. They're eating turnips and potatoes for breakfast, lunch and supper back there, my girl says.' He stepped over the dead quartermaster, and I and the Tommy followed. 'Look at this then. They do themselves proud.' We found boxes of candied fruits, sweet biscuits, canned tongue and ham.

'Fuck you, Jack, I'm all right, eh?' said the Tommy.

'*Ja*,' Eisenmann agreed. 'For the senior officers.'

There seemed a lot in what Eisenmann said. I found a stout pack in there and quickly began to fill it. Why not? I knew where the bastard senior officers lived, sleek and fat, in the chateaux way behind the lines. Me and mine, we went high in the sky to freeze, until a chance bullet set us alight, and we burned, all the way down. Hell, yes, they could spare me and Hilde something. They owed it to me.

The Tommy was obviously of the same opinion. '*If you want to find the general, I know where he is, I know where he is,*' he sang softly.

'*If you want to find the general,*
I know where he is.
I've seen him, I've seen him,
Miles and miles behind the line,
I've seen him,
Miles and miles and miles behind the line.'

Eisenmann was a resourceful man. He had a knife with a corkscrew, and deftly opened a green bottle of Reisling. He took a swig and passed it on, we had it inside us by the time I had my pack filled.

Eisenmann tossed the Tommy some chocolate and a big round tin of cigarettes. We all lit up and went outside, walking down to the crossroads, trailing aromatic smoke.

The Tommy started to sing again, softly and plaintively, and

we joined in, for we knew the song now, even in English.
> '*If you want to find the old battalion,*
> *I know where they are, I know where they are,*
> *If you want to find the old battalion,*
> *I know where they are.*
> *They're hanging on the old barbed wire.*
> *I've seen 'em, I've seen 'em,*
> *Hanging on the old barbed wire,*
> *I've seen 'em,*
> *Hanging on the old barbed wire.*'

I always wake early. Rheumatism does that for you. I don't go to bed any more, I sit in my chair by the fire and doze off. But before it's dawn there's a combination of testy joints and the ghosts that are getting up to go and fly that gets me up too. Sometimes it's the smell that wakes me; sometimes the combination of dope and oil, of crushed grass; sometimes the violent chemical stench of *T-stoff* – but that is from twenty-five years later, although it all seems like yesterday, to me.

When I am lucky the air is clear outside, and I see the sky turn cinnamon grey, then blue, and the sun climbs over the mountain peak behind me to paint the far slopes of the deep valley in all their glory. I am out by then and have let the chickens from the coop. I gather eggs, if there are a few. I sit out on the porch with strong coffee and my pipe, and watch the hawk hovering into the air flowing down the slope; she can go backwards if she wants to. See the sudden dive as she spots breakfast; see her fly away to her roost to eat. The squirrels are out by the trees that line the meadow, looking for nuts. In the quiet I can hear the icy stream rushing in the ravine. My pipe smoke drifts away with the air, down over the meadow, silver for as long as I can see it, and vanishes where the slope falls away into the valley. I am perched up here, on a ledge.

I have a new purpose now that I am putting down all the memories. All the people jostling, grinning and joking at my elbow and reminding me of their presence, that they should be written in as well. And the others, the ones who stood in the shadowy fringes of my mind, in their uniforms, ready to step out into the light of day where I might see them once again. But no, I shall let them stand there awhile, since I am with my comrades. And since I can remember Hilde so clearly, just as she was then. It is pleasant, that. I shall put off thinking of the others until later.

I can see them all as clear as I want, though. It is curious: people of fifty, sixty, seventy years ago, I can see them as though they were with me minutes before – and yet show me a man I met yesterday and I cannot remember his name. This carob-crunching policeman, I can barely remember what he looks like and I have already forgotten his name, although I feel sure he told me what it was. That is what I told the other policeman, the one who drove up as I was drinking my coffee and puffing on my pipe in the morning light.

He drove up in a different car, one with markings on it proclaiming its driver to be of the something police, and a blue lamp upon its roof. The other one, the lentil-lover, he drove a car without markings, though it had a blue light he could attach to the roof by a magnet, but he was, if I remember, a detective.

This one wore a uniform, although he looked barely old enough to put on long trousers.

'Herr Wolff?'

'*Ja.*'

He took off his peaked cap. 'I have some bad news,' he said diffidently.

'I know,' I said. 'My accountant Willi.'

'Yes ...' He seemed rather relieved at not having to go through it. It is a nasty business. I have done it too many times. 'A friend mentioned that he came to see you. There was a telephone number but –'

'It does not work,' I finished for him.

'No. The funeral arrangements ...'

'They are being taken care of?'

'Yes, yes. But you will be wanting to attend. We can have a car –'

'No,' I said quietly. 'I shall not be going.' I held up a hand. 'This may seem odd to you, but I do not like funerals. Some time ago I made a decision not to go to any more in my life. I have been to enough. But I will ask you to buy me flowers.'

I went inside, and got some notes from the desk. He was still there, looking about him, and I gave him the money.

'You live all by yourself here, Herr Wolff?'

'I do.'

'Is it safe?'

'Who would want to harm me?'

'Somebody wanted to harm your accountant and his family,' he said soberly. 'Do you have any idea why it happened, sir?'

'*Ja.* To be certain, they were killed by a maniac. I have lived a very long time. I have lived through times in which millions of people died in ways that they would have not chosen for themselves. Each and every one, they died because of maniacs. One maniac, just one, can kill millions if they get into the killing place.'

He frowned. 'The killing place?'

'That is it. Let me tell you. I too have killed people. I was a pilot in the two great wars. Up there, there is a killing place – you must get into it to shoot down your opponent. But my killing place was small. I killed only one, two or perhaps at most ten people at a time if it was a big bomber, poor devils. To kill millions you need a maniac. He stands like us here on the mountain, above all humanity, and he rains down death upon those below, and always, in the most horrible manner. That is how poor Willi died, his wife and the two little girls. It was not a traffic accident. It was a maniac.'

'Yes,' he said quietly. 'It was. They were ... badly mutilated, Herr Wolff. Whole ... pieces of them were missing. I do not know why, or where the parts are ...'

We stood silent for a few moments. It is very quiet there in the valley. It is remote, of course, which is why I live there. There are no ski slopes – the sides are too steep for that. The road is but a lane that goes nowhere but my *völkisches* dwelling that no peasant ever lived in. Well, I was not about to ask Le Corbusier or Van der Rohe to make me some splendid crisp white glassy item of *Zweckmässigkeit und Sachlichkeit* any time after 1933, was I? The rabbits in these parts don ivory coats in winter to disguise themselves, and I had been no exception.

'I had better get myself back,' he said. 'We are all on extra duty, looking for Mother Nature.'

The bizarre nature of this remark brought me back from reflecting on the past. Looking for Mother Nature? A surreal image of uniformed policemen singing like *Wandervogel* in the mountains, songbirds fluttering about their heads while rabbits cavorted at their feet rose up in my mind.

'Mother Nature?' I questioned.

He looked at me, seeing that I had not understood him. 'You have not seen it on the television?'

I gestured at my house, free of aerials.

'Ah ... then you do not know of this group. They are eco-terrorists.'

I waited for him to explain.

'A terrorist group that is very concerned about the environment. They say that the technologies of industry and farming, the desires of the consumer state, the military-industrial complex, are bringing about the end of the world through exploitation and pollution. They demand the abandonment of the industrial state and a return to an age in which there was no war and when men lived in harmony with animals and nature.'

'When can that have been, I wonder?' I mused. 'But I should say that they may demand all they want; it will not change things a jot.'

'Oh, *ja*,' he agreed. 'But they are, as I say, terrorists. They do not just lie down in front of tractors and sing songs. Last year they kidnapped Herr Solmitz, the chairman of Solmitz Foods. A very big food manufacturer. The company has global links – with Africa, Latin America, the Far East. They demanded the total destruction and abolition of the company.'

'But the company is still in business, at a guess?'

'To be sure. The shareholders were not enthusiastic about the idea.'

'And this Herr Solmitz, he was released?'

'In a manner of speaking, yes. When the workers turned up for work one morning at the factory, they found some pigs tethered to the gate, and a note saying that they had brought Herr Solmitz with them. Since nobody could see Herr Solmitz it occurred to someone – I am not sure who – to kill one of the pigs and open it up. Inside its stomach were, to be certain, chopped up parts of Herr Solmitz.'

'They do not sound very nice, these Mother Natures.'

'No,' he agreed. 'Last week they kidnapped a chef. A man with his own restaurant, very famous. Which is why we are on extra duty. Hoping not to see pigs.'

'I wish you luck, then, in catching these people. I thank you for coming,' I said, 'and for arranging the wreath.'

He left, and the burned smell of his exhaust drifted down the slope. I went inside and got out my exercise book and pen, filled with ink. I opened my wooden-framed window. My peasant's house is comfortable enough to live in. I am very used to it, and nobody really remembers it was all pure symbolism, not even me, sometimes. Speer knew, but he's dead, and nobody remembers him either.

1918

The pack was very heavy; the mud of my clothes had hardened to the quality of armour-plate and, as I heaved myself up the rickety staircase, it shattered and ground, sending explosions of yellow and brown into the air, so that looking down the well I could see a swirled trail like that of a doomed scout, marking my passage upwards.

I reached the top. Sunlight was leaking in through a skylight. I knocked on the door. Footsteps, light, soft, came running. The door opened and someone looked out. A small face framed by short, glossy, jet-black hair looked seriously at me. It was topped by a rakish scarlet beret and tied underneath by a huge and flamboyant matching silk scarf. Blue eyes looked doubtfully at me. 'Hans?'

I looked at her, for a second equally uncertain. 'Hilde?'

She knew my voice. She beamed, her arms flailed in sudden uncertainty, wishing to embrace, but seeing the impossibility. 'You are completely, from your head to your feet, covered in mud,' she said seriously. 'What have you been doing?' She poked her head back inside the doorway. 'Erna! Erna! Come and see a mud-man.'

Another short-haired young girl appeared, and grinned at the sight of me. She too was bedecked in scarlet.

'Hilde,' I said. 'Do your parents know you two are going about dressed like this?'

'Our parents!' Erna cried. 'My parents are dead.'

'Dead? What happened?'

'Oh, not *dead* dead,' Hilde said dismissively. 'Just dead. All part of that rotten corrupt primeval culture that is dying all about us. But we, we are the new life!'

'*Ja, ja,*' I said, 'very possibly. But in the meantime I am still covered in mud.'

'This is true,' she admitted. 'Look, you cannot bring all that in here. We shall have to take it up on the roof and beat it. Start taking your clothes off.'

'*Here?*'

She giggled. 'In the new world, all those old-fashioned notions will be gone,' she explained. 'We shall glory in the beauty of our bodies, not hide them away in bourgeois shame.'

'We may also get cold,' I said.

Erna giggled. 'I'm going out,' she said. 'I shall leave you to get the mud-man clean, Hilde.'

I eased off the pack, as she went down the stairs and swung it inside the door. 'We may get cold, but not hungry or thirsty, for I bring gifts from the old world.'

'Oh, wonderful,' she said practically. 'I am so sick of potatoes.'

'Save some for me!' Erna called as she clattered gaily down the bare staircase. 'For I, too, have eaten enough potatoes. Turnips, as well.'

I managed to clamber out of my leather greatcoat. It was totally stiff. I stood it up on the floor. Hilde looked at me in amazement. 'But you are muddy *underneath*,' she exclaimed. 'What have you done?'

'I crashed.'

'You've been bathing in the stuff,' she said, accepting my Iron Cross as I took it off.

'Yes.'

'Hans,' she said, in a small voice. 'There is blood all over this.'

'*Ja,*' I said wearily, 'there is blood in the mud as well. I crashed in between the lines. In the middle of a British attack. I had to fight.'

She was quiet, watching as I piled up the clothes. 'I'll put water on for a bath,' she said.

At the level of my skin I was simply stained with the stuff, not actually armoured by it, and I went in, shutting the door behind me and carrying my pack to the table. The room also had a skylight like the landing outside, and in its radiance Hilde had set up a large easel, on which she was painting a dramatic poster. There was a lot of red in it, and what looked like machine parts, and people with clenched fists against high factory chimneys.

I opened the pack and took out a bottle of brandy. I tipped some into two tumblers; wonderful, scented, powerful.

'What is it?' I asked.

'It's the future,' she said.

We drank and tears shot into our eyes. When I could see again I peered more closely at the painting. 'Are those bodies they're standing on?' I asked.

'That's the old order. It must be crushed totally, made extinct.'

'We're fighting the French and British at the moment,' I observed.

'All the old order!' she cried. 'To be swept away by the irresistible force of history!'

'What does your father think of this?'

'Oh, pooh! He shall be swept away too.'

She looked critically but approvingly at her painting. There were little smears of scarlet on her hands. It was very good, like nothing I had seen before.

'It's a change from still-life,' I ventured.

'All that's in the past!' She swung round and finally embraced me. 'Oh, Hans! It's happened at last. Just a few days it took in Russia, and now it's coming here! A whole new world, and we're going to be part of it! I can't wait, I can't wait . . .'

Wisps of steam were issuing from the bathroom, and she pushed me that way.

'You got some bath salts from your generals' store – I've put some in.'

'I grabbed anything that looked good,' I admitted.

I sat in the warm, soapy, scented water and she poured more over my head as I washed. 'You were very grubby,' she said. The bottom of the big, claw-footed white bath began to resemble the lining of some slow-moving African river.

Brandy fumes swirled inside our heads. We held tight to each other inside the white sheets. Her scarlet accoutrements were pooled next to us. She was warm and smooth and springy. My hands were possessed of their own life, almost unable to believe that they were not gripping the cold hard tools of killing, the throttle and joystick, rifle, spade, club.

'Don't go back,' she said.

'I have to.'

'The war will soon be over. From the ruins our new world will spring, fresh-formed and wonderful.'

'You are wonderful.'

'I am serious,' she wriggled.

'So am I.'

'If you are killed you will not be there to enjoy it with me.'

'I am enjoying it with you now.'

'Don't go back,' she entreated, taking hold of my hands.

'But I must. I cannot desert. I am an officer.'

'There will be no officers or private soldiers after this war.'

'Somebody must lead the troops.'

'Don't you believe that there will be no wars in the new world? How can there be? So many have been killed. Stay here with me. Who are you fighting for? The Kaiser? That butcher Ludendorff?'

'No . . . but the boys are going up every day. Each time, some do not come back. In the new world, when the fighting is done and I meet them, perhaps without legs, or blind, or burned, or in the mad house, what shall I say? That I stayed at home waiting for the new world to come, while they went up without me?'

She was silent. 'Pour us more brandy then,' she said at last, and let my hands go.

We lay in bed and ate delicate pink ham and chicken breast in aspic, the jelly quivering gold as you lifted it up to your mouth. We peeled quails' eggs and spread soft aromatic cheese on to flaky baked biscuits that came in a cylindrical tin bearing the coat-of-arms of the Kaiser. We nibbled on chocolate shaped like butterflies, and washed it down with golden green wine.

'Hans . . . why did you say that, about the boys – without

legs, or blind, or burned, or in the mad house?'

'It is the way it is,' I explained. 'We fire bullets from machine-guns at one another. The bullets arrive in clusters. If you get hit, you may live, if you do not pass out on the way down. Six or seven bullets through your legs will smash you up pretty good, even if you manage to put it down.'

'Burned?' she asked quietly.

'*Verbrannt, ja.* In every combat there is smoke, black, spiralling smoke. The aircraft, you see, they catch fire very easily. Those machine-gun bullets open up the fuel-tanks. These are in the nose, in front of you. Also in the nose is the magneto, which provides the spark for the engine. It sets the fuel alight.'

It was gasoline, or petrol, though we never called it that. Hell-brew, Orange Death, Witches' Water, Infernal Liquid.

'There's a pretty big wind since you are doing maybe two hundred kilometres in a dive. The fuel sprays back over you and soaks your clothes. The magneto keeps turning, and if you are lucky, it sets the aircraft and you alight. If you're unlucky, it may *not* set you alight.'

She frowned. 'I don't understand.'

'You may be high, very high, when this combat happens. It can take ten minutes to pilot your aircraft down – it is crippled, too. It is like ten years. The nerve of the boys may go, they may crack – end in the mad house.'

'Is there nothing that can be done?'

'There is, yes. You can wear a parachute. That is what the gunnery men in their observation balloons do. When we set the balloons alight they jump out and float down under their parachutes, like big umbrellas.'

'Well, why don't you get parachutes?'

'Not allowed. High Command says so. Bad for morale.'

I poured some brandy into the tumblers. She took mine and with a finger painted her breasts. 'You can drink it like this, today.'

I bent over her, brandy and beautiful Hilde.

'I am here for you always,' she said clearly. 'But you must come back for me too. The new world is coming. Then there will be no rules, no High Command, no war.' She moved so that I might take the liquor from the other side. 'I want you whole,

Hans. With your legs. With your eyes. Not *verbrannt*. Not in the mad house.'

I sat at my old desk, lost in the memories, more real to me than the present. I rummaged in my drawer and there was my old medal bar. I took it out, looking at the different crosses. Then, the present made itself felt. The dim noise of an engine – I am somewhat deaf – the burnt smell of an exhaust. I was suddenly enraged. Hilde had slipped away from me. I had been happy in her company. Who was it that had driven her away? Why was I being persecuted like this?

It would be an exaggeration to say that I bounded to the door, for I have not moved much above a shuffle for some years, but I made as much haste as I was able. It was him! Lentil-Gas. I goggled with annoyance, and he beamed. Vitamin-blind to boot.

'I was passing, Herr Wolff, having bought some very fine organic potatoes, and it occurred to me that I should share them with you.'

'Are there no criminals for you to catch?' I howled. 'Do I like potatoes, organic or otherwise? No, I do not! I took a great aversion to them years ago and have not eaten them since. Why do you persecute me with these wretched tubers? Eh? Answer me that!'

He looked at me, the smile dying from his face. 'I am sorry you do not care for potatoes,' he said with some dignity. 'I personally am very fond of them, especially these organically grown ones. I am only trying to help, Herr Wolff. You are an old man and without relatives who may care for you. What will happen to you? Have you thought of that? You are an independent person, and would not care to spend the rest of your days in the old people's home. I am only trying to provide some assistance if it is in my power.'

The rage left me like air going out of a balloon, as is the way with me. I saw that I had allowed myself to be discourteous. 'I am sorry,' I said formally. 'I did not mean to be rude. I have been putting down reminiscences of the past, and I was remembering how it was at the end of the war, when there was little but potatoes to eat, or even drink. We made both coffee and schnapps from them.'

'Ah, *ja*?' he said, interested. 'That was the Hitler war?'

'Oh, no,' I explained. 'I am so old that I fought in both of the great wars. I was remembering the days of 1918. Had there not been potatoes we should have all starved. But it has left me with little affection for them. But here, come in. I am about to make coffee.'

'I do not imbibe, I'm afraid,' he said, stepping inside anyway.

He looked around the big room, seemingly fascinated by the many objects and machines there. All along one wall I had a workbench with my tools in their places on the wall and pieces of equipment – a small lathe, a drill press, a shaper and a milling machine – as well as pots of varnish and glue, solder and wire, metal sheet and shaped blocks and strips of wood.

'You are . . . an engineer?'

'Engineer, model-maker, artist. Many things,' I said.

He bent to peer at a half-finished model. You could already see what it was; its gossamer wire frame gleamed in the light like a spider's web in the morning, tiny blobs of solder at the joins, glinting like dew.

'A little aircraft?'

'Fokker VII,' I replied. 'The best scout we had in 1918. I flew it.'

'You make it from a kit?' he hazarded.

'No, from plans I drew up. I first made a model like that when I was thirteen years old. An Antoinette, it was, as delicate as a butterfly. The war was only a gleam in the eye of the Kaiser. My mother and father were dead and I was living with an uncle. I took to making models and have never stopped.'

'So many strange things . . . ,' he said. 'What are they? They are not all models.'

'I was a pilot,' I told him, 'in both wars, and sometimes in between. But also, I became an inventor of sorts. I hold a number of patents. I have always been fascinated by technology.'

'Patents?'

'Several,' I assured him. 'Everything from coffee-pots to self-sharpening scissors.'

He was peering at a device on a table. 'And this? What does

this do?'

'Guess,' I said. Nobody does.

'Well, it has three cylinders in the shape of a star,' he said, not unintelligently. 'It is perhaps some kind of model aircraft-engine? But then, why does it have this reel, and a kind of spade?'

'That is right. In a war, you see, much equipment is often abandoned, because it cannot be moved. It breaks down, or is damaged. It gets bogged in mud. This is all very wasteful. A tank, for example, is a very expensive and valuable piece of battle machinery. If it could be moved once it had broken down, one may save it for another day. But for that winches are required, and another heavy machine. Unless one has one's own portable winch. A prime mover of one's own.'

He frowned, peering at the little engine. 'That cannot move a tank,' he said flatly.

'It can't,' I agreed. 'Although I made one not much bigger that did. But it would move your car with ease.'

'It's too small.'

I picked it up. It is quite light. I used aircraft alloys. 'Let me demonstrate.'

We went outside. About twenty metres from the front of his car I stopped and put the spade on the ground. It is like an entrenching tool with the blade at right angles to the haft. I put one foot on it and it sank into the ground with ease.

'It will cut into even the driest ground,' I explained. I picked up the engine and its ancillaries and walked to the car, the clear line paying out behind us. 'The line is simply fishing line. This one will hold a marlin – it is ocean line.'

I saw a frown flicker over his face, and then it was gone. 'How do you attach the machine to the car?' he asked.

'Hold it anywhere you want,' I said, doing just that. 'And start it up.' I flicked the cylinders and the engine started with its usual pleasing roar. The machine was stuck as if welded to the car, the cylinders whirling in a silver blur in the centre, and the reel began to pay in. It took up the slack and, without any hesitation in the steady drumming beat, began to haul the car forward.

'How does it stick?'

'Electro-magnet energised by the engine,' I explained simply. The car was rolling forward at a great pace. As it came up to the spade I turned the little hidden switch that cut off power to the spark plugs and removed the apparatus as the cylinders whirled to a stop.

'And the final thing . . .' I lifted the handle of the spade, and the cam at its far end smoothly pushed the wide blade from the earth, as easily as pulling a carrot. 'A half-trained team can make two kilometres in an hour,' I said. 'You don't have to shut the engine off either. I designed one with two winches for maximum speed. Not that it saw production.'

'Why was that?'

'German tanks of the Hitler war only had forward gears,' I said. 'So to speak. They were under orders to go only forward. Why do you need equipment to rescue tanks from the battlefield if they are going forward?'

'I see that . . .' he said thoughtfully. 'The leader says something and everybody has to obey.'

'For a long time so many people thought Hitler was infallible,' I said, 'that he was the sleeping hero-Kaiser, the reawakened Frederick Barbarossa, come to save Germany. The God-sent Führer, chosen by history.'

He looked at me intently. 'And was he?' he asked. 'You were there, were you not?'

'In the end, Hitler believed it himself and brought everything down about our ears. I myself never believed a word of it.'

'There are many false prophets,' he said strangely.

'I knew how it was put together. I knew Goebbels. I have lived through ideologies of Kaisers. Kaiser Wilhelm, Kaiser Stalin, Kaiser Hitler. The greater the Kaiser, the more people he kills; and at the end, all is for naught. There is more truth in a bottle of good wine than in any of them. That is what I said to your companion who was here today.'

He looked startled. 'My companion?'

'*Ja*. The other policeman who came in a police car. To tell me of the death of Willi.'

'Ah . . .' He looked at me, like a fox that suspects you have a gun somewhere to hand. 'We are no more efficient than anyone else,' he said apologetically.

'I told him I already knew,' I said, as we turned back towards the house. 'He was in a hurry to get back anyway. He has extra duties. And you, you have extra duty?'

'For what?'

'These... terrorists. What was it he called it? I can remember the serial number of the last Fokker I flew, and I cannot recall this morning...'

'Mother Nature,' he said quietly.

'That is it, *ja*. Mother Nature. Who are these strange people?'

'Ecologists.'

'They kill people,' I objected. 'Did they not feed this industrialist to some pigs? This is not pleasant.'

'They are the militant arm of a more widespread movement that calls itself the Children of the Earth,' he explained. 'You have no doubt heard of the IRA?'

'Yes. The Irish terrorists.'

'They would say freedom fighters, but yes. They are the militant arm of the political group, Sinn Fein.'

'Ah, I see. So Mother Nature does the killing, and the Earth Children present a good face. But feeding industrialists to pigs is still not right.'

'They would disagree with you. I wonder if you are familiar with the British opera, the *Mikado*? By Gilbert and Sullivan? There is a character there called Poo Bah. He is the Lord High Executioner, and he has a list of those he is going to punish. In a special way. For he likes, he says, the punishment to fit the crime.'

'This industrialist provided food and jobs. Is that a crime?'

'The animals would say so,' he said softly. 'I am speaking as one of them, you understand. For their argument is that these food companies exploit animals. Only humans benefit. So those who organise such exploitation must pay, in a suitable fashion to fit the crime.'

I nodded. 'It does not surprise me,' I said, as we re-entered the house. 'There are always people in the world ready to believe anything, however strange. In fact, the stranger the belief, the more attractive they seem to find it. If you can get people to believe that Adolf Hitler is the Messiah, or that Jesus Christ died, rose again on the third day and was sent to atone for your sins, then you can get people to believe anything.' I paused, trying to remember what the other policeman had said. 'Ah, *ja*. They have kidnapped another man. A restaurant owner, I think.'

'Herr Haffner,' he said, nodding. 'He runs a gourmet restaurant. He has just written a book about ways to cook game.' He glanced around the room. 'Boar, and so forth. Like that one on your wall.' He got up. 'Well, I must go, Herr Wolff. Duties call. I thank you for showing me your things.' He paused by the desk. 'May I?' he asked, indicating my medals.

'Please do.'

He held them up. 'So many medals . . .' He looked up at the wall. My boar's head seemed to fascinate him. 'They gave you these for killing animals?' he asked. I was not sure if he was joking or not.

'No,' I said shortly. 'People.'

'Ah, *ja*. Of course.' He smiled strangely at me. 'Much better.'

I saw him out. He paused by his car – some modern creation with big knobbly tyres like the Führer used to have on his six-wheeled Mercedes.

He paused to look about him. 'A beautiful place,' he said approvingly. 'Is all this yours?'

'What you see,' I told him. 'From the wood over there to the ravine; from the high slope down to the river. I am tucked into a fold of the mountain here. I am overlooked by no one. It will snow soon. I must make my rounds of the land while I am still able to move.'

'How wonderful,' he said, 'to have nobody able to see you at all.'

November 1918

It was cold and dark. A single kerosene lamp hissed to itself, hanging from the wall of the maintenance hut. It illuminated the pitifully short line of scouts. I kept my hands stuffed into the pockets of my flying-coat, and huddled down into the sheepskin collar. My chin touched the elegant but icy cross at my throat, as lovely as a piece of jewellery: the Blue Max, *Ordre pour le Merite*. It was the highest award you could earn as a pilot. It was very expensive. You had to kill men who were trying to kill you to get it. I had shot down my thirty-seventh enemy aircraft – one of the very dangerous British Camels – the previous week. Somebody up there, back where the generals decided these things, had noticed.

Krefft, my chief of maintenance, stood next to me in the dark light before the dawn.

'If the gasoline does not come soon the British can turn up in an old spotter plane and machine-gun us where we stand,' I grunted.

From somewhere out in the blackness we could hear the faint sputtering of an engine. Through the bare tree in the distance we saw the slightest yellow flicker of automotive lamps.

'That had better be it,' I said morosely.

'It's a lorry,' Krefft said, with an expert ear.

I walked over to my own Fokker, my boots slapping through the grass, heavy with almost-frozen dew. God, it would be cold up there! The only advantage was that the cold air was thick: it gave power to the engine, bite to the planes, to the controls.

I tapped my hand on the linen covering of the plane nearest to me. It should have responded like music, like a fine drum, taut and ready, but all it emitted was a dull *thwack*. It hung between the ribs like the skin of a starving cow.

'Look at this!' I snarled. 'It's like trying to fly a barge, up there.'

The cold air gave more power to the enemy, too, more bite to his planes, his controls.

'I know, Herr Hauptmann,' Krefft said as soothingly as he could. 'We have simply had no supplies of good dope for the fabric. Without it, we cannot make them tight.'

'I know that,' I said. 'I wish the generals knew it too. I'd like to take one up there.'

'Show him how it flies without proper dope, eh?'

'*Nein*, I'd like to take him up and drop the *Schweinehunde*. From about eight thousand metres. Let him think about it on the way down.'

'*Ja, ja,*' Krefft said approvingly. 'Ah, here it is!'

A dirt-brown lorry bearing a big cylindrical tank on its back drew up with a rattling gasp of its engine. The fitters suddenly swarmed out of the hut under Krefft's bark of command. The pilots came shuffling out of their tents, muttering as they felt the icy fingers of the rising breeze penetrate their clothing, fumbling with buttons, pushing up collars. I hardly knew any of them. The *Jasta* looked the same, but it was like an ancient piece of tapestry hanging on a castle wall, an old battle flag, patched and darned so many times that no original threads remained. The slaughter had been so great that the oldest surviving member rose to command. It happened to be me. In a few days it would probably be somebody else.

'No smoking!' Krefft yelled, and the fitters nipped out their home-made cigarettes with work-callused fingers, tucking the ends into their pockets to be relit when we had gone up. There was a clanking and a glugging and the raw smell of aviation spirit on the cold air.

'Have we still got enough schnapps?' I asked Krefft urgently. 'We cannot fly without schnapps.'

'*Ja*, Hauptmann,' he said soothingly.

We needed it. We needed it to keep ourselves from the cold, to revive ourselves to do it again, to anaesthetise the pain of it all. I was tired of killing people.

The Fokkers were hung with clusters of grey bombs arrayed like strange fruit under the bottom planes. It did not seem so long ago that the old Taube and Avros had fluttered about above the battles observing the struggle below. The air was one place men did not kill each other. Now we set each other alight at altitude, and when we came down low, it was to drop bombs on the people on the ground.

'You're sure of that? Plenty of schnapps?'

'Plenty, Hauptmann,' he said again, reassuringly.

One after the other we strapped ourselves in, the metal of the machines icy to the unwary touch, hands and feet already half-numb even inside our sheepskins, goggles forming frozen circles around our eye-sockets. One after the other the Mercedes engines started, the harsh exhaust notes ripping the silent still air. I looked up, and the sky was starting to brush over the faintest dove grey, the colour of Hilde's eyes.

Down by the hut pinpricks of red and gold glowed like fireflies, as the fitters sucked on their tobacco. I opened the throttle, and the Fokker rolled forward over the sodden grass, slowly at first, and then gaining speed, until, with a last thump through the undercarriage I was aloft.

It was still dark. I concentrated on my simple instruments, holding the nose down as my speed built up, then pegging it on a hundred and ten kilometres as I climbed, taking up and keeping my compass heading out to the battle area delineated on the map and aerial photograph clipped to the board strapped about my left thigh.

I flew into a bank of mist pushing through in the wind, damp and dark. I concentrated on the airspeed and the bubble, the little spirit-level mounted in front of me. I felt cold air begin to rush over my left cheek, and kicked in a little left rudder to keep the aircraft straight, to kill the beginnings of the lethal, ever-tightening spiral dive that had claimed so many pilots in cloud.

Then I was out, and above was the dove-grey sky beginning to turn the faintest tinge of golden, like a girl's hair. I twisted about in my cockpit and saw in a rough vic that the others were with me. I looked above and below, skidding the Fokker about, making sure there were no enemy planes creeping up on us. The British got up at the same time as we did.

It had become easier to find your way about. This, of course, we did by use of a map and our eyes, looking out at the ground below from our cockpits. The problem before had been that war alters the landscape: something confidently predicted to be there on the old peacetime map – like a tower, an orchard, a wood, a village or a small town – might simply have vanished. You could be flying in the correct place all right, but you were flying over shell-cratered mud that had obliterated the whole thing, covered it in pools of stinking water and nameless slime, done it up like the devil's Christmas present in ribbons of rusting barbed wire, decorated with rotting men. But now, as the sun crept up and illuminated the land below, it sent long shadows marching across the meadows from the trees. Cows ran in panic as you came down low. Roads were marked clear and the rivers shone clean.

We had been going backwards towards Germany for months.

The sun lit my scarlet *Jasta* leader's streamers standing out taut from the struts between the planes. Ahead, the road was wrinkled green, moving like the sea at altitude. The meadows

were full of brown tents, lorries, dumps of shells, tanks.
Whoomph.
Whoomphwhoomphwhoomph.
White clouds slapping us, the smooth air suddenly rough.

I checked the map and photograph one last time. There it was, the church tower, there the river and bridge, there the road leading towards us, with the British coming down it, there their camp and arms-dump, there the guns that were trying to kill me.

I put the nose down, steeper and steeper, the wind starting to howl in the wires, screaming at me, the ground getting larger and larger, trees, men running, guns firing, prickles of light all aimed at me.

Whoomphwhoomph.

Out of the corner of my eye, a sudden heap of blazing rubbish tumbling down out of the sky.

I picked out some vehicles – tanks, yes, tanks. Great dirty green boxes abristle with guns. I kicked rudder, skidding into line, coming back on the stick, the centrifugal forces pushing me into the hard seat. They vanished under the front of the plane and I pulled the lever once, twice, three times, the Fokker jumping as it lost its load, and I was whizzing over their heads, the guns so close they crackled and snapped in my ears. And behind me, the crumping roar of the bombs going off. Twisting my head round, I saw a tank rising up, clear of the ground, an Albatross smashing into some tents, a ball of scarlet-centred smoke.

I was over the road. Men. Vehicles, horses and carts. I went down it, weaving, firing bursts from the machine-guns, the Fokker rocking and bumping in the turbulence from the wind swirling through the trees. Men tumbling like the toys I'd played with as a boy. A sudden ripping through the plane, fabric streaming. Back on the stick, full power, going for the sky.

Camels.

Small, short, chocolate devils. They had altitude on me, they were between me and home. I twisted in my seat looking for help, but behind there was just streaming black and grey smoke, the glow of fires. The smoke was standing out, fanned by the November wind.

I clung to my climb as the Camels circled like deadly, watchful buzzards ahead and above, black against the sun. I wanted as much height as possible. I might be able to dive and run if I could escape their gauntlet. The linen was tearing where the machine-gun bullets had hit the planes; it was poor stuff – you wouldn't use it to sack up chicken feed, let alone clothe a scout. But it was all we had.

Down below, the river gleamed like polished silver – I would have much preferred to have been down there fishing. I put such thoughts away as I gained as much height as I could before the waiting Camels tried to slaughter me. The torn linen was letting in the wind, ballooning the fabric. It was tearing away in strips, flapping uselessly from the trailing edge of the plane.

About two thousand metres. Here they come.

A curling demon. Bastard. Fucking bastard. A vertical turn, the planes shuddering, and he shot by. I tried to get my sight on him but he snap-turned away, like only the Camel could.

Ratatata.

Another, diving down from altitude. I saw his tracer and kicked rudder, trying to keep out.

Ratatata.

Sudden ripping through the planes. A terrific burning in my leg, something screaming about in the cockpit with me, a mad bird, smashing my instruments. Glass, bits of leather in my nostrils.

A Camel.

Smack in front. I squeezed the triggers desperately and sudden oil sprayed from him.

Ratatata.

Full stick back, right into my stomach; full left rudder and the Fokker reared up like a horse; left planes dipping, right sweeping over, stick over to help it. A Camel whizzing under me, the pilot staring right into my eyes, half-rolling, snapping round so fast with his rotary torque. The Fokker spinning, the world going round and round, the Camel with me, diving round in a spiral with me, *ratatata, ratatata*, I'm going to die.

There he is. Full right rudder, stick all the way forward, gripping on to the dashboard with my left hand, heaving it out of the spin, the centrifuge slamming me against the coaming; blood in my nose, a darkness in front, firing, the scent of the guns.

Down to eight hundred metres. No idea where the lines

are now. Left, right. A half-loop, the Fokker shuddering. Bits flying from the plane, things screeching in the fuselage, Camels everywhere – above, below, behind, at the side. *Ratatata*, my boots slipping on the pedals, blood.

Something hit the Fokker so hard that the stick struck my hand like a whip. There was a screaming of broken steel from the engine, a sudden howl of runaway pistons, a tremendous bang as parts broke inside, oil lacerating my face, boiling hot.

Sudden silence, just the moaning of the wind in the spars, whining in the rigging, the throaty engines of the Camels somewhere about me.

Gasoline.

Witches' water, Hell-brew, infernal liquid.

It was harsh and pungent in my nostrils. I could see it streaming across the engine cover in front of me, behind the clacking, uselessly whirling propeller.

The ground, where was the ground?

There it was, green below. The Camels were clustering about me, watching the wreck. Smoke was streaming from somewhere, gushing through the cockpit. Frantic fingers fumbling in the gauntlets, scrabbling at the wide belt.

It came loose, and I stood up, out of the fuming oil.

Whooomph.

The gasoline exploded. A ball of fire enveloped me.

I stood high, the world spread about me below, and I jumped.

The air blasted me, tumbled me over, the world whirling about me. Its cold blast blew into my mouth and out of my nose. It tore off my goggles, it ripped my helmet from my head. It spun me over and over, my flapping arms reaching for the strap that whipped and stung at my neck.

There it was. I heaved, and it came loose. For an eternal moment, I plunged towards the green world that reached out for me, and then suddenly something punched me in the stomach, whipped my shoulders back like a schoolmaster, slapped me across the sky like a shuttlecock.

The breath rasped in my throat, and I hung like a dying chicken from the plaited silk cords of my parachute. It billowed white and round and beautiful above me, and I drifted like a giant dandelion seed across the sky.

The Camels whirled about me, one after the other. They waved, and I waved back, and then they were gone, leaving only the lingering scent of castor oil in the air.

One of my boots had come off. My foot was cold. I looked down and it shone pale, splashed with sticky, congealing blood.

The world was getting bigger. A field, some trees, the river. Troops looking up at me. I was travelling sideways as well as down. The wind. I could see it, sweeping a polished sheen on the grass, bending the trees.

I hung on to the straps that were fixed to the silk cords. I was coming down at a great rate. It was like jumping off a haystack as a boy, but nothing soft to –

Whump.

Grass and dirt in my nostrils. Suddenly on my hands and knees. Voices not far away, shouting. I pushed myself up, and suddenly, something yanked me off my feet, dragging me across the meadow. It was like a runaway horse, pulling me with it whether I wished or not. For a moment it slowed, and I saw that the wind had a hold of my parachute, was playing with it like a kitten, filling it with air. It took in a deep breath and the silk ballooned mightily, whipping me from my feet again as I struggled desperately with the fastenings. It dragged me down the hill, across something wet. Reeds slapped me in the face, and something pushed me under the water.

I came up like a drowning cat. My boot was heavy, filled with water. It dragged me down; frantically, blood drumming in my head, the breath like steel bands about my chest, I pulled at it, working in glue. It came free and there was sudden air.

There were voices. Something tugging at my shoulders, hands pulling me to shore, laying me out like a flounder. I arched, spewing up river water, gasping and rasping.

Voices, rough and coarse and wonderful.

'What you got then, Dusty?'

'Fuckin' 'un, isn't it?'

'Fuckin' 'un? Frow 'im back.'

'Don't be like that. I'll 'ave 'is parachute. Lovely bit of silk, that is. The missus can make French drawers out of that.'

I felt efficient, callused hands stripping me of the harness. I was looking at the sun.

Somehow, it was darker. We bumped along a road. I was lying on the floor of an ambulance. A Tommy with his arm in a sling was sitting along the side, smoking a cigarette. He saw me looking at him.

'Hello, Fritz.'

'Hello.'

'War's over then,' he said cheerfully.

'I suppose so. I am a prisoner.'

'No, mate. War's over. We won.'

I looked at him, bewildered. 'What do you mean, you won?'

'We won, you came second,' he said happily, 'and I'm back to Blighty. Honest, ceasefire in two days.'

'Ceasefire . . .'

The Tommy produced a small mouth-organ and began to play a tune. In between snatches, he would sing a verse.

'Why should 'e wiv all 'is money
Mix wiv 'er wot is so pore?
Bringing shime on 'er relitions,
Makin' 'er into an 'ore.'

He blew on his harmonica, and some of the others bumping down the road took it up. Ceasefire . . . I heard the words as though drunk.

'Nah she's standing in the gutter,
Sellin' matches penny-a-box,
While 'e's riding in 'is carriage
With an awful dose of pox.'

Ceasefire. I fumbled at my throat. Sharp-edged and cold, there was the Blue Max. What the hell would I do now? I had been trained for only one thing – to kill. I had only one hope – to live. My horizon had been the next day's patrol. *Ceasefire.* I was eighteen years old. The horizon had moved and I was staring out into something I had never seen. Ceasefire.

The Tommies' voices swelled up in chorus.

'See 'im in the grand theayter,
Eating apples in the pit:
While the poor girl what 'e ruined
Wanders round through mud and shit.'

I stared up at the swaying white roof of the ambulance. *Ceasefire.*

Berlin, December 1918

I got off the S-Bahn at Alexanderplatz and walked out to Unter den Linden as the train rattled away behind me. At least it was still running, that at least was normal. God knew, little else was. I still had my flying-coat, long and lined with sheepskin, and some British boots the Tommies had given me.

Hilde was gone, the little room bare and airy under its skylight. We'd been going backwards for months. I hadn't had a letter since June. On the wall was a scarlet clenched fist that gripped, powerfully, a hammer and a sickle, done in her new style.

There were shops open, taxicabs sputtering along powered by some sort of charcoal. Streetcars clanked by and thin, half-starved horses dragged old *Droschken* over the dirty packed snow. From somewhere in the city I could hear rifle fire, the occasional crump of a grenade. Still, there were people about, shoppers and peddlers selling crude Christmas decorations and hot chestnuts.

I was hungry, but what little money I had I knew I must keep. The Tommies, with a generosity born of victory, had given me a round gold tin of cigarettes, and I decided that soon I would let myself have one to dampen down the pain.

Down near the Schloss, the royal palace, I saw a procession of factory workers go by, women amongst them. They carried red banners and were chanting some slogan I couldn't hear. It was cold and the street-cleaners hadn't been out. I stumbled over piles of snow, my wounded leg giving out twinges of protest.

The Schloss was dark, with what appeared to be a red blanket flying from its flagpole. Some dirty-looking men in unkempt sailors' uniforms stood outside, rifles slung from their shoulders, muzzles pointing down. The Kaiser would not have been pleased, but he was not there. He was in exile in Holland and was not expected to see his palace ever again, sailors or no sailors. Crudely-lettered paintwork over the Greek temple of a guardroom proclaimed it to be the home of the People's Naval Division, whatever that was.

I was completely bewildered. I had that feeling of walking upstairs in the dark and finding the next step not there. *What was going on?*

There's a new world coming, Hans. I could hear Hilde's

passionate voice. I could feel her, too, warm and smooth under the sheet. It sent a tingle over me under my sheepskin coat. Where was Hilde? And was this it, this mess, dirt and hunger and slogan-chanting rabble – no order, no nothing? If it was, I wanted no part of it.

I saw a man staring at the Schloss and its ill-disciplined sailors at about the same time as he saw me. He was wearing a field-grey overcoat and a steel helmet, the coal-scuttle type the Tommies mockingly called 'Jerries'. An MP 18 machine-pistol was slung about him and he was peering intently at the palace. He caught sight of me, and just as he was going to look away again he paused, taking a second glance. A hesitant smile came on to his face. '*Herr Flieger*?' he asked uncertainly.

'Hauptmann Wolff,' I said, glad to use my proper title.

'*Ja, ja*,' he said beaming. 'You remember me? I am Huber, Rudolf Huber. You crashed near our trench. Adolf the *Meldegänger* brought you in – you fought with us when the Tommies attacked.'

I beamed. 'That's right, Rudolf. That's me.'

God, it was good to find somebody I knew in this blasted mad house.

'What are you doing here, Hauptmann?'

'I'm not sure I know! I was shot down, you see, right before the ceasefire. The Tommies took me to the hospital – I was wounded in the thigh – and when I was better they let me loose. I've made my way here but I can't find anyone I know. My unit's been disbanded, I don't know what the hell I'm doing, and the whole place is in a mess.'

He nodded vehemently. 'That's right, Hauptmann. That's what you get when a bunch of Jews and Bolsheviks and Spartacists stab decent fighting men in the back.'

'Spartacists?'

'Jewish filth,' he explained. 'People like that whore Rosa Luxemburg, and Lenin's agent, Liebknecht. Agitators. The rear are all about us here – the rear. They can't stand up to them, they're planning revolution. Look down there at the old Imperial Embassy. Covered in red flags now. Calls itself the Soviet Embassy now. Well, we're having no Soviets here, let me tell you. We're the *Frontkämpfers* – we'll put a stop to that.'

I knew what he meant. I was one myself. For us, the front fighters, it was all either the front or the rear. We at the front got killed, burned, maimed, went mad. Those at the rear were the civilians, those who'd made so much money in the war factories, never got near a bullet. The fat men in their Mercedes laundalettes, and soft, scented women, the bankers and financiers, the pacifists who'd wanted to stop us winning the war, the 'November criminals' who'd signed the armistice.

On his steel helmet was a strange kind of hooked cross, daubed on with black paint. 'What's that?'

'Swastika,' he said proudly. 'We're the Freikorps. All *Frontkämpfers*, Hauptmann. Some of us put on the swastika to distinguish us from the regular army. We're the ones who're sorting out this mess.' He looked at me intently, a thought having come into his mind. 'Here, what are you going to do now?'

'I don't know,' I said frankly. 'I'd join my unit but as I said it's disbanded.'

'That's settled, then. Join us. I saw you in the trench – you know how to fight. Come on. There's decent food and a clean barracks. You hungry? Course you are. Here, I'll buy you a beer first.'

I needed a home to go to. A unit. 'Very good,' I said.

He led me down Leipziger Strasse. The place was total bedlam. Drunks and beggars and swindlers mingled with prostitutes both male and female. Young pickpockets slipped through the crowds, and I put my hand firmly over my purse. The air was filled with a strange, not unattractive, caterwauling music.

'What's that?' I asked. I noticed that all the civilians gave way to the tough young soldier in his steel helmet.

'Jazz,' Huber said in disgust. He spat on the filthy snow. 'Amerikaner jazz. That's what we've got for being stabbed in the back by the November criminals. Filthy nigger music and Jews. But we'll sort them out soon enough, you'll see.'

We went into a bar and Huber quickly had a couple of tall steins of dark beer in front of us.

'Now that's better,' I said appreciatively. Some black bread and fine sausage arrived, and I ate eagerly. Huber watched me approvingly. There were young women in the bar and I saw with amazement how skirt lengths had risen. You could see their ankles! Some of them were showing off flesh-coloured stockings. Maybe the new world had something to recommend it after all.

I gave Huber one of my British cigarettes from my round gold tin, and he breathed in the smoke appreciatively.

'Not bad,' he said. 'Not bad at all. The Tommies know a thing or two.' He leaned forward. 'You know,' he said conspiratorially, 'I never hated the Tommies. They were *Frontkämpfers* like us. What we should have done is got together and killed all those bastards at the rear. But here, let me tell you, in our mess you can have beer like this, food too, that's free – two hundred grams of meat, seventy-five of butter, a quarter litre of wine, all free – plus cigarettes for just about nothing. It's a good place to be while we're sorting things out. Pay, too. Forty marks a day. But the best thing of all, Hauptmann; good comrades, men you can trust. Fighting men like you and me.'

A pretty girl went by, showing her calves. Huber looked at her legs, suddenly angry.

'Whore,' he muttered. 'Can you imagine your sister going about like that? Your mother?' Then he brightened. 'The Spartacists, they have Red women in their ranks. Red whores,' he confided. 'You've joined us just in time. They're sending us in next week.' He looked at the legs of the young woman and grinned savagely.

'We'll show them,' he promised. 'We'll teach them to stab us in the back.'

The big imperial room stank of cordite. Dirty black dust drifted through in the icy breeze from the tall shattered windows. My nostrils wrinkled. For a second I was in the air, looking for the Tommies in their SE5s and Camels. It was *our* shells, our ack-ack. The Freikorps knew how to rip up an enemy position: you shelled it first.

Now the room where the Kaiser had received ambassadors, where he had sat on his military saddle at his desk in full cavalry fig, even to sign his correspondence, all was ruined by a single 77mm shell, one whizz-bang, one pip-squeak.

I paused, rifle in hand, trying to get my bearings. I was no blasted infantryman, whatever Huber might have thought.

This filthy dust-laden air made it difficult to breathe. I wished I was in a Fokker. From above there was a short savage crump as a stick-bomb went off. A whole section of ceiling blew off above me, showering me in gilt plaster. The chandelier swayed dangerously and I ran for the tall doors, askew on their hinges. The *Freikorpskämpfer* were way ahead of me. They knew how to slaughter the enemy in their dug-outs; you massacred them while they were dazed by the shelling, you winkled them out of their hideyholes with a nice grenade or two.

A rising scream of terror made me jump back in the grand hall, with its huge winding stair. A young man in the uniform of the Imperial German Navy landed where I had stood with a noise like a sack of wet sand falling off a building-site scaffold. Blood spattered my boots. He was wearing a non-regulation issue scarlet neckerchief. A Bolshevik, a Spartacist.

The *Freikorpskämpfer* knew how to deal with the enemy.

I took a deep breath of dusty, stinking, chemical air and made a run for it up the grand stairway, where counts, barons and duchesses had paraded in their finery. A gigantic portrait of some archduke hung gashed and adrift on the wall.

On the first floor there was a rattle and rip of machine-pistol fire, another crump of a stick-bomb. A set of tall doors slammed back on their hinges, dust and smoke belched into the high, domed corridor. Something squealed like a dying pig.

I heard a yelling from the room at the head of the stairs. I poked my head round and saw Huber and some others quickly ripping through chests of drawers and cupboards, expertly grabbing anything of value, any silver, any silks, lace – anything that could be stuffed away fast.

'Come on!' he yelled, stuffing a handful of sheer stockings inside his jacket. 'Plenty for all here.'

He yanked open a cupboard. There was a sudden high-pitched scream, a noise of bubbling hate, a flash of steel. Something went at him like a ferret on a rabbit, something blue and red and black. But you couldn't do that to someone like Huber; he'd been there before you – a lot of people had tried to kill Huber and had failed. He swayed back away from the attack and his rifle swept up, smashing the knife from the sailor's hand, reversing to smash into the stomach, and a small blue figure tumbled retching to the carpet.

The sailor had long black hair.

Huber reached down in savage, joyful triumph, and heaved the girl up by her hair with one powerful hand. A scarlet scarf was tied round her slim neck. 'Well well well!' he jeered. 'What have we here? A bolshie whore! A fucking bolshie whore, lads!'

Breath rasped into the girl's chest in a moan. Blood was running down her chin from her mouth. She spat it all over Huber. '*Schwein*. Fucking bastard *Schwein*!' she yelled. The others had her arms twisted up behind her back, laughing, and she screamed in agony as they snapped her light bones.

'You've got a dirty mouth,' Huber said seriously. '*Dreckig*, it is. A filthy Jewish whore's mouth.'

I opened my mouth to shout, for just a second. I knew the girl. I shut it with a snap. If Erna was here, so was Hilde.

For Huber, life was clear. There were those of the front, and those of the rear. The ones of the rear had sent the ones of the front off to be killed, had betrayed them, let them down, were traitors, and now the *Frontkämpfers* had been told, had been given permission, had been ordered, to redress the balance.

Huber had his fighting knife in his hand, and he hit her across her pretty young face with it. Blood bubbled up through smashed teeth. She tried to cradle her face in her broken hands, and Huber stabbed her between her thighs. She collapsed, screaming, and they bayoneted her, one after the other, in a leisurely fashion, until she stopped jerking and whimpering, just a small heap of sodden blue serge on the cream carpet.

I went on up the stairs. It was silent up there, just the sounds of the *Freikorpskämpfers* smashing things and looting below. Perhaps I knew what I was looking for. I pushed a door open with my boot, probing the room inside with the muzzle of the Mauser. Huber would have berated me for a fool. He knew how to clear a room; you chucked a grenade in it first.

'Hilde?' I called softly. But the room was empty. Erna. Hilde's friend. Small, fiery, anarchic. And dead. Again, more urgently, for they would be coming: '*Hilde?*'

Hilde would go up high. She was an artist, a person of attics and skylights. We were birds, both of us, lovers of high places, of the air.

Another room, a bedroom of some kind. The valuables were all below, they had slowed the progress of the soldiers. But they would be here, given time. *'Hilde! It's Hans.'*

A door creaked. A pistol pointed at me, in front of a small face, screwed up tight with fear and determination. *'What are you doing here?'*

'Never mind,' I hissed. From below, the sounds of destruction and revelry were growing in equal parts. They'd found the Imperial cellars. 'They're killing everyone. They've just killed Erna.'

'We were separated ... when the shelling started.' She was in the stupid sailor's uniform, pea jacket, trousers, striped vest, scarlet scarf.

I shoved her back into the room. A wardrobe, some simple dresses. I grabbed one, threw it on the bed. 'Quickly,' I ordered. 'Get that on.'

'I cannot –'

I yanked her pea jacket from her back in fury. *'There is no time,'* I snarled. 'You can be a traitor to the revolution later.'

She scrambled out of her clothes in a flurry of long legs, delicate arms, round breasts. Huber and his comrades would have enjoyed themselves, hacking her to bits.

I dragged the dress up over her shoulders, did up the pearl buttons, kicked the revolutionary outfit under the bed. The dress was a cream linen which dropped to her ankles.

We came down the stairway. I saw Huber leaning against a bust of the old Kaiser. His eyes were glazed with sated lust but he wasn't drunk. His pack bulged with loot.

'The bastards took hostages,' I proclaimed. 'I found this fine young lady tied up upstairs, a prisoner.'

'The bastards...' he breathed, and stood aside to let Hilde by. Dead sailors and Spartacists littered the corridors. Tears glittered in her eyes and, as we went out, ran silently down her cheeks. I picked her up and carried her away across the snow, out over the *Schlossbrücke*. The artillerymen were standing beside their 77mm field-guns in the Alexanderplatz.

'I'll get you some shoes,' I promised. It was cold, freezing, the sweat and fear congealing like ice on us. 'God, what were you doing there?' I demanded. Through the shattered windows somebody the *Freikorpskämpfers* were killing screamed a horrid, bubbling yell.

'We could not but be a part of it,' she said, suddenly passionate. 'The old order is dead. There is a new world coming. We were making it. I saw it.'

'It's here,' I said. 'This is it.'

Munich, May 1920

Goggles, again. But no glass in them. Steel rims through which I peered out at the enemy as intently as ever I had looked for Tommies in SE5s. A combat was a combat, even if nobody was actually to get killed.

Steel spectacles, padded canvas waistcoats, long, slender sabres of shimmering steel, sharp as razors. A referee, a doctor, a second. Only certain blows allowed. Not two heavy machine-guns, no quarter and anything goes.

The long hall was cold. Shreds of hair and dried blood spattered the ceiling; this had been going on a long time. At a trestle table the surgeon had unpacked his bottles of antiseptic, his needle and thread.

'*Silentium!*' the umpire called.

My feet were well set on the sawdust-covered floor.

'*Los!*'

My opponent and I, we lunged forward and back, free hands clasped in our belts behind us, our blades clashing, violent vibrations shivering down into the cupped guard, stinging our sword hands. The harsh commands of the referee, the heavy breathing in the ancient duelling-room.

'*Halt!*'

I put down the point of my sabre. The doctor stepped forward, checked the blood forming from a line of pinpricks beginning to trickle together and down the temple of my opponent, a young man with a near-shaven head like a pink, furry apple, of the Alemanians fraternity.

'*Alles in Ordnung! Los!*'

Foot forward, the clash of steel, back and lunge.

Bang.

I remembered that. The *noise* it makes when you are hit. Blood now trickled down *my* face, like a warm splash of rain, tickling.

Back and forth, gasping for air, a flicker of sparks as the blades clash, intent eyes, *bang*, back and forth ...

The bout was finally halted. Two rounds. Blood spotted the fresh sawdust on the old dark boards. It spattered our canvas waistcoats, it ran down our cheeks and necks onto our collars in rivulets, it hung in shivering gory stalactites from our chins.

We bowed formally, the young furry pink apple and I, with our respective seconds, and went off to be stitched. My opponent sat down on the wooden chair as his second, a slight, bespectacled young man called Himmler, collected his accoutrements. Pink Apple bent over a tureen of steaming water as his wounds were cleaned, and it began to turn the colour of oxblood soup. He sat rock steady as the military doctor sewed up with a heavy needle the gashes I had inflicted, the kind of thing a saddler uses. He passed the needle to and fro as if sewing canvas and the boy uttered not a sound.

'*Selbstbeherrschung!*' Himmler cried approvingly. It was. Iron self-mastery was what it was a test of, more than just a contest of technical skill. An ordeal to be withstood without flinching, that was the point.

'We are the descendants of the Teuton knights,' Himmler commented. Blood was still running slowly down my face and along my neck, down onto my collar. 'Do we not search for the truth as they did?' he asked me, peering into my eyes. The wounds hurt fearsomely, and I assumed that this prattling idiot was but a part of the test of self-control.

'That may be so,' I said.

'Have you read Hesse?' he enquired as I sat down to be stitched myself. '*Siddhartha*? I was very struck by the Ferryman's sense of will and duty. Detach oneself from suffering and do what is right.'

I too sat as still as agate as the needle sliced in and out of my skin, the doctor pushing each time to get its bluntening point through, like puncturing a tomato. The tugging of the expert knot that drew the lips of the wound together, a buzzing of rage from the flesh, recovering from the stunning of the blow.

'I think it not unlikely that such as we are reincarnations of the ancient knights,' he went on. 'We are but mortals, painful examples of all that is transitory. Yet none of us die; we only change, are reborn with a new face, only time stands between one face and another...'

'*Selbstbeherrschung* ...' Himmler said again, with quiet, almost envious approval. I had noticed that his face was free from scars.

Well, to be sure. I was a man who held the Blue Max. I stood up, thanked my opponent formally, and he me, for having slightly maimed each other with each other's approval.

Himmler paused for a moment. 'You will be off to the *Gasthaus*?' he enquired. Each fraternity or brotherhood had its own beer-cellar or inn, the *Kneipe*, and distinctive coloured cap and ribbons, much as we had decorated our scouts. There, dark beer was consumed by the stein until it veritably leaked from the pores, and the entire brotherhood shook the whole *Kneipe* in song, roaring out the old verses of knights and giants, of chivalry and wine and honour, the songs that had been sung by Germans for centuries. Blond titans, towering white castles, misty forests, blazing valhallas, Teutonic knights, ivory-skinned women with eyes of ice blue...

'Tomorrow,' I said. 'Tonight I am invited to a military reunion.'

'Ah, *ja*?' he said, with envious interest. 'Your flying *Gruppe*?'

'Not the *Jasta*,' I said. 'Some soldiers of the 16th Bavarian Regiment. Near the end of the war I crashed close to their part of the line and I was involved in fighting with them. They have invited me to join them.'

He bowed in approval. 'From a duel to a reunion. It is very fitting. Are you interested in reincarnation? I am. I have a most interesting book in my room I could lend you. *Das zweite Gesicht, Second Sight*. It gives a most interesting account of such truths as astrology, hypnotism, telepathy and spiritualism. I am thinking of gathering together a small group to discuss –'

'I have to go,' I said politely. My wounds were buzzing.

'Should you change your mind...'

'Perhaps another time.'

Selbstbeherrschung indeed, to have to listen to that kind of crap, I thought, and I stepped out for the inn.

Hoeppner saw me come in and beckoned me to sit by him in the wooden-framed booth. He stopped a waiter and a lid-topped, heroically-decorated tall stein of beer was almost instantly forthcoming. He peered with disbelief at my dressed wounds. '*Duelling?*' he asked.

I shrugged. 'It is important to know, from time to time, the state of one's nerve.' I explained.

He nodded. 'I can understand that, I suppose, in a warrior.' He glanced calculatingly at me. The former line Leutnant, the commander of the sector into which I had dropped, was wearing a good suit; he was cleanly-shaven, well-fed.

'I am training as an engineer,' I protested.

'I saw you in the trench,' he said. 'You are a warrior. You dropped from the sky into a battle on the ground. You fought like a wild animal. It's in your nature. I heard – somebody told me – that you were with the Freikorps for a while.'

'Only a while,' I said, putting back some of the marvellous, nutty beer. 'I was desperate for somewhere to go, when the war stopped. My unit was disbanded. I bumped into Huber – you know, one of your former soldiers.'

'*Ja*, I know Huber. You could have stayed,' he pointed out, looking to know. 'The Freikorps still exists. Huber is still there.'

'Their concept of . . . life was not perhaps mine,' I said.

'Very tactfully put,' he said quietly. He looked around. 'But to the taste of many in these parts, I regret.'

'That matters to you?' I asked curiously. 'What are you doing these days?'

'I'm in government,' he said. 'My family are known in these parts. For my sins I represent Weimar here.'

'My girl is in Weimar,' I commented. 'Studying art at the Bauhaus.'

'The Bauhaus?' he said, his eyebrows rising. He laughed. 'I can see why you didn't stay with the Freikorps. The Bauhaus is everything they hate. The new culture, *die neue Sachlichkeit* . . .' He looked around again. 'These are bad times for men of reason, Hans. Can I include you in that? *Ja*? Here am I, one who represents the government of Weimar, a social-democrat government, a republic – a *democracy*. Born in defeat and revolution, tainted by both, and yet ... and yet, the only way forward. But loathed by many. On the right, the old ruling class, the nobility, the officer corps of the army and navy – you were a *Flieger*, Hans! – the judges, the top civil servants, the big businessmen. On the left, the communist leaders, the radicalised *Lumpenproletariat*. Marxist fighting bands every bit as violent as the Freikorps. Both despise us! The right yearns for a restoration of monarchy. The left longs for a dictatorship of the people on the Soviet model. What have we to offer but a system of what seems to them some sort of messy compromise. But this is democracy!'

I steadily consumed my tall stein as I listened, about which lusciously painted grapevines curled in profusion, the fine beer soothing my wounds.

'For the time being, the right co-operates with us when they must, to maintain order. Give us a communist uprising and the army and Freikorps will put it down, always with the most extreme violence on both sides. There are many who are becoming used to warfare on the streets ... I tell you, Hans, it's easy to be a *Schwarzseher* these days, see nothing but gloom.'

'You think the republic will last?' I asked. 'People seem to be hankering after a leader, someone who can get us out of all this mess.'

'A hero?' Hoeppner said quizzically. 'Shall Frederick Barbarossa awake from under the Thuringian mountains?'

'What about Italy? That Mussolini looks popular. They say he may take over.'

'A new Caesar? Shall he be surrounded by cohorts of steely men, as Spengler thinks? Those who look not for personal gain but to service? And shall it be an age of cruel wars in which civilisations shall rise and fall, as so many feel?' He shook his head. 'It will simply be a new dark age, Hans. And yes, the republic *must* survive, it *will* survive. You want to know why?'

'Tell me.'

'Democratic countries don't make war on each other. Dictatorships, of the people or otherwise, do.' He collared a waiter, summoned up more beer, stared intently at me. 'It mustn't happen,' he said with certainty. 'We can get out of this.'

The beer came, we toasted each other again.

'How long are you at the university?' he asked casually.

'Another two years.'

'The Freikorps, you left without rancour?' he asked artlessly.

'To be sure. I am not one who deserts.'

'He's here tonight. Huber. He's hanging about with Korporal Hitler.'

'The *Meldegänger?*'

'The runner. He's out of the army now – gone into politics! The little rat's an agitator.'

The *Bierkeller* was noisy, but for some reason Hoeppner had dropped his voice. I leaned forward to hear him better.

'He's taken over some rag-bag group of mangy dogs. God, Bavaria crawls with them! This little band of sweaty, rabid creatures and that one . . . Sometimes you feel like taking a bath when you get home, to get the invective off . . .' Hoeppner sank a portion of his beer.

'Who are they?' I enquired. 'This particular lot?'

'The German Workers Party. No, hold on, the National Socialist German Workers Party. They call themselves the Nazis. Apparently the little bastard can speak! – If you like bile and abuse, and they do. The worst sort come and hear him.'

'What is it you want from me?' I asked, and he smiled, gratefully.

'Just keep an ear to the ground. Tell me what's going on among the radicalised sort, out at the university. You're a war hero, a duellist too; you were in the Freikorps. You have respect.' He drank some more beer. 'I have to *know.*' he said quietly. 'I have to know what's happening.'

I stood up, drained my stein. 'I call by here of a Friday night,' I suggested. 'You can usually find me here then.'

He smiled in acknowledgement. 'See you then.'

Moving about in the smoky air I came across Huber. He was delighted to see me, flinging a comradely arm about my shoulders while berating me for leaving the Freikorps. 'We smashed up plenty more of those filthy bastards,' he assured me. He peered at my dressed wounds. 'Ah, but you're an officer,' he said, as though this somehow explained my behaviour.

I saw that he had an armband on over a brown shirt, some remnant of tropical army issue. The armband was a kind of red and black thing. 'You're wearing your *Hakenkreuz*,' I said, peering at the hooked cross.

'The swastika!' he said proudly. '*Ja*. I'm with Adolf now.'

'Adolf?'

'You remember – Hitler, who was Korporal with us.'

'The *Meldegänger*?'

'That's it. He doesn't run with orders any more. He *gives* them.'

'Ah, *ja*, I've heard about it. Doesn't he lead a party?'

'*The* party,' Huber said proudly. 'We're Nazis. We're getting Germany back on the right road. We'll smash all these filthy bastards. All these enemies within the *Volk*! Fucking socialists, commies, Jews – all those who betrayed us to the French. You see if we don't.'

The knuckles that gripped his stein were cut and bruised. 'Looks like you've started already,' I said, half-joking.

'We have!' Huber yelled happily. 'Me, I'm in the *Sturmabteilung*.'

'The Storm Squad?'

'That's us! All *alte Frontschwein* like me. God, it's good, Hauptmann. You should be with us. We're there when Adolf makes his speeches – you should hear him tear into all those filthy bastards – and if any of them object we give 'em the old one-two, smash their fucking teeth in, we do. Then it's out on to the street in the lorries and cars, and we know where the Marxist cellars and halls are: it's out with the staves and clubs, down the stairs like we used to at the front – fast as you can. Some of the Marxists, they're old front-swine like us, and we give each other what for with the clubs and broken bottles and chairs – no quarter asked and none given, let me tell you. God it's good – all blood and broken bones and screaming people – we know how to clear up filth, we do. That fucking bolshie Jew Lenin says terror is a weapon of the revolution and by God we give 'em terror!'

He was breathing hard as though he was in there doing it, his breeches bulging with joy, his eyes staring into his memories.

'God, I love smashing them up,' he whispered. 'It's like fucking a whore but better.'

Then he came back, and grinned at me with his savage, insane happiness.

'And you know what, Hauptmann? Those Marxist *Frontschwein*, when we beat them, they're the first ones to join us the next day! It's what Adolf says, you see.' He paused, an uneducated man getting his facts straight. '*Ja*. Adolf, he teaches us too. We're political warriors, we are. How has man become great? Through *kampf*, through struggle. Whatever goal man has reached is because of his originality, plus his brutality.' His seamed, scarred young face split in a beam. 'That's us! And this. He who wants to live must fight, and he who does not want to fight in this world where eternal struggle is the law of life has no right to exist.' He delivered the words like tasty morsels, enjoying their flavour. Then he peered at me. 'You remember Adolf, don't you?'

'Only briefly,' I said dryly. 'I was covered in mud and fighting the Tommies most of the time we were together.'

He roared with laughter. '*Ja*, great times! Here, why don't you come see him some time? Look, we're going over to Austria next month, quite a lot of us.'

'Why Austria?'

He grinned. 'We're going to listen to Wagner, like the rich folk.'

Werfenstein Castle, Austria

They were a peculiar lot to see at a production of *Siegfried*. You could tell by the broken noses, the scarred faces, the rough hands more ready to grip a stave and a club than a pair of opera-glasses, by the concealed bafflement as to what was going on, that they were, indeed, much more at home breaking heads and pouring beer into their bellies than imbibing culture.

They had sat, however, as quiet as mice, as inoffensive as church-goers. In the next decade I saw them regularly, at the great festival of Bayreuth – those that survived the night of the long knives, of course. Those that did, you could see them at Bayreuth in their SS uniforms, and they were there for the same reason that they had come to Austria to listen to Wagner in full bellow: because the little man in the *Lederhosen*, red-and-blue checked shirt, blue jacket bagging over his bony frame, wanted to be there. And where he wanted to be, so did they.

It was something that puzzled me, as I too let the big yowling voices and tremendous crashing music break over me: the power this vaguely starved-looking individual with the protruberant blue eyes was exerting over the others. A corporal. And yet the sergeant-major, whom I remembered too, a tough one-armed fellow called Amman, was deferential. There was some other fellow there, one with mad eyes and a neck that flowed over his collar like melted candle grease, called von Liebenfels, who had the wet lips of a pornographer. When I learned he was a defrocked monk I wasn't surprised. I overheard him talking of racial purity to Huber, who clearly didn't understand more than one word in three. Huber and the other *Frontkämpfers* I could fathom in their devotion to Hitler, but there was also a tough, scar-faced officer veteran, a short, big-bellied soldier-of-fortune type with the air of the bugger about him – Röhm, his name was – and he, too, paid attention to the little man. Only Göring seemed in command of himself, quite at ease in the grand operahouse, but then Göring moved in high society without problem. Which was in itself strange. What was my former senior officer, commander of the *JG Richtofen* doing there, with types such as Huber and Korporal Hitler?

I wondered why. When it was over, and the Nazis – it was a strange word, back then – were back in the fantastic gothic castle they had taken over for the few days they were there, I got an inkling.

He was at home with them, of course, with the simple, rough elements, and they worshipped him as one of their own done good. Done good! Why, how far did a man want to go . . .

Huber had introduced me, or rather, reintroduced me – I had done that the first time by crashing into *Meldegänger* Korporal Hitler's own patch of slime at the front – before the visit to the theatre. He was deferential, that man of bruised knuckles and certain hatreds; he had waited until he was sure that Hitler was free from other preoccupations, standing outide the high gothic architecture, impossibly slim white towers thrusting into the blue sky above us, the Danube swirling icy and strong below.

'Führer,' he said. It was the first time I heard the title. 'Führer, I have a comrade from the front. Hauptmann Wolff, the flieger.'

The pale-blue eyes stared at me, and then he smiled. '*Ja* . . . of course! I found you in the mud . . .'

'You did. I was grateful to have someone who knew the way!'

He peered at my duelling scars, and his face cracked into a kind of smile. The little man had a strange, obsessed look about him – seeing him smile was like watching an underfed doberman become amused. 'Still fighting!' he cried. '*Ja*, me too. I'm fighting for the *Volk*! All we good Germans hounded by all those bastards. Bolsheviks, Jews, Slavs, the November criminals! You and I, we're *Frontkämpfers*, we know how to fight, don't we? We know what we're fighting for, don't we? The *Fronterlebnis* . . .'

The blue eyes were misty, thinking of the past.

'The best time of our lives!' he shouted, and those nearby lifted their heads, wondering what their leader was talking of. 'War is for man what childbirth is for a woman: a time of hardening of the will. From callow youths we become veterans of steel, whom nothing can shock, steely warriors impervious to pity!'

The eyes focused again.

'The war . . .' he said. 'We shall set it all to rights, one day.' He moved on, nodding abruptly. He had no manners to speak of, as you would expect from someone of his rank.

But he left me vaguely uneasy. How had he known about my inability to come to terms with the war? How I had hated and loved it at the same time, how nothing else quite matched up? Nobody had told him that, they couldn't – I didn't tell anyone, not about the dreams, when I was back in the cold sky, the scream of the wires, the gulp of air before falling, the chocolate crosses in the sight, castor oil and blown grass, the rip of the machine-guns.

'What do you think?' a voice said at my elbow. I turned, and it was Göring, grinning sardonically at me. I'd seen him about at the university from time to time. He dabbled at it, and had a rich Swedish wife. His fine Mercedes was parked not far away, and he was dressed in a beautifully cut lounge suit. Somehow he didn't seem that comfortable in it. I remembered from the war that he had always loved a magnificent uniform.

'I don't know,' I said. 'I came to listen to Wagner.'

'You'll have to listen to him too. *Der Korporal*,' he said, drawing on an English Dunhill cigarette. 'Want one?'

'Thanks. What are *you* doing here?'

'Maybe I came for Wagner too. But a man does well to keep his options open. Interesting times, you know. Men like us, we were great ... gods, we were, not so long ago.' He looked thoughtfully down at the rushing silver water. 'Heroes of war have a difficult time of it, when peace comes,' he commented. 'We all have to try to work out our destiny.'

There was a clattering of boots coming down the stone stairway, announcing the arrival of Huber and the other *Frontkämpfers*.

Göring smiled. He seemed amused. 'What will they make of *Siegfried*?' he asked me, with raised eyebrows.

What indeed? But they all sat through it resolutely, because Hitler was there. I shouldn't think they understood a word.

Back at the castle as the sun went down in glory through the gothic spires, they had laid on food and beer. It was good, very good, in times when a lot of old *Frontschwein* were standing on street corners in broken shoes that let the icy rain in, trying to sell matches, watching the profiteers go by in their warm, dry cars. Smoked pork and beef, pickled eggs, fresh bread and salty yellow butter, ten kinds of sausage, hot meatballs spicy and pungent with thyme, a hot beef stew the kind the *Frontkämpfers* would walk that extra kilometre or two for, coming out of the line. There was *Apfelstrudel* like their mothers used to make, cut in great slices from the big plate, and drenched with cream scented with lemon and cinnamon. There was a whole roast pig, golden brown, that had been turned steadily on a spit. It now lay in state on a giant serving dish, and people helped themselves to the crisp crackling and tender meat. All washed down with rich, dark-brown beer and green yellow riesling.

We all ate and drank with a will – all, that is, except the Korporal. He was shovelling back some muck-spaghetti with a vegetable sauce – and drinking water.

As the beer penetrated their minds and they belched and helped themselves to some more, Huber and some of the others round a table in the great wood-and-stone-lined hall were striking up verses of the Freikorps Erhardt Brigade marching-song. I was at the long table where Hitler was getting through his slop, along with such as his bodyguard, Ulrich Graf, a huge, bull-necked young man, who was a butcher and wrestler by trade. He could eat more than anyone I ever saw. Amman, the sergeant-major, was there, eating and drinking, his one arm moving deftly and quickly. Röhm too, his eyes flicking about for the handsome young men. Göring was nearby, a napkin tucked into his collar to protect his fine suit.

The monk, Lanz von Liebenfels, was there too, and when he had swilled enough riesling he began rambling in a high-pitched voice, pausing frequently to wet his lips. I heard some reference to anthropology. Pleasantly numbed by the good food and wine, of which there was not enough about in those days, I vaguely assumed he was talking about monkeys. Then I saw that a change had come over Hitler. Instead of mechanically filling his belly with the gunk in his bowl, he had put down his fork and was listening, his pale face intent. He looked like some formerly inert powered doll to which one has applied electricity. Göring glanced at me as though to remind me that I should, indeed, have to listen to the ex-corporal.

'Anthropology!' Liebenfels yelled squeakily. 'What does that mean to you, eh?'

One of the *Frontkämpfers* nearby let loose a liquid belch. Somebody chuckled. The merriment was instantly cut dead by a single savage glance from Hitler.

'Anthropology,' the former monk said again. 'I'll tell you what it means for us, for us here. *It means the preservation of the European master race by the maintenance of racial purity*!'

Hitler, sitting opposite, gulped like a pig that had swallowed too large a lump of swill, his face suddenly flushed.

'Does a farmer allow his prize herd to breed with inferior beasts?' Liebenfels yelled, his voice suddenly loud, his eyes bulging at us. 'No, no, a thousand times no! What does he do? Does he not take his knife and slice the testicles from those contaminating creatures that would sully and pollute the purity of blood in his herd? Should we be any different? All about we pure Aryans they lurk in the dark places, seeking to pollute the crystal water of our blood pool!' He pushed himself up, leaning forward, his claw-like hands scratching at the table. 'Shall we not extirpate the animal man? Whole classes of the unfit, whole races of the unfit. We must exterminate them and propagate the higher new-man. *Let us wage the race-struggle to the hilt of the castration knife!*'

Hitler jerked to his feet, his eyes bulging, his face flushed red, and the chorus of the Erhardt Brigade was cut dead. Göring put down his fork. 'Struggle is the father of all things!' Hitler screamed. Fragments of unnamed vegetables and spaghetti flew in the air, some landing on me. His mouth clear, Hitler continued. 'Virtue lies in blood! Leadership is primary and decisive. We shall fight! Anyone who will not fight in this world where eternal struggle is the law of life has no right to exist. We shall destroy them, cut off their balls, trample them into the dust of history. What is this age we live in? It is not the age of the Greeks and Romans. It is not the Middle Ages, when German values flourished. It is the age of the capitalist West, which is sick and in decline.'

Hitler looked about the audience of half-drunk men, all now suddenly sober. His eyes sought out theirs, seeking some kind of communion, and they gave it to him. I saw Göring's eyes flicking about the room, assessing Hitler's power.

'Why do great cultures die? Why do great empires crumble into so much dust?' he asked, dropping his voice, almost beseeching, holding out his hands to them. 'Why?'

Liebenfels had sunk back into his seat, but his eyes were still fixed on Hitler's, his wet slash of a mouth working in agreement.

'They decline and die because of contamination. Because of pollution. All the great civilisations of the past became decadent because the originally creative race died out.'

He searched the audience looking for support, and they gave it to him.

'Why? *Because of contamination of the blood!*' He screamed out the last words, his face suddenly mottled and swollen with rage. 'Its race value becomes sullied, weak, impure. The source of a people's whole power does not lie in its possession of weapons or in the organisation of its army but in its inner value – that is, its racial value. It is this that has to be defended against the deadly poisons of internationalism, of egalitarianism and democracy, and of pacifism. Any people that incorporates these vices immediately loses its racial value.'

He paused, calming himself.

'Poison is not in the air. Poison comes in a container, in a bottle, a jar that holds it tight until that moment it can be spilled into pure clean water. What racial container can this be, what race holds tight these evil contaminants?'

Just a moment's pause.

'*The Jew*! The parasite! Is not the ultimate goal of the Jewish struggle for existence the enslavement of productively active people? Do they not seek to denationalise, to promiscuously bastardise other peoples, to lower the racial level of the highest peoples and domination of the resulting racial mish-mash by the extirpation of the *völkische* intelligentsia and its replacement by members of its own poisonous race?

'The Jew has done it before – now, should he succeed, with the help of his Marxist creed, in conquering the nations of this world, his crown will become the funeral wreath of mankind!' His arms thrashed the air furiously. 'Is there any form of foulness, any shady undertaking, especially in cultural life, in which you may not find the Jew? Put the probing knife into that kind of abscess and, like a maggot in a putrescent body, you find the Jew.'

Liebenfels nodded feverishly, some saliva running down his lip.

'Look on it!' Hitler screamed. 'A nightmare future in which hundreds of thousands of pure German women shall have their blood sullied by the seduction of the repulsive, crooked-legged Jew bastards, hiding there in the dark places.' He looked about, as though for somebody, breathing hard. 'Why did we go to see the *Siegfried* today? To receive a message. Does the hero not show the way to the tasks awaiting us? What did we see but the Teutonic age of war! Does it not give us the model we shall need to revitalise the German *Volk* in this sick age of decline?' Once again his voice sank, and all leaned forward to catch his words. 'A man is coming ... a man shall step forward, a man of the *Volk* ... he shall be wearing the mantle of Siegfried, and he shall lead the *Volk* as they destroy their enemies!'

He suddenly threw himself back in his seat, as abruptly as he had jumped up. There was a roar of applause, a thumping of fists on the table, a drumming of boots. When they were sure he had finished, they began to sing the marching-song of the Eberhardt Brigade once again.

Von Liebenfels' face was as sour as if he had swallowed a lemon. 'It is amazing what some people can learn from other people's books,' he muttered acidly.

Hitler shot him a look that could kill, but the man was attending to some crackling.

Göring picked up his fork and impaled a chunk of fine pork. He put it in his mouth, and raised his eyebrows questioningly at me.

I had a little car, an Opel with a rag top that folded back over the cramped rear seat. I was up not long after dawn, having swallowed some rolls and coffee. The day was going to be fine. I took the sticks and canvas apart, rolling it back for the journey through the mountains. In the courtyard, I could smell the oil and burned gasoline of Göring's Mercedes, just make out the fine note of the engine going away in the early light. We were pilots, we were used to rising early; the air was at its best then, smooth as silk. Göring's was a fine machine. We all assumed he had money, as did those of society in whose ranks he swaggered. Style and the Blue Max opened all doors. In fact, he was living off his wife's jewellery. Avarice, lust and ambition drove Hermann, all his life.

Somebody else was up – the monk, von Liebenfels. He was in full fig, in his white robe with the red double-swastika *Hakenkreuz*. He waddled across the courtyard, beaming in an oily fashion at me, rubbing his hands together. 'Good morning, good sir, good morning,' he said. 'I'm glad to have caught you.'

'What can I do for you?' I asked. His change of manner, from the near-contempt with which he had regarded Huber and the *Frontschwein* as they bawled out their marching-songs to the fawning way in which he regarded me was unpleasant to behold.

'You are, sir, if I may say so, practically racially pure.' He stared at me in some sort of admiration.

'Really?'

'Yes, yes,' he assured me. 'I have spent long years evolving my own theory of race. I publish a very popular magazine –' He reached into the folds of his white gown.

'Here, *mein Freiherr*, please –' He thrust a copy of a magazine into my hand. A violently drawn titan had his mailed foot on the throat of a dark-skinned, hook-nosed creature that clawed ineffectually at him. '*Ostara!*' he said proudly. 'The magazine for blond, blue-eyed supermen such as yourself.'

I stuffed the rag into my pocket and began to clean the windscreen. I am obsessed, as all fighter-pilots are, by having my glass completely transparent.

He moved round so that he could still see me, peering through his small, oval glasses. 'I was, as a younger man, as blond as you are,' he assured me.

'Does it matter?' I said.

'Matter?' he expostulated, suddenly shocked. 'Dear sir, you do not know of what you speak. We are the chosen ones! The racially pure, within whom the pure essence of man resides. I have, you know, founded my own order, so that we pure Nordic men may propagate the race, and drive the *chandalas*, the negroes, the half-castes, the Jews, from the face of the earth. We are the New Templars.'

I thought, briefly, of the many millions of negroes, half-castes and Jews that there must be in the world. 'It would take some doing,' I said, somewhat derisively. I wished Huber would get up out of his hangover and stagger down to the car. I was giving him a lift back to Munich. I have always disliked being trapped in conversation with people who are borderline or actually barking, who, perhaps, believe that small green men from Mars are taking over the world, or that the essence of Germany can be found in a pair of blue eyes.

'Certainly,' he agreed seriously. 'The pure types must breed. And the *chandalas* must be suppressed. Yes, to the hilt of the castration knife if need be! This is war between the light and the darkness! The pure must breed. In my new order, all pure, Nordic Aryan men will have the duty to inseminate as many pure Nordic women as possible. I wonder if you –'

'Look, Herr Liebenfels, you would probably do better to enlist Herr Hitler in this order of yours. He seems to be more interested in this kind of thing than I am.'

'*Him?*' Liebenfels drew his robes about himself

contemptuously. '*He* is not racially pure at all. He came to see me, many years ago, before the war – a ragged, dirty creature, he was – to beg for some issues of my magazine that he had missed. I gave them to him – I saw in him some useful qualities, those of an underling ... I invited him here with his gang of ruffians because I considered he might be of use. And what does he do? He has the temerity to lecture *me* about race! *I*, whose theories these are! Pah! I shall be glad to see the back of him.'

With relief I saw Huber lurching down the steps, rubbing his face. 'I have to go,' I said. 'I thank you for your hospitality.'

'You will not join us?' he asked, somewhat wistfully, like a fisherman watching a particularly plump salmon swim by out of range.

'I have more things to do than impregnate women.'

'You are married, perhaps?' he asked hopefully.

'I am.'

'Then you must have many, many children!'

'I have one.'

'Blond, blue eyes, as yourself?'

'Yes,' I said shortly. 'Now I have to go.'

'Ah ... it is a start!'

Huber slept in the back most of the way back to Munich. As far as I could see, he had occupied the previous night vying with his fellow Storm Squad members to see who could drink the most beer. He lay on the ribbed leather seat in his brown shirt and his breeches, sweating it out as he snored. The cold at the top of the pass through the mountains woke him at about the same time as the altitude made the radiator boil, and I pulled up outside a *Berghof* for lunch. Göring, who had set out not long before us in his magnificent Mercedes, was probably back in Munich by now, his mighty engine devouring the kilometres, defeating the efforts of the mountains to hold him back. The little Opel was not in that class, and I felt it deserved a break.

Huber peered at the *Hof* in gratitude. 'My mouth's like the sergeant's underpants,' he said, and we went in. He was in his uniform with the *Hakenkreuz* armband, not that anybody took any notice. In those days everybody from clerks to post office workers wore uniforms, and they probably thought he was someone from the Ministry of Works. The Nazis were nobody outside Bavaria, back then.

The *Hofmeister* in his wide white apron brought us beer and *Schinkenbrot*, fine thick slices of ham on fragrant bread and yellow butter. We were hungry and attacked them with zest. Huber had the true *Frontkämpfer*'s digestion: he could drink or eat at any time, after a drinking bout or sober.

'Do you wear that all the time?' I asked, referring to his uniform.

'*Ja, ja*. The Führer, he insists all party members wear uniform. You get some bastard employers who don't like them – not that many of us have jobs as such – but we wear them for all duty.'

'I didn't realise he hates Jews so much.'

'Hmm?' he said, through a mouthful of bread and ham. 'Oh, *ja*, he hates the fucking Jews all right.'

'Do you hate them?'

'Well, there's a lot of the filthy bastards. More than before the war – you see them all over the place. The forces of evil are spreading, Hans. That Lenin, he's a Jew.'

'Is he?'

'*Ja*, let me see: Issachar Zederblum, that's his real name.' He chewed and swallowed. 'Look, what the boss says is good enough for me. All I know is that not so long ago we were defeated. Us. The greatest nation on earth, brought to our knees by the November criminals, the Jews, the Bolsheviks. Now we have the boss who's showing us the way, so that our nation can be *wieder ehrlich*, honest again.'

He leaned forward, his scarred face totally sincere.

'The boss, he says he is just *der Trommler*, just the drummer, building up support for the great leader who will come, who will be the Saviour, who will lead Germany from darkness into light.' He shook his head. 'I know that the Führer is that man,' he said softly, with complete belief. 'No *Trommler* he. He has been given by fate to the German nation.'

The Opel had cooled down by the time we finished lunch. I topped up the radiator with a jug from the *Hof*. Huber got in the back to catch up on his sleep and we rolled down the winding pass through the carpet of flowers, over tiny stone bridges under which silver streams splashed, until the land flattened out and we put on speed towards Munich.

Huber woke up and came to sit by me. In the city we came through the good quarter, with the big town-houses and wide streets, and Huber looked across. 'Fellow I want to see round here,' he said.

I pulled over. 'I need to stretch my legs. I'll be here for a few minutes if you want a lift on.'

'I won't be long,' he agreed. He pulled out a jacket from his bag, putting it on over his brown shirt, concealing the swastika armband, and hurried away.

He was as good as his word, and as I was getting back into the Opel he came trotting down the street. He took off his jacket as he got in, and put a small wad of notes into his pocket.

'Got paid?'

'There's a fellow I know who lends me money. One of us, a *Frontkämpfer*. You remember him? Eisenmann, the machine-gunner.'

'He's got money?' They were bad days, back then. I was fortunate – I had a rent income from property left to me by my parents. For many, there was little work, and hunger in their bellies.

'Of course. Him and his brother, they work for their father. They're Jews,' he said casually. 'The Jews always have money. He helps me out as an old comrade.'

'You cover up your armband.' I observed.

'Oh well, no need to offend an old *Frontschwein*.'

'He's a Jew,' I said mildly.

'Yes, but he's my Jew. We fought together.'

I let him off near the *Hofbräuhaus*. He was refreshed and looking forward to going and smashing up some meeting of Reds that Hess, Hitler's organiser, had on the list for brawling with that night.

A few days later I bumped into Hoeppner at the *gasthaus*. The stitches were out of my duelling scars, and all that was left were some precise pink lines. We found a quiet corner and I told him about my visit to the castle.

'The Korporal, he's rabid about the Jews,' I said. 'He hates a lot of people – Bolsheviks, Slavs, Poles, capitalists, democrats, Frenchmen, Englishmen, you name it. He doesn't really talk – more spew out abuse and bile – but he really hates the Jews.'

That seemed to please Hoeppner, strangely enough. 'There's not so much mileage in that,' he said. 'Russia is the land of the pogrom, not us. Plenty of people are anti-semitic, but not so much that they want to actually do anything physical about it.'

'The students at the university don't like them,' I told him. 'They banned them from duelling last year. You know the *Hochschulring* movement? They're just about the same as the Nazis. They have half-a-dozen full-time workers in the university; they're students but they don't study – they're paid to get recruits. I heard one speak a while ago. He said that there were only two pure races in the world, the Germans and the Jews. God flourished in the Germans and the Devil in the Jews. Both pure races; one good, one evil, both possessed of an implacable will to power; eternal enemies.'

Hoeppner grimaced. 'You can find all kinds of intellectual detritus about these days. But that's all it is – shit.'

'The students loved it. They poured more beer inside themselves and, when they were good and ready, they went out and half-killed some Jews they found! What's more, the rector did nothing about it. The authorities never do.'

'I know, I know. We need prosperity, and then people will stop looking to the extremists for solutions. What was your impression of this Hitler, then? Do we take him seriously? Or is he just one more fringe lunatic?'

'I don't know . . . He's half-educated, or self-educated. When he tries to quote from some book he's read, or make an argument from some theory he hasn't really understood, he's pathetic. Any second-year student at university could pull him apart. But I saw him speak when it simply came from the heart, when he sensed the atmosphere of the men about him, when he . . . responded somehow to what *they* were thinking, what *they* felt, and then it was just different. Then he wasn't just some scrawny beerhall braggart, he . . . *shone*, somehow. He didn't come out with policies or anything. He just got their emotions. He took them out as though they were his, and gave them back even stronger than before. You can say that all he does is spew out abuse and hatred, but somehow it works. There're so many people out there today who are fearful, resentful, who despair, who want someone to blame. *He* feels that way, too; he's brimful of hate and spite and he tells them that they're right, that there are unseen enemies out there who are responsible – capitalists, democrats, socialists, Jews, financiers, foreign imperialists, Bolsheviks, you name it. He can be all things to all men, when he speaks. He's not very impressive person to person. But he has this gift . . .'

I recalled how the man had strangely known about me, about the war.

'He deals in emotion,' I said. 'I can't explain it any better. Not policies, nothing concrete. Emotions. Fear, envy, hatred, desire, revenge. And somehow, he gets it right.'

I awoke in my chair. It was dawn. The seventy-odd years that had passed since Hoeppner and I had tasted our beer and talked of Hitler had left me stiff. The strangest thing had happened: in my nostrils was the smell of the roast pork they had consumed at the castle – I couldn't get rid of it. I could see it; golden-brown crackling, tender meat, Göring wiping his mouth with his napkin (for he was a gentleman), Huber using his sleeve (for whatever Huber was, it was not a gentleman). There it was, the scent of it, just as though all the years had not passed – roast pork and apple. Göring put a slice of apple pie on his pork and ate it that way.

I opened the window, thinking the fresh air would blow the memory away, and it did, only from somewhere I could smell wood ash – someone on the mountain making a bonfire, no doubt, before winter came. I stood looking out, down the steepness of my meadow. Far below in the valley I could see the twinkling lamps in the village. The sun had not dipped down there yet; people were making breakfast in the dark while I stood in the pale dawn light. Old Fegelein had the store down there – or was it his son? I decided to get the policeman, Cabbage-Gas or whatever his name was, to drop off a letter for me, and have him deliver supplies, now that Willi would be coming no more. Maybe once every two weeks, that would do. And it would enable me to get rid of blasted Vegetarian-Features. I had gone to spend my old age in my *völkischen* mountain retreat because I did not want to see people. I did not want to have them drop in every time they were on their way to some beetroot-tasting session.

I put some wood into the stove, and a kettle on to boil. I

raked out the ash of the fire. When the wind sweeps down the mountainside I put the ash out and the breeze blows it all over the meadow. I have fine wild flowers; they are like a wonderful carpet of colours.

When I had it done, and had washed and dressed, the kettle was whistling. I made tea and ate some black bread, some sausage and cheese. The smell of roast pork had vanished. I can't eat like I used to – it's one of the disadvantages of getting old. Not that I could ever eat like Göring. He was a big man even back then, after the war; he'd been lean when we flew, but peace made him put it on, though nothing like later, when Himmler, who was thin and spavined, used to call him *der Dicke*, the Thick One. They loathed each other, though not as much as they did some of the others. They were always ready to get together to stick a knife into an enemy.

I could see Göring's face, grinning as he tore into the pork, eyes ever alert and calculating as he listened to this strange corporal spouting. A swaggering braggart he may have been, but he had fine judgement when it came to that kind of thing. Göring was on board really early; he walked with Hitler towards the rifles that day they, the *alte Kämpfer*, the old fighters like Huber, thought their time had come.

I was there too, but not as one of them. Like Hoeppner, I'd heard that a *Putsch* was nigh, that Hitler, like Mussolini to Rome the year before, was to march on Munich, to take over Bavaria.

It was a mess. Hitler proved indecisive and was outmanoeuvred by the Prussian officers. Röhm and his Storm Squad got surrounded over by the War Ministry – my duellist opponent's second, Himmler, was down there with him, carrying the *Reichskriegsflagge*, the banner they had invented – and Hitler, Ludendorff (the old army commander) and Göring led a ragbag column to 'take over the city'. They got through a cordon or two by threatening to shoot the Jews and socialists which they had taken hostage – Göring's idea – but came up against one across the Odeonsplatz. The police simply opened fire. Göring went down, holding his side, blood spurting through his fingers. He looked indignant, annoyed that anyone had had the temerity actually to hit him. Richter, who had linked arms with Hitler, fell down dead, along with many others. Ludendorff walked through, confident that nobody would shoot him. Hitler escaped and the entire march collapsed in total disorder. It was a fiasco.

Fiasco... that was what Hoeppner said. He was well pleased to see Hitler fail, despite his performance at the trial, when he used his rhetorical skills to such effect, and got front-page treatment in every newspaper in Germany. His closing speech was a *tour de force*. I suppose we should have listened. On his way to the prison he finished up by saying: 'The man who is born to be a dictator is not compelled, he wills it.'

He was sentenced to five years, but they let him out after less than one. As far as I knew, he practically vanished from sight – him, Huber, Göring and the rest. I met up with Hoeppner in Weimar, the political capital, in 1925. I was there because Hilde was at the Bauhaus, doing a set for Brecht's new play. Hoeppner took the trouble to look me up, he was in the national government by then, a young and successful politician. I was spending my time inventing things. I had a small workshop, and in my spare time I was teaching young men how to fly gliders up in the mountains.

The Versailles Treaty so hated by nearly everyone had eradicated our air force, so those pilots of the future made do by learning to fly gliders. They were taught by the best, by old aces like me. I say old but, of course, I was only as old as the century; I was only in my twenties.

We were forced into this situation. The British, who won the war, could go and fly something like a Hermes Moth, powered by a war-surplus four-cylinder engine. We who had lost it had to hurl ourselves off mountainsides in unpowered gliders. However, the skills involved in attempting to maintain altitude in such aircraft are such that we produced very fine pilots, who could turn their skills to devastating effect when given something designed by Kurt Tank or Willi Messerschmitt.

In the mountains I had become involved with the design and contruction of the gliders themselves, for we were beginning to realise something extraordinary; that certain conditions of weather and topography created rising air, which a suitably designed and contructed unpowered aircraft could use to maintain altitude, to become not merely a glider but a sailplane. This rising air could be found as a standing wave off a ridge, or was convection- or thermal-generated, and as we gained in skill as pilots and designers we were able to stay aloft for longer and longer periods, and sometimes even gain altitude.

It was 1925 before I met Hoeppner again. We sat outside and had a light beer. It was a fine summer's day. Cars and buses and lorries growled on the street, people bustled by, the girls pretty in their light, colourful dresses. There was plenty going on; the theatres were packed, the news-sellers bulged with magazines, the streets full of bookshops and art galleries and the new cinemas; there were clubs where you could see naked black dancers, listen to American jazz and dance the foxtrot and quickstep. The Nazis called it 'negroised' dancing, which probably increased its attractiveness. There were huge department stores packed with the best of everything from Paris fashions to machines from Chicago. There were exhibitions of sculpture and posters of the new art, and strange and wonderful new buildings made from concrete, steel and plate-glass were springing up everywhere. You could sit in these buildings on chairs made from tubular frames and canvas – I know, I designed one myself. It paid for me to spend my weekends aloft, circling silently like a hawk, seeking out the thermal currents which would carry me ever higher.

The republic was a cultural phenomenon. It was everything Huber and his ilk hated.

In 1925 it was all coming right for Weimar. The currency was good and the economy was starting to boom. Hoeppner sat in his shirtsleeves, looking as content as a politician ever does.

'A fiasco,' he said, consigning Hitler and the *alte kampfers* to the dustbin of history.

'You don't hear anything of him now,' I agreed.

'We made sure of it,' he said with a measure of vindictive satisfaction. 'We've banned the little swine from speaking in public throughout Bavaria. See how he likes *that*.'

'Hasn't he written some book or other?' I asked.

'*Mein Kampf*! *My Struggle* – God what a pretentious little prick he is.'

'What's it about?'

'I don't think I've ever read anything that manages to be more turgid and more repulsive at the same time. I bought a copy, I did, just to see. It's not easy to get hold of – I suppose he makes his diseased little followers purchase it, if any of them can read, which I doubt. It's written like he talks: violent, vulgar, abusive, nasty, megalomaniacal and wrong.'

He took a pull at his lager, frowning, not seeing the cheerful bustle all about.

'It's bad enough Hitler scribbling this filth. He's a nasty little uneducated thug with a chip on his shoulder. But you get people who should know better! Schmitt is the leading legal philosopher in the land. He pours out a stream of books and articles, all promoting the demands of the state! What about the freedom of the people, for which he appears to care nothing? And Van den Bruck – did you see his book? He calls for the purging of capitalism and liberalism from society entirely. From this a new state will somehow emerge that will embody everything that is finest about the German race. This state will last, he claims, for a thousand years. Want to know what it's called? *The Third Reich.* I ask you . . .'

He came back from his thoughts, looking about him, and he smiled at me.

'These blasted easterners! Everything that's finest about Germany? Let me tell you, Hans, we're doing it right now! Our architecture, our music, our literature – even the printing, Hans! – our theatre, art, cinema! It's all, what, thirty years ahead of any other nation in the world! You know, losing the war was the best thing that could have happened to Germany – look how far we've advanced now that the people are free to think, to act, to create for themselves.'

'You sound just like Hilde,' I said, amused.

'Yes!' he agreed. 'Is she well?'

'Doing the sets for Brecht's new play,' I said proudly.

'And your son?'

'Kurt? Marvellous. Would you believe he's four already? He's with his aunt, Hilde's sister. I must go and pick him up later.'

'What about you? Still designing?'

'Did you see my chair? Chromed tubular steel. I have a version that's got padded leather, as well as the canvas one.'

'That's what you want to do?' he asked casually. 'Be a chair designer?'

I hesitated for just a moment. It was why I had arranged the meeting, after all. 'No, not if I don't have to,' I said quietly. 'You know how it is with me. I still have this thing about the air, about flying. These are interesting times in aviation, Claus. The war brought about a great jump in technology for us. We went from paper and string to 200 kilometre-an-hour aerobatic scouts. Now there's the challenge of all-metal monoplanes, of gyroscopic blind-flying instruments, of long-distance radio navigation, of jettisonable fuel-tanks, variable-pitch propellers –'

'Enough!' Hoeppner held up his hands, laughing. 'I believe you, although I hardly know what you are talking about.'

'The Americans, the British, the French, the Italians, all of these countries are investigating these matters. The Americans have their aerial mail service; they hold various altitude and long-distance records; the British are developing very long-range flying-boats to service their empire. The Japanese – the Japanese, Claus! – have ships that carry aircraft, floating airfields, and so do the British. There's a Spaniard who's making rotorcraft! Yes! The wings are like blades, they go round and round above his head. It can land in a back garden. The American, Mitchell, sank a battleship by using aerial bombs. His compatriot, Doolittle, won the Schneider Trophy for the second time this year. What a machine! Nearly six hundred horsepower from a Curtiss engine: that's 360 kilometres an hour! They say someone will fly the Atlantic solo soon!'

It all poured out of me. I subscribed to American and British flying magazines and I yearned to be a part of it all.

'And us! What are we doing? Nothing.'

'We aren't allowed to,' Hoeppner said mildly. 'The Versailles Treaty forbids all forms of military aviation in Germany. The Ambassadors' Conference of three years ago places severe restrictions upon civil aviation.'

'I know. But are we to stay on the sidelines forever? When, as you say, we lead the world in so many other spheres?'

'Maybe not,' he said noncommittally.

'I heard . . . that we are involved in some things abroad –'

He looked up, his eyes sharp. 'And you want to be a part of it.'

'I'm a flyer,' I said simply. 'And an engineer. I need to get back in. It's my world, just as art and the theatre is Hilde's. I'm still at it, as much as I can. I'm involved in flying and designing gliders.'

'You might have to go to some funny places. Months at a time.'

'I know.'

'Ever heard of Lipezk?' he asked.

'No.'

'It's in the Soviet Union. We're starting a training school there.'

'With the Bolsheviks?'

'We have some joint interests . . .' he said vaguely. 'After all, they feel threatened by the West; they supported the Whites in the civil war.'

'I instruct now,' I told him. 'I teach with a gliding club.'

'And you were an ace in the most famous fighting group of all,' he said thoughtfully.

'Will it lead to development work?' I asked.

'Of course. That's the main reason we have to establish a base out of Germany, so the Allied Aeronautical Control Commission can't poke its nose in and tell us to stop. There are some interesting designs coming through, I'm told. Rheinhold Platz, you have heard of him?'

'Of course!' I said warmly. 'He designed the Fokker I flew.'

'Also someone called Messerschmitt.'

'I'd like to get in on it if I can.'

'I'll see what I can do, then,' he promised.

I left him not long afterwards and went to pick up my son. On the way home we stopped at a café, and I bought him an ice-cream. He was a lovely little fellow, with blond hair like mine used to be, and Hilde's grey-blue eyes.

He looked solemnly at me with them as we sat waiting for the ice-cream. He liked raspberry. 'Go on, then,' Kurt said.

'What?' I smiled.

'You know, the café.'

'Oh . . . all right.' I recited the poem for him.

'I dreamt last night that my favourite café
was on an island with palm trees overhead.
Myself, I always sleep in my own bed,
but dreams like to roam far away.'

He giggled at that, he found it very funny, the thought of one's dreams strolling about wherever took their fancy.

His ice-cream came and he ate it carefully. I often think of him when he was young like that. It is a happy memory.

Hoeppner was as good as his word, and not long afterwards I was asked to go and talk to some people at the Technische Amt, the Technical Office of the RLM, the Air Ministry. I wore my medals, including the *pour le Merite*, and it transpired that I was just what they were looking for.

For the next six years or maybe a little more, I spent much of my time in Lipezk, only returning to our apartment in Berlin on leave. Hilde moved us there from Weimar when her artistic and theatre career really took off. We had a nice place within walking distance of *Unter den Linden*. With both Hilde and I working, we could afford to send Kurt to a good school, and we planned for him to move on to a university preparatory school once he reached secondary level. I used to write to him, from Lipezk, and he wrote back, in a steadily forming hand.

I used to do three months duty at a time and then spend a month at home, and I would see as much of him as I could, taking him to the wonderful Berlin parks and lakes, to the funfair. Often, in the evenings, Hilde's sister would babysit for us if I had to go to see anyone. Hilde was often out at the theatre, or sometimes at the cinema or a gallery. That was her world, and I could not join it.

Sometimes I would have a drink with Eisenmann, the machine-gunner of 1918, who had come up to Berlin in business. He and his wife had an apartment not far from us.

The month's leave would always be up too soon, and I would be back to Lipezk, sometimes flying a new aircraft out there for us to test. But that was my world, as the *neue Sachlichkeit*, the wind-tunnel culture of Weimar, was Hilde's.

She was most envious of me, working in the Soviet Union. She was always more politically-aware than me, and for the left-wing intelligentsia in those days, the world's first communist state was something golden, a holy grail in an imperfect world.

The truth was that I never saw the outside world at all when I was at Lipezk. I met some Soviet pilots who came to the base, but that was all. It was a huge training range stuck out in the middle of nowhere – which was the whole point. We Germans weren't meant to be doing it at all, according to the Versailles Treaty: we were to have no tanks, heavy guns or aircraft, nor even a general staff, so we did it where nobody could see us.

This was sound thinking, because what we were doing was fashioning the tools of a new form of warfare. We were taking up where we had left off in 1917–18. The stalemate that had so marked most of the war had been caused by the stranglehold defensive measures and firepower imposed upon offensive mobility. The offensive doctrine developed first by us and then taken up by the Allies was what we were interested in, and what made it possible was the use of the internal combustion engine in the armoured fighting vehicle, or tank, the ground-attack aircraft and the truck.

We were not alone in working out the lessons of the last war – it is what military men are meant to do in peacetime after all, to predict how the next will be fought. There were, largely, two schools of thought about it all. The first was that artillery was dominant – that artillery neutralised – while infantry and tanks occupied. This was the view the French had come to, and also the British, who actually disbanded their own experimental mechanised force. The French went off to build a chain of gigantic artillery forts, the Maginot Line.

Which left us Germans and the Russians working out how to combine tanks, ground-attack aircraft and motorised troops with the right communications, in places like Lipezk. Some very interesting people were to be found there. Ernst Udet, who had shot down more aircraft than anyone in the previous conflict except Richtofen, but who had also survived, was there, as I was. On the ground there was a man called Guderian, who acquired the nickname 'Hurrying Heinz'. It was he who came up with the phrase that summarised what we were building: '*Klotzen, nicht kleckern*'. Smash, don't tap. The Russians had Tukhachevsky, who was actually marshal of their army, and *he* said: 'Only a decisive offensive in the main direction concluding with persistent pursuit leads to the complete annihilation of forces and means of the enemy.' He and Guderian understood each other.

But Tukhachevsky and his best men were all slaughtered by their own leader, Stalin, in the middle of the 1930s, along with a large proportion of the rest of the population, which meant that only we Germans were left. But I am going on too far. When I was there in the late 1920s and early 1930s, all that was in the future. And if we were planning this new, devastating doctrine of fighting, it certainly never occurred to any of us as a part of that future war that any leader of a nation would voluntarily massacre his most able officers. If Tukhachevsky had still been there with the world's largest mechanised armed force in 1941, you may be certain that Barbarossa would have remained simply the name of King Frederick. But again, I digress; it is an old man's habit.

As a young man back where he needed to be, in an aircraft, I played a large role in the development of what we called the *Sturzkampfflugzeug*, the dive-bomber. We considered that such a machine could attack difficult targets such as bridges and supply columns far more accurately and successfully, and at a greater range, than artillery. We had several prototype aircraft out there from such manufacturers as Henschel, Curtiss and Junkers. The result of our labours, in the mid-1930s, was an aircraft called the Junkers Ju 87, better known to those who endured its menacing, bent-winged silhouette and wailing Jumo engine as it came at them in a near-vertical dive as the Stuka.

But again, I am travelling on too far . . .

In my wooden peasant's dwelling, at my desk, as I wrote down these memories, I suddenly stopped. I put down my pen, puzzled and slightly alarmed.

My telephone had rung. It let out one full *brrriiinngg* and then went quiet.

I got up, staring at it. It is an old black bakelite affair, and I have not used it in years. When I told the phone company to disconnect it, I simply left it there, still plugged in to the socket but not, as far as I knew, to the rest of the network.

I shuffled over and picked up the receiver, holding it to my ear. For a second or two it was, I knew, connected to someone. It held that strange, hollow sensation, like a sea-shell. Then it clicked and went dead, and I was, once again, simply holding an old, inert piece of moulded black bakelite on the end of a twisty cord.

I peered at it, held it up to my ear again, but it responded to me not, so I replaced it in its cradle. As I headed back to my desk to continue writing, I paused to look out over the valley, as I like to do. The far slopes were splashed and spattered with the russets and golds of autumn.

Nearer to my house, a man moved, over by the barns. His car was parked nearby but I had not heard it come. From the look of it, he had taken the bottom road, which would account for his silent arrival. I think he saw me at the window for he waved and walked up the slope towards me. It was him, of course, Cabbage-Gas, the policeman.

'I was passing,' he called. 'I thought I would see if you needed anything.'

I was, I suppose, about to be somewhat short with him, for one does not retire to one of the remotest parts of Germany because one wishes to be persecuted by cud-chewing, spaghetti-swallowing, lentil-laden enforcers of the law. Then I remembered that I wished to contact old Fegelein at the village store, or his son. I had the letter already written.

'It so happens you may help me,' I said as he came up. I went and opened the door, giving him the letter. 'It is addressed as you can see. If you take the track back all the way to the road you will eventually come to the village you can see down there. There is a store there – perhaps you would be so good as to give this note to the man who runs it.'

'I will do that for you,' he said, taking it.

'A strange thing has just happened,' I told him. 'My telephone, which has not been connected for years, has just rung.'

He looked at me impassively. 'Who was calling?' he asked, finally.

'Nobody. It is now dead.'

'I saw some telephone engineers working on the poles when I came up,' he offered.

'*Ja.* That is undoubtedly it.' I looked down to where his car was parked by the barns. 'You are in these remote parts a great deal,' I said.

'It is a part of our search for the eco-terrorists.'

'Oh, *ja* . . . what were they called again?'

'Mother Nature,' he said softly.

'You have found them?'

'No.'
'And what of this ... chef, was it?'
'Chef and cookery writer.'
'You have found him?'
'Yes. We have found him.'
'That is good, then.' There was something about his face. 'It is not good?'
'He was found by staff at his restaurant one morning when they came to open up,' he told me. 'They found a long table fully set as for a meal. On three large platters, as though ready for carving, they found the chef. He had an apple in his mouth. He had been prepared, basted and roasted on a spit.'
I was silent for some moments. 'What harm had this unfortunate gourmet done to these lunatics,' I finally burst out, 'that they should murder him so horribly?'
'They left a notice saying that they had warned him against involvement in the Holocaust.'
'Holocaust?' I repeated, puzzled. 'He was nothing to do, surely, with the concentration camps?'
'The Holocaust is what Mother Nature has called the entire process of producing animal products for food.'
'Farms?'
'Everything. Farms, fishing, restaurants that cook meat, supermarkets that sell meat, butchers ... This is known as the Holocaust.'
'We are to starve?' I enquired.
'They demand that we all become vegans,' he said. He gave a wry smile. 'Like me, for example.'
'They appear to wish to change the entire nature of the human race since we emerged from the primeval swamps,' I said. 'Fishing, you said?'
'A fishing-rod is an instrument of torture akin to a medieval rack.'
'I see. Pets? A dog or a cat?'
'Slavery. Identical to the slave system of the pre-Civil War American South.'
'These people take hallucinogenic drugs, perhaps?'
He shrugged.
'Industry, modern technology?'

'Must be abolished, before pollution destroys the living earth itself, and everything in it.'

'One sees that they desire a transformation in human society – across the globe, one imagines, yes? – that will make any previous revolution, such as the Bolshevik one, let us say, seem like a change of council government. What is to happen to the animals that are now farmed in various ways, or hunted, for food?'

'The world will return to the golden age of Mother Nature, when mankind did not interfere.'

'Yes,' I said testily. 'But we have *always* modified, created, planted, nurtured. The world is a better place for it.'

'They would disagree with you.'

'I understand that. They disagreed with the restaurateur. But do they have the slightest idea what it is like for an animal in the wild? It is not as it is portrayed in a Walt Disney film, let me assure you. I understand how it is; I have been close to the land all my life. The young, I believe, think that food comes wrapped in cellophane in a pack on a supermarket shelf.

'Life in the wild is a terrifying place in which something is always wishing to eat you. Summer and warmth and plentiful food gives way to winter and bitter cold and agonising hunger. Disease inflicts you with pain and weakness. The competition for food, for shelter and warmth is violent and brutal from birth to death. A crow may eat you alive, a fox hunt you down and devour you as you struggle, a hawk tear out your living entrails. And no creature dies of old age out there. They die of cold, they die of hunger, and they die because they are too slow or too enfeebled to run away in time, and a predator gets them.

'In contrast, a farmer must look after his animals if they are to produce food of high quality. He must protect them against disease, he must provide them with warmth in winter. A farm animal has a life its wild cousin would envy.'

'But it is killed for food.'

'Yes, it is killed. It dies. We *all* die, and taking herbs or eating strange diets will not alter that. You will die, I will die, the chickens in my run will die. What all of us want is to have the best life possible while we are alive.'

I peered angrily at him.

'These mad people, they want the world to descend into a

maelstrom of horror? It is only civilisation that has managed to lift life on to a higher plane, to relieve the terror of the wild. These crazed people – they want the other?'

'It's Mother Nature's way,' he said quietly. Then he shrugged, spreading his hands. 'That's what they'd say,' he said.

'I know them for what they are,' I said fiercely. 'They are ideologues. Ideology is religion. Those afflicted by it *know* what is true, and do not require proof, nor will they listen when they are shown to be wrong. I don't care whether they are those who have burned each other at the stake for believing the Holy Ghost to be something somebody else does not, or those who thought that all evil resided in members of a different class or a different race, and slaughtered as many of those people as they could, or whether they are these latest ones who believe that the devil exists in toxins and in eating meat – they are all the same.'

I looked angrily over my valley. I had come there to spend the rest of my life quietly, and yet the world and its insanities pursued me even there.

'Well, you had better get off and find these lunatics. We do not need new maniacs in Germany – we have had enough in the past. Let there be an end to it.'

He got up from the porch step where he had been sitting. 'You're right,' he said, and held up my envelope. 'I'll deliver your message.'

I went back inside and a short while later I heard his car driving away. I picked up the phone but it was lifeless, as it was supposed to be, and I went to the stove, making some coffee before I sat back down at the desk.

I found it difficult to shake off the image of the roasted man. Instead of continuing my story with the work we did in the second half of the 1920s, my mind jumped to, let me see, about 1931 or 1932, it must have been. We had been told that diplomatic relations between Germany and the Soviet Union were deteriorating, and that it was not unlikely that the joint testing and development site at Lipezk would be closed. For that reason we pressed on with a number of projects while we were still able. One of these involved high-altitude photography of various parts of the Soviet Union. For this, we were using the cover of long-distance flying in a prototype Messerschmitt.

It was later produced as the 108 Taifun, a very fast passenger aircraft and the predecessor of the famous 109 fighter. We had it fitted with internal fuel-tanks – we should have developed external jettisonable ones, the 109 needed them – and with silenced exhaust and quiet propeller. The underside of the aircraft was painted a pale, bluish grey. And, of course, it was equipped with a Zeiss camera. It was a very effective spy. When you were up at nine thousand metres, those on the ground could not know you were above them. But you were, taking crisp, clear photographs. We anticipated aerial surveillance by many years, but that was our fate. We developed the guided missile, the stand-off smart bomb and the jet fighter, for that matter, as well as the high-speed snorkelled submarine. Not that it did us any good.

I was the pilot on a number of these flights. The one I remember in detail took me, on my homeward leg, over the Ukraine. It was a June day and I had been in the air for some seven hours. A haze had built up and seeing the ground below was like looking into a dirty pond. I hoped that my early photographs would be clear. The sky ahead was darkening and I could make out the menacing outlines of building cumulo-nimbus clouds. I was well aware of their power, the updraughts and downdraughts within which often exceeded full-control movements. To fly into a mature thunderstorm was to risk being whisked up and down inside like an ice-gathering yo-yo, until finally falling to earth, a glittering, solid lump, *sans* wings.

The sky seemed clearer over to the west, and I took a cut of about thirty degrees on the heading, letting down to get under the cloud layer. At about two thousand metres, the ground below was quite clear, as was the way around the approaching front.

Then I caught a glimpse of something.

That was all. I was at cruising speed, some two hundred and seventy kilometres. I simply caught the slightest sight of something white, and it hit the aircraft with a terrific thump, the smack of an anti-aircraft shell. The entire airframe shook and shuddered, the dials dancing in their panel. It is very unpleasant, being hit by things in the air. You cannot, for example, pull over to the side of the road and examine the vehicle for damage.

The aircraft was still flying. It was still level, and the controls responded correctly when I made gentle movements. Much relieved, I continued my course under the cloud layer. But then the cylinder-head temperatures began to rise. The oil temperature did likewise, and the oil pressure began to sag. The engine was starting to overheat. The logical end to this would be that it would get hot enough to melt various working parts into a nasty, unmoving whole and I would then plunge to earth. I decided therefore to land while I still was able to exert some control over the plane. I throttled well back and, looking at the land below in a series of s-turns, identified what appeared to be some sort of dirt road below. It was straight and, thankfully, had no power or telephone lines alongside it. No walls formed its edge. It simply cut through some kind of scrubby-looking meadow or field. It was certainly my best bet. It might be rutted, but the field could just as easily contain potholes that would stand the aircraft on its nose or tear the gear off.

I lined up the plane. There didn't seem to be much wind. I dropped the undercarriage and throttled back some more. The oil temperature was in the red. I touched down with a rumble from the tyres, keeping the nose high. The road was no rougher than I had expected, and I rolled to a stop, a cloud of dust pursuing me and overtaking me. I cut the mixture and switches and the prop sputtered to a halt. I climbed out, extremely stiff, to see what it was that had hit me.

It was a duck. Its corpse and feathers were comprehensively stuffed into and around the oil cooler. It was all very hot. I opened my toolkit and began to remove the semi-barbecued, high-flying avian from my machine.

As I did so, I glanced about me. I had been forced to land in a truly desolate place. The field on both sides of the road had clearly been cultivated, but it was simply a mass of weeds pushing up through last year's rotting brown growth. Some distance away was a poor version of a peasant hamlet, a gathering of primitive wooden dwellings.

Nobody was about, no cows, goats or sheep. No chickens or pigs. It was very desolate indeed. I continued to scrape and poke away at the macerated meat, clearing the oblong oil radiator's honeycombs so that the air could flow through it.

There was a vague rustling in the long grasses, a wheezing like an elderly and leaking steam-engine. A very thin, very old –

he seemed to be old – man shuffled towards me. He wore dirty clothes, as peasants do, that had once fitted him better. He smiled, however, showing bare gums.

'Water,' he said in Russian. He spoke it about as well as I did. I think he thought I was a Russian. He was a Ukrainian peasant. 'Water,' he repeated. 'Have some water from the well.'

It was very hot, stickily hot with the approaching thunderstorm. My hands stank of dead duck's entrails. I was very thirsty and the engine would benefit from cooling down some more.

'Thank you,' I said in my bad Russian, and he muttered something in his, pointing over at the nearest wooden hut.

We made our way over there. We did not move fast – he did not seem able to, his chest heaving, his mouth open as he dragged air into his lungs.

There was a strange musty smell in the air. It was silent, with none of the normal sounds of a farm or smallholding. We were outside the hut, a simple single room with a beaten-earth floor, I knew the kind of thing. He gestured for me to go inside the door. It was half-open. I stepped inside, and the musty smell was intensified. For a second my eyes could not see in the gloom, and then I saw that an old woman lay against the far wall, as desiccated as a mummy, rags sticking to her body, just a sack of bones. She was very dead. The room was quite, quite empty. There was nothing in it except for the dead woman.

Behind me the old man gasped in an exhalation of enormous output of energy. I whirled away from him and he fell through the doorway, the knife in his hand missing me. He recovered and staggered at me again, desperately slashing the air as I danced back away from him, moving almost in slow motion.

Then the door was at my back and I jumped through it. In the yard outside, other skeletal creatures were shuffling towards the house. They bore knives, sickles, axes. As they saw me, their sunken eyes – men or women, I was not sure – shone with a desperate need. They cried out hoarsely in their language, all moving as quickly as they could towards me, their eyes focused only on me, raising their killing instruments in ultimate want.

I ran. I ran as fast as I could around the hut; I ran into a latecomer carrying a scythe and knocked him down, his desperate fingers scratching at me like claws. I ran back across the field with the gang of skeletons after me, their breath bubbling and gasping in their chests, their desperate voices crying out as they saw me getting away, running so much faster than they were able to.

I heaved myself up into the cockpit, and quickly set the switches and controls. The prop jerked and then spun into a blur. I applied full power and the aircraft began to roll. The tail came up as one of the creatures staggered on to the road, his face working, shouting something. He walked straight into the wing and it hit him with a bang, throwing him like a sack of rubbish. And then I was airborne, lifting up and away from the desolate dark ground.

I pulled up the gear, gaining speed. On some impulse, I swung around, flying back over the road and the gang of zombies that had pursued me, had tried to kill me. They now paid me no heed, not one of them wasting the energy to look up at the aircraft above their heads. They were gathered about the dead man, hacking him to pieces, the first-comers frantically carrying off their joints before the others could take it from them.

Berlin, November 1931

I heard Eisenmann come puffing up the stairs and I let him in.

'Am I late?' he asked. 'Hello, Hilde, it's nice and warm in here.'

'Hoeppner's just come,' she said. 'Stand by the stove, it's very cold out there.'

'I'll say,' he said, hanging up his overcoat on a futurist hat-stand that somebody at the Bauhaus had made for Hilde. He stood gratefully by the baroque stove, as colourful as an altar in its bright, shiny tiles. The place was a strange mixture of the old and the new. There were fantastic lamps made to look like pressure-gauges, thermometers, switchboard dials cast round splashes of light on the ornate plasterwork of the ceiling. Half a wall was a cupboard with doors out of a gothic cathedral, fitted with stained glass. Next to it, Hilde had hung the big painting which Anton Raderscheidt had given her. Two big blonde nudes swung from parallel bars watched by a gloomy man in a bowler hat. A black-

and-white spiky caricature by Grosz hung nearby, his Prussian generals as violent as ever, his capitalists as bloated and pig-like.

The capitalist Eisenmann warmed his hands as Hoeppner came in from washing his. I poured everybody a drink – a cocktail in the New York fashion – from a shaker.

'I thought I'd walk over,' said Eisenmann. 'I heard there was going to be a riot on the Leipziger Strasse; if you leave your car out when those bastards come by, they smash the windows.'

'That's because it's a Mercedes, Karl,' Hilde said.

Hilde had come back unexpectedly that afternoon. She had been gone for some time, out in the world which decorated her walls. At some point she would put up some new painting, some new piece of sculpture, some new writing that had seized her passion. They hung there, filled the shelves; she collected them like scalps.

Kurt was over with her sister, Clara. My own hours were erratic, even when I was there, and she felt it was more stable to leave him with his aunt.

'So?' Eisenmann demanded. 'The communists hate me because I drive a Mercedes and the Nazis hate me because I'm a Jew. It's a nightmare. Only yesterday things were normal, and now it's like after the war again. Everywhere you go, there they are, brawling or bawling out that ridiculous song about Horst Wessel. Who the hell is Horst Wessel, anyway?'

'Was,' said Hoeppner. 'He was a pimp who happened to be a member of the SA at the same time. The two went hand in hand. He was killed by a rival pimp in a sordid squabble over prostitutes' territory.'

'What do you say, Claus?' I asked Hoeppner. 'Is this depression going to get better soon?'

'It's the death throes of capitalism!' Hilde cried cheerfully. 'I welcome it. We want struggle, friction and sparks. At last, a new world!'

'Careful what you ask for in this world,' Hoeppner warned her unhappily. 'You may get it. And no, it isn't.'

'Which means more rioting, more fighting on the streets,' Eisenmann said. 'You never saw the SA out there, not in the last five years, not since they threw Hitler into jail. Now they're back, and getting bigger all the time. They go looking for people who're out of work – they offer them a uniform and hot food, new leather boots, if they'll join.'

'People are frightened,' I pointed out. 'Look what happened after the war. Five years of it! Defeat – and that after all the losses we took – then Versailles and the reparations, no Kaiser, practically civil war and revolution, inflation so bad you needed a suitcase of money to buy a sandwich – and then some kind of order. Things looking good. And now – here it is again!'

'That's it,' Hoeppner agreed. 'The people have become irrational. They are willing to believe irrational things. Now we face the *Ermöglichung*.'

'Possibility?' said Hilde. 'Possibility of what?'

'Your new world, Hilde,' Hoeppner said, smiling crookedly. 'It exists already, in the Soviet Union.'

'Yes! That's what we want.'

'Except I think Korporal Hitler will deliver it.'

'You take the little bastard seriously?' Eisenmann asked, rather anxiously.

'Unless the economy gets better suddenly. Which it is not going to do.'

'Pity he didn't collect a stray one when we were in the trenches.'

Eisenmann reached into his pocket and fished out a sheet of brownish paper. On it was a scrawl of black ink in an uneducated hand. He gave it to Hoeppner, who read it and passed it over to me.

'*Karl Eisenmann.*
Watch out! We shall settle the score with you and all the other filthy Jews. You have twenty-four hours to get out of Germany, otherwise you'll get what's coming to you.'

Underneath was a crudely drawn swastika.

'That's awful!' said Hilde. 'What are you going to do? Have you told the police?'

'Hilde, my dear, the police would get very tired of me turning up every week with my little bundle of letters. We get three, sometimes four a week. I ignore them. I am a Jew; we are used to the signs of pogrom. But I cannot deny, I would prefer it otherwise.'

'Hitler and the SA are simply what gets thrown up when capitalism is in its death throes,' Hilde said seriously.

I wondered who she had been with in the past couple of weeks. They discussed things like that with the burning ferocity of clerics trying to determine the number of angels filling the head of a pin, as they lay in bed with silver-grey cigarette smoke coiled up towards the high ceiling, like the trails of destroyed scouts.

'You're missing the point,' Hoeppner said sharply. 'Hitler is *popular*. And popular *without policies*. We are living in bad times, and he offers something to believe in – for both young and old, for both conservatives and radicals. For Protestants in need of something to believe in, for atheists looking for the true way. For all Germans who want a moral and spiritual renewal of the nation. For there are plenty out there that these renewed times of trouble have made mad. They are not rational, and now they are willing to *believe*. And everything the Nazis are doing is designed to get people to believe. Have you seen him perform? It's not normal politics, it's a mixture of theatre and religion. You ought to understand that, Hilde. Look at what he does. Symbols, dramatic uniforms, rituals, flags, lighting, loudspeakers, parades and rallies, all centred around this Führer myth. It is hard for boring, plodding, ordinary politicians whose job is running things to compete. Hitler offers himself as all things to all men. People think that he will give them what they need.'

'It is effective,' Hilde admitted. 'But the KPD, the communists, will smash him on the streets.'

'They won't, you know!' Eisenmann cried. 'Did they manage it after the war? The Freikorps massacred them. Rohm's back, you know. He runs the SA again.'

Hilde didn't answer that. She went into the kitchen and started putting plates on the table: wurst, mountain cheese, smoked ham, a bowl of sausages very hot from the pan, the ones with the skin that let out a jet of water which stings you when you stab them with a fork – rolls and pumpernickel bread, sauerkraut and pickled eggs. Whenever she came back, she was, for a while, the very *hausfrau*, almost *kinde, kuche and kirche*. It always lasted for a few days.

I took the corks out of the bottles Eisenmann and Hoeppner

had brought and put them on the table as well. 'Hitler's not going to attempt a *Putsch* again,' I said. 'Not after last time. The generals don't like him. The Reichswehr are real soldiers; they'd cut the SA up into pieces.'

'That's true,' Hoeppner admitted as we sat down. 'And he'll never get an electoral majority. I place my hopes on his supporters getting tired of no success. Right now he has their hopes up, but if we can keep him out . . .'

For a little while there was simply the clink and clatter of us preparing and beginning to eat the meal.

'I didn't get that,' said Hilde, who always liked to provoke Hoeppner, 'when you said the new world would come, like it has in the Soviet Union, yet Hitler would provide it. What on earth can Hitler have in common with communism? They hate each other.'

'Well, yes – but I have this strange suspicion . . .'

'Yes?'

'I think they *need* each other. Who do they both hate? Us. The democrats.'

'But communism is the democracy of the people. Hitler and the Nazis, they hate democracy, of course they do. Communism is the democracy of the new world. How many times do I have to tell you?' She grinned mockingly at him over a sausage.

Hoeppner turned to me, all of a sudden. 'Hans, you know how you took pictures of places in the Soviet Union? High-altitude shots?'

'Yes, of course.'

'Did you ever see any?'

'No, the film was taken away.'

He reached inside his jacket. 'I brought some over. I thought you ought to see.'

I peered at the grainy black-and-white shots. The clarity was impressive, given the altitude. People. People like ants. A kind of construction project, a gigantic scar in the ground. A camp of some kind, long wood huts. People, people like ants.

'What is it all?'

'Prisoners. Forced labour. Very big camps to keep them in. Shiploads of them sailing off somewhere.'

'Claus, don't be naïve,' Hilde said sharply. 'You know

perfectly well that the new world in Russia is threatened by subversive elements. Western spies and reactionary monarchists. They have to be re-educated to understand the new order, to play their proper part in building the future.'

'Hundreds of thousands?' Hoeppner asked doubtfully. 'Millions, maybe?'

'Look at the map!' she cried impatiently. 'Have you seen how big the Soviet Union is? What are a few malcontents being made to do an honest day's work compared to building a new and clean world? I just wish we had the Bolsheviks in here to do the same for us.'

Hoeppner scooped up his photographs and tucked them away again. 'They're coming,' he said. 'They're called the Nazi Party.' He smiled suddenly as Hilde opened her mouth to object. 'But no!' he said. 'I come to this apartment to bathe in culture, not to talk politics. Don't you agree with me, you two? Now, what about *Emil and the Detectives*? Have you bought it for Kurt? Of course . . .'

Lipezk, 30 January 1933

I couldn't find Krassin anywhere. It was freezing cold but clear, and the next day promised to be a good one for flying. I was anxious to get the week's programme agreed with the Russians, and Krassin was the one I had to do it with. Only he wasn't there; his office remained obstinately empty. I decided to go to my room and wait for him. If he came in, we could still organise things before supper.

My small room was at least warm, being close to the boiler. The further out you were, the chillier it became. I had a workbench set up along one wall. I spent a certain amount of time making models of aircraft, partly for my own amusement, partly to try out new ideas. I believed, for example, that for very high-speed flight, it might be advantageous to sweep the wings back – or even forward – and I was making various models to try out my ideas. Of course, back then we knew nothing of the drag and compressibility effects of such speeds, but I am still pleased to note that I was correct.

I also had a radio. I had made it myself from parts taken from our store. It was quite unglamorous, simply a collection of valves and condensers on a bare baseboard, all hooked up to a R/T speaker. But with it I could hear not only stations from home in Germany but others from as far away as England or America.

While I worked I switched it on, tuned to, the American voice told me, station WGEA, an international broadcast station owned and operated by the General Electric Company of Schenectady, New York. They played dance-band music, and a girl singer crooned into the microphone while horns wailed softly behind her, and I cut wing ribs from flat sheets of balsa, using the templates I had designed. I fixed them together in neat rows to the spars with tiny globs of scented glue.

While it all dried, I lit a cigarette. I wondered if Krassin was in his office yet. The dance music came to a stop and somebody told me of the virtues of some washing-powder, so fresh and clean, and such terrific value that no housewife could afford to be without it. Some very well-meaning people began to talk about the efforts of the WPA in alleviating poverty in South Carolina, and I decided to see what was on the long-distance station at Cologne.

I thought I had tuned it wrong. The Cologne station employed very staid announcers, men with calm and objective voices, speaking clear and good High German. But what was gushing from my R/T speaker was the voice of some fanatic, filled with a kind of unsavoury, burning joy. He was excited – he might have been giving a commentary on the winning lap of Carraciola's Auto-Union at a motor Grand Prix.

'A procession of thousands of blazing torches... They have marched through the Brandenburg Gate, the brown columns of the SA, victors in a long and arduous struggle, a struggle that claimed many victims. The banners glow blood-red, and against a white background bristles the swastika, symbol of the rising sun! A glorious, an inspiring sight!'

Thousands of miles away, I listened in disbelief. What in hell was going on?

'The torches sway... Everywhere torches, torches, torches and cheering people! One hundred thousand voices shout joyously, "Sieg Heil! Heil Hitler!" into the night!

'The Führer – *yes it is the Führer*! Adolf Hitler – the

unknown soldier of the World War, the unyielding warrior, the standard-bearer of *freedom*!

'His eyes gaze out into the distance. Surely he is now thinking of the long years of struggle, thinking of those who fell for the Movement, of the long march and its privations – and *now* – yes! yes! A thundering chorus swells up toward the young Chancellor from one hundred thousand voices – the German anthem! From the shores of the Maas to the banks of the Memel: *Deutschland, Deutschland, über alles!*'

Chancellor. Adolf Hitler was Chancellor of Germany?

'Like a prayer it rises towards the heavens, like a hymn of gratitude and rejoicing! And *now*: *Yes*! *Yes*! Now the crowd strikes up the fighting song of the National Socialist Movement, the Horst Wessel Song!'

I could hear them. Horst Wessel. Who would have believed it. Horst Wessel, a dead pimp.

'*Oh, raise the flag and close your ranks up tight!*
SA men march with bold determined tread.
Comrades felled by Reds and Ultras in fight
March at out side, in spirit never dead.'

Horst Wessel, doggerel poet and dead pimp.

'With one accord, as far as the eye can see, one hundred thousand arms are raised in the German salute. The billowing crowd salutes the Führer with faith and gratitude, and at the same time honours the unforgotten victims of the struggle, comrades shot by the Red Front and the forces of reaction. Yes, truly they are marching in spirit among the ranks!

'Many there are in that crowd who furtively wipe the tears from their eyes, tears of gratitude and rejoicing! *Hail to you, – our Führer, hail to the German Fatherland*! sing their hearts; and the little old grandmother there in the crowd on the pavement speaks what they are all feeling, all the men and women down there, and also the stalwart men of the SA and SS, marching past in long columns beneath the swastika banner: *Thank you, Almighty God, for letting us live to see this day*!'

I sat by the radio, quite shaken. How had *this* happened? The new announcer was still ranting on, so I tuned the radio elsewhere. The Stuttgart station came in and in steady tones gave me another, more measured, account of what was going on. Hitler was indeed Chancellor, but only as a part of a coalition government together with the Nationalists and Conservatives led by Hugenberg and Von Papen. The Nazis had only two ministerial posts out of eleven. I smiled wryly when I heard that Göring was one: the fat man would love strutting about in a position of power. I wondered how long the coalition would hold together – about as long as it took everybody to realise Hitler was no damned good, I thought. I recalled Hoeppner telling me how he had given him an Iron Cross rather than promote him beyond the rank of corporal, the very limit of his leadership potential.

Somewhat relieved, I switched off the radio. I was hungry. I decided to go and get something to eat and see if Krassin had come in.

Ahah! The light was on in Krassin's office. Good!

I poked my nose round the corner with a smile. It died away when I saw a man in a green military hat stare coldly at me. He was searching Krassin's desk. Even stuffed away in the very outer sticks, I knew what a member of the Secret Police looked like. This man was OGPU.

'Yes?' he demanded.

'Sorry. I was looking for Major Krassin.'

'Prisoner Krassin was arrested yesterday.'

'Arrested? What for? Did he get drunk?' Krassin loved his vodka. He had a peasant father who made his own, flavoured with apricots.

'Prisoner Krassin has confessed to being a British spy.'

My mouth flapped like a codfish for a second or two. Krassin, a spy? 'But ... how could ... I mean, he is just a liaison man. What on earth could he tell the British?'

'Secrets. Secrets of the state,' the man said certainly. 'He confessed this morning.'

'Confessed ... look, if anyone needs to get in touch with him, where shall I tell them to write?'

The Secret Policeman's mouth twitched in a small demonstration of ghoulish humour. 'They may write wherever they like,' he said. 'Prisoner Krassin was shot this morning, after implicating several other officers.'

Back in my room, I looked out into the darkness. Over by the hangar containing the dive-bombers, a solitary lamp was burning. Methodically, I began to clear things up, to put them away in boxes. I had the feeling that we would not be staying in Lipezk much longer.

A couple of days later I turned on my radio and this time I heard an 'Appeal to the German People'. Hitler spoke in solemn, reasoned tones. He sounded almost like a statesman. He talked about the national government, and didn't mention the Nazis at all.

'The national government will preserve and defend the foundations on which the strength of our nation rests. It will take under its firm protection Christianity as the basis of our morality, and the family as the nucleus of our nation. Standing above estates and classes, it will bring back to our people the consciousness of its racial and political unity, and the obligations arising therefrom. It wishes to base the education of German youth on respect for our great past and pride in our traditions. It will therefore declare merciless war on spiritual, political and cultural nihilism. Germany must not and will not sink into communist anarchy.'

I nodded to myself, and began to pack some more things. We surely would not be staying in Lipezk.

'Fourteen years of Marxism have undermined Germany.'

I had to smile at that, thinking how annoyed Hoeppner would be at being described as a Marxist.

'One year of Bolshevism would destroy her.'

Yes, indeed, we would be going home.

Berlin, May 1933

We flew into Tempelhof Airport, finishing the last leg of our long journey on a warm spring afternoon. From the air you could see the broad boulevards and parks, the sun shining on the lakes, the city crowding up all around the airfield. It was a unique enitity, back then. It seemed to embody the future for us, being able to fly directly into the centre of the greatest city in Germany. All was brand new, the runways white, the buildings all designed by

Kosina. I knew him – he was at the Bauhaus with Hilde.

I taxied in, having flown one of Messerschmitt's prototypes. I cut the mixture and switches outside one of the wide, airy hangars Kosina had made. I got out and breathed in the Berlin air gratefully as I stretched. Berlin has a kind of electric smell all of its own.

I didn't have to do much then. There was a ground crew to take care of the aircraft as they came in. I was tired after the long flight, and I wanted to see Hilde and Kurt. I had not been able to tell them I was coming – whatever change in the diplomatic climate between us and Russia that had called a halt to our collaboration had also brought about a cessation of mail. And as for telephone calls, it was not possible to call outside Lipezk, let alone to another country.

I took my bag and walked across the ramp area with its Lockheed, Junkers and Handley Page aircraft of various types, and to the main building, where I knew I could get a taxi into town. As I came in, a uniformed SA man standing in the concourse stared at me – rudely, I thought – as though examining my face for mud. Whatever it contained satisfied him and he looked away, his eyes tracking about for other people. I walked through to the taxi rank and thought little more about it.

Berlin was the same as always. The traffic flowed down the big, wide boulevards, the flowers bloomed. Yet it wasn't the same. I sat forward in my seat as I became aware of it, much as one might smell something in the air. I wasn't sure what it was. To be sure, there were a lot of Nazi flags about, while the black, red and gold banners of the republic seemed to have vanished. The Nazis had always hated the colours of the liberal visionaries of 1848. There were plenty of SA men about too, but there always had been, ever since 1929.

No Reds.

There were no men of the Red Flag, or children of the Red Falcon. The KPD – communists – were conspicuous by their absence, at least to my eye. When I got out near our apartment I stopped off by the news-seller in his canvas hut, the papers and magazines laid out for sale all about him.

'Heil Hitler,' he said wearily.

'Heil Hitler to you,' I replied, and I saw his eyes flicker left and right, as if to see if anyone had heard.

He had a really poor selection of journals. Like the streets, his shelf was lacking anything tinged pink. *Die Linkskurve, The Left Turn*, was not there, nor the *Internationale*, though *Der Angriff, The Attack*, with its screaming scarlet banner, was in evidence, its headlines yelling something about Jews. What did it say? I turned my head sideways. *The Jews Want to Kill Hitler*. Its editor, Paul Josef Goebbels, was in with Hitler. *Rote Fahne* was no more visible than the KPD. The *Völkischer Beobacher*, the Nazi organ, was in a big pile, along with the SA's own *Stürmer* and a rag I hadn't seen before, *Das Schwarze Corps*. It had a cartoon of the Pope buggering a choirboy, his pontificals hitched up about his waist.

'Not much of a selection,' I complained.

The old paper-seller took in my bag, my arrival in a Tempelhof taxi. 'You've been away,' he said.

'What's that got to do with the papers?'

'*Gleichschaltung*,' he said expressionlessly.

'Bringing into line? Who?'

A horny and print-dirty finger flicked the small Nazi flag standing on the shelf in front of him.

'Who?'

'Everything,' he said. He had a few copies of *Vossische Zeitung*, the cultural paper – an institution, really, it had been going for two hundred and fifty years – and, rather grumpily, I bought that. Everybody knew it as *Tante Voss*.

I walked the distance to our apartment block, glad to stretch my legs. The bell sounded with its mellow Bismarckian ring as always, but the door did not open, so I used my own keys. The apartment was completely quiet. Neither Hilde nor Kurt was at home. It was rather stuffy, so I opened the tall windows to the balcony.

It was good to be back. I put my bag and *Tante Voss* down and strolled about. Hilde had some new prints and originals on the walls: Dix, Beckmann, Reiderscheidt. A record of *Weintraub's Syncopators* lay on the turntable of the gramophone, rather dusty. I wiped it carefully and put it on, listening to the jazz like a flower reviving in water. The Russians did not approve of anything like that.

The bookshelves were still full. Jack London rubbed shoulders with Wilhelm Speyer and Mark Twain, Erich Kastner sat alongside Thomas Mann and Upton Sinclair. Feuchtwanger, Tucholsky and Neumann, Erich Maria Remarque, Romain Rolland, Arnold Zweig.

The clock on the wall, made from pieces of modern industrial technology, ticked visibly but silently. I wondered where Hilde and Kurt had gone. It occurred to me that I might have to wait some time, if Hilde was involved with an affair. With some other *trommler*, some other drummer of the Left. I had proved a signal failure as a husband. I found the political thought that so entranced Hilde and her friends tedious. And for Hilde the *neue Sachlichkeit*, the whole new culture that had sprung up, which had burned with such intensity in Weimar, was her life. Much more so than being married to a faded war hero, an engineer, a test-pilot.

We shared the same apartment was what it was. And a son, whom neither of us saw as much as we should. Kurt was probably with his Aunt Clara. I knew that was where Hilde put him when she became involved with someone. Her affairs were like her passion for the new world she thought was coming – all-consuming while they lasted. Then, like a drunk, she would be sober for a while. Whatever it was that Hilde was looking for, I did not provide it. But, then, nor did her various lovers, if their turnover was anything to judge by. Her failure to find it did not stop her from searching for it, though.

I sat on the sofa, and read *Tante Voss* while I waited. If nobody showed up soon, I would walk over to Clara's and see if Kurt was there.

Reading through the paper brought back the strange feeling of driving through the city in the taxi. It simply wasn't the same. Near the back, after the social commentary by Bella Fromm, I came across a plain, unexplained section marked 'In Custody'. Under it there was a list of names. I had heard of some of them – they had been important people the last time I had been in Berlin.

There was also something called 'Forbidden'. This list had something to do with an organisation I had never heard of, the Ministry of Popular Enlightenment and Propaganda. The newspaper's editor, Goebbels, a Nazi rabble-rouser and

Jew-baiter, appeared to be in charge of it. My mind was beginning to boggle. What the hell was going on? The lunatics were taking over the asylum. Under 'Forbidden' I could see a number of the papers I had been looking for on the news-stand.

Finally, next to the religious service list of the Berlin Jewish community, I found a small headline: 'Shot While Trying to Escape.' Somebody had apparently been shot somewhere near Munich, while trying to escape from a place called Dachau.

I put the paper down, rather alarmed. I decided to help myself to a drink. There was always wine and lager in our advanced, ceramic-coated white refrigerator.

There was. There was also food in there, all of it covered in green-grey mould.

Hilde and Kurt had been gone much longer than I had thought.

Immediately I thought of Eisenmann and Hoeppner. Surely they would know what had happened. I picked up the telephone, but it was dead, cut off. I went out into the hallway where the post-boxes were, and there were letters in there that went back weeks, and unpaid bills.

It was getting dark. I locked up the apartment and went out. Eisenmann lived not far away.

At his solid, imperial block I went in and took the lift upstairs. I rang the bell. There was silence, I thought that he was out but I rang again, and I heard somebody moving inside. Heavy steps came to the door, and Eisenmann opened it. He was fully dressed, with a hat and coat on, and he had a suitcase in his hand. Very pale, he stared at me in sudden relief. He had pinned his war decorations in a broad ribbon on his coat.

'Hans . . .' he breathed. 'It's you.' He put down the suitcase with a thud. It was packed. 'Come in, come in . . .' He began to peel off his coat with hands that shook.

'Who did you think it was?' I asked, closing the door behind me.

'The auxiliary police . . .'

'Who the hell are the auxiliary police?'

'They're young thugs. The kind the old police used to arrest.

Now *they* arrest us. They are SA.'

'I've just got back from Russia,' I told him. 'What the hell is happening?'

'I was in Ossietsky's a few nights ago,' he blurted out. 'I dropped in to have a drink while I went through some papers before going home.'

Ossietsky's was Eisenmann's local, the restaurant and bar he had frequented for years.

'In a booth not far from me were some Brown Shirts – a Sturmführer, somebody from the Kreisleiter's office, a journalist on *Der Angriff*. They were drinking together but I took no notice of them – I had work to do. I ordered a stein and got on with what I was doing. Then the waiter came over. He looked worried and was white in the face. He gave me a note from the Brown Shirts. It said: "Get out, filthy Jew!" They were all staring at me. In Ossietsky's!'

He had collapsed onto the edge of the sofa and sat staring at the wall, remembering it.

'Get out, filthy Jew ...' he whispered. 'You know, I was angry! I know their sort. No more than rabble – they've never done anything good in their lives. I was angry, Hans. I jumped to my feet, red as a beet. I shouted at them: "I was a *Frontkämpfer*!" I yelled. "I was wounded twice, at the Somme and Verdun! I have the Iron Cross First and Second Class! I do not have to put up with abuse from you!" I showed the note to the other people there, but they were embarrassed, they stayed silent. You could hear just the clatter from the kitchen. Then the Sturmführer got up and bawled, "Get out, you Jewish pig! Or shall we throw you out?" They all brayed with laughter, the brown ones, they just laughed at me and the others looked down into their beer or their plates. I got up and I left, Hans. When I got back home I sent Irma and the children over to Greifswald, where her parents are. I've stayed here, I have to run the business, but I am afraid ...'

'Hilde is missing, with Kurt,' I said bluntly. 'For some weeks, it looks like.'

'Oh, no – you see, Hans, the brown ones, they've been taking it out on everyone they don't like.'

'But *how*? There has been no *putsch*, no revolution, surely? I know Hitler's Chancellor, but there is still a government, surely?'

He looked at me with pity. 'Didn't you listen to Hitler? He said it often enough. "Once we possess the constitutional power, we will mould the state into the shape we hold to be suitable." Well, this is it, Hans.'

'So where are Hilde and Kurt?'

He shook his head. 'I don't know. She was an artist, a member of the KPD, just the sort they would go for. Maybe she got out, Hans. Maybe she has taken Kurt and they are keeping their heads down somewhere. Perhaps she will get in touch.'

'The telephone is cut off,' I said. 'I'll go round and pay the bill, and then she could call, if you're right.'

'Yes, that's a good idea. And ask the neighbours, perhaps, or try her friends.'

'There's her sister. I'll go over there.'

'Yes. Best of luck, Hans.'

I left him sitting on the sofa in his heavy blue coat, the medals on his chest blazing like a kingfisher, staring at the wall.

Hoeppner. As I left, I thought of Hoeppner, who always knew, and I altered my steps over to where he lived, not far from Wilhelmstrasse. When I rang the bell, and the door opened, I got another shock. Hoeppner was in the uniform of a captain in the Reichswehr reserve.

'Hans, Hans. Get yourself in.' He opened two bottles of beer without a word and gave me one in the kitchen of his apartment.

'What's this?' I asked, gesturing at the uniform.

'Protective colouration,' he said briefly, cynically. 'Most people are up to it in one form or another.'

'I've just been over at Eisenmann's. He says Hitler and that lot have taken over.'

'That's right. Hitler is having his revolution, the way he always wanted, with the power of the state on his side, and it's too late to do anything about it. Most people are too frightened, and most think that it's just a passing phase, and anyway, the Nazis are getting on with the "national rebirth", that there'll be work again, employment, that Germany will be given back her pride.'

'Hilde's missing, with Kurt.'

'Yes? Yes, of course.' He looked grimly at me. 'Do you know if she got out, or if they took her?'

'I only got back today. She's been gone for a few weeks.'

'Try and find out if she's in hiding. If she isn't, you'll have to try to find out who took her away. You see, Hans, it could have been quite a few people. It might have been Röhm's SA – that's very likely. But, equally, Goebbels is the new Culture Minister – he decides what's acceptable, and anyone to do with *Zivilisation* and the old order is out. Then there's a new body, that's Göring's *Geheime Staatspolizei* – most people call it the Gestapo. They're over on Prinz Albrechtsrasse. Then there's the SS, the boys in black; they're up and coming, mark my words, we haven't heard the last of that little creep Himmler.'

'I met him once, a long time ago. At the university.'

'So pull some strings,' Hoeppner urged. 'You flew with Göring – why not start with him, once you're sure Hilde's not hiding out.'

'Right,' I said. 'I met Röhm, too, in the castle, you remember, when you asked me to let you know what the Freikorps lot were up to. God, it seems a long time ago.'

'Listen. Whoever you go and see, just make sure you join the Party first. Whatever you do, have an armband on.'

'Yes, of course . . .'

Suddenly I was exhausted. I had spent eight hours in the air that day. I still had to start calling round. There was a phone booth in the restaurant down the street from the apartment. I decided to get something to eat and make my calls from there.

Wearily, I said goodbye to Hoeppner, and trudged back out on to the street, walking along under the lamps. Our block came into view, and further along the lights of the restaurant.

Suddenly, something small came running out of the darkness, and piled into me. '*Papa, Papa!*'

It was Kurt. I bent down, clutching him to me. 'Where have you been?' I demanded.

'With Aunt Clara. Mama told me to go.'

'Where is Mama?' I said anxiously.

'They came and took her away. Early in the morning. She hid me, and the men took her away.'

Röhm hadn't changed much. His surroundings were better, though – he had a nice place in the diplomatic quarter south of the Tiergarten. The previous owner's gothic paintings were still on the walls and his silk-covered furniture still filled the rooms; Röhm sat behind his desk.

The little man was slightly redder in the face than when I had last seen him. The bullet scars still creased his cheeks and his neck was still thick. A blond rent-boy in a close-fitting SA uniform showed me in and Röhm stared unabashedly at his groin.

'Yes, I thought it was you,' he barked, transferring his attention to me as the young man left the room. 'I never forget a face. You were with us at the castle, when Adolf wanted to listen to Wagner, right? So what can I do for you? Where have you been all these years?'

'Flying aircraft,' I said baldly. 'Developing the new fighters and stukas out in Russia. I've only just got back.'

His small, piggy eyes gleamed with approval. '*Ja!*' he shouted. 'You were the fighter ace. Good for you. And now you've come to take part in the new Germany. We'll show them what for! We'll crack a few more heads before we're through. This is only the start, Wolff. The Second Revolution's on the way, and we stormtroopers will head it. We'll smash all those smug gentlemanly bastards, the Von this and the Von that! We'll break all the money-grubbing capitalists like they've done in Russia – they'll be begging on the streets while SA men lie in luxury in their great houses. Oh, yes, this is just the start!'

He had on an armband like mine, but he was in full uniform as head of the SA. He had three million men under his command, and was probably more powerful than the head of the Reichswehr.

'Have you come to join?' He didn't wait for a reply but immediately went on in his hoarse, quick voice. 'I'm a simple man. You're for me or against me. I love soldiers, hate civilians. I love men, hate women. Want to know what was rotten at the core of Weimar? Women. It was a democracy; it allowed women a high place in society. That's why we could push it over so easily! Women have only one place – on their backs having male babies who'll grow up to be soldiers.' He squinted at me under knitted brows. 'You one of us?' he demanded. 'I can't remember.'

I raised my arm to show the swastika.

'No, no,' he said impatiently. 'You're a Nazi, of course you are. No, are you one of *us*? We're creating a new order, a higher man. Men like me. My boys are proud, they're arrogant, they can drink and fight. They smash windows and heads for the hell of it. They can kill and slaughter and sleep well in their beds. Men like me. Men who love men, not women. Straights are soft, they aren't up to it. Did Alexander the Great ever get stiff for a woman? No, of course not. Frederick the Great? Never! He was a bugger, the same as me.'

The door opened, and the rent-boy put his head round it. 'Car's ready,' he said, and Röhm jumped to his feet.

'Come and see me when you're ready,' he said. 'We'll go and crack some heads.' His hand darted into the youth's groin. 'I might even let you fuck Ernst,' he said.

Göring was bigger, fatter, and wore a uniform he had bought at a theatrical tailor's, about two sizes up and three across. His medals rippled over his chest in a blaze of glory. He guffawed when he saw me come in and embraced me like a bear, cologne billowing off him.

'Where the hell have you been?' he bellowed. 'This is no time for heroes to hide out in the woodwork! Come and get some of it!'

'I've been in Russia. With the new warplanes.'

'Ah ... *ja*! Udet mentioned it. Listen, we're having a new airforce, a Luftwaffe. Mine! I need good men. You'll join me.'

'Of course ...'

I looked at the seemingly jolly fat man in front of me. He was the boss of Prussia, and Berlin was in Prussia. Many of the people who were missing were missing because he, Göring, had had them taken away. The cars that squealed to a halt in the dawn to disgorge agents and suck in bewildered, terrified suspects were his cars. The cellars of the Colombia Haus where they screamed and sobbed and answered the questions that were put to them were his cellars.

Hoeppner had told me, as I left. Göring made no secret of what he was doing, he had stood up in public and told them all: 'A bullet fired from the barrel of a police gun is my bullet. If you say that is murder then I am the murderer.'

'I need a favour,' I said. 'As one *Flieger* to another.'

'What?'

'My wife is missing. While I was in Russia. Some officials took her away, apparently.'

He stared at me, his eyes hidden in the folds of flesh suddenly cold.

'It is clearly a case of mistaken identity,' I said clearly.

He suddenly grinned, once again the jolly buccaneer. 'You were always a silly bastard,' he said. 'You never could think straight. But you could fly, Hans!' He seized one of the several telephones littering his enormous desk. 'Get me Diels,' he barked. He looked at me. 'Name? Your wife?'

'Hilde. Hilde Wolff.'

'Rudolf,' Göring said affably into the phone, 'have we got someone called Hilde Wolff? *Ja*. Call me back.'

I sat for some while in the opera set Göring called his office, while he worked on his papers and issued a stream of orders. Finally, the telephone rang again. He listened in near silence, and then put it down. He stared at me.

'We haven't got her,' he said. 'But I know who has. Himmler. Some of his SS picked her up for Goebbels. You didn't tell me she was a commie, Hans.'

'She is an artist,' I said flatly.

'Well, Goebbels doesn't like artists. He's cleaning them out.'

'Where is she?'

'In a camp. Himmler's got a camp near Munich. Place called Dachau.'

'How can I get her out?'

Göring rubbed one of his several chins thoughtfully. 'It won't do any good *me* asking for you. That little crippled prick hates me. Himmler – he was at the university with us. Did you know him?'

'I fought a duel with someone who had him as a second.'

Göring slapped the desk with a hand like a ham. 'There you are then! I'm having a party on my new estate. Karinhall. Up on the Schönheide. Next weekend. We're going to do some shooting. Himmler's coming. The little creep doesn't want to – he gets the collywobbles when he sees blood, wet little fart! But he never stays away when he thinks there's a bit of politicking in it for him. Him and Goebbels, what a pair. That's it! You come too, and you can approach him there.'

'Thank you,' I said sincerely.

'Now you owe me,' he said genially, and sincerely. He looked at me, assessing something. 'You should be all right,' he said. 'Himmler – you remember him, he hasn't changed much. He's still weedy, still looks like a bank clerk and can't hold his liquor. He's got a thing about Nordic types. You know, fellows like you, blond hair, blue eyes. Surrounds himself with young men of that type, all a head taller than him. Sucking up to the Führer, of course – Adolf's a bit funny that way and we all have to go along with it.'

He frowned, trying to remember.

'Don't you have a son?'

'Yes, of course. Kurt. He's twelve, a strapping fellow.'

'Blond, blue eyes?'

I nodded.

'There you are!' Göring beamed. 'Himmler will never believe your wife's a commie if she produced a child like that. I tell you what, bring him along with you. That'll be proof.'

'Thanks. I'll do that.'

'Did you hear the new joke that's going around about me?' he asked, his eyes gleaming with glee within the folds of fat.

'Which one?'

'I'm late for luncheon with an English friend. At last, in I dash, all apologetic: "I'm so sorry I'm late, Sir George, I've been out shooting." And Sir George looks at me, and says, poker-faced: "Animals, I presume?" Eh? Isn't that good?'

Göring slapped his huge thigh, roaring with mirth, and I laughed too. It was always a good idea.

'Animals, I presume ... Yes, Hans, we've cleaned up the country all right ...'

I decided to collect Göring jokes. They were currency. He poured me an enormous drink and I put it away in one. Göring didn't like people who couldn't take their liquor.

Karinhall, Schonheide

It was a beautiful morning. Under the trees surrounding Göring's *völkische* hunting-lodge servants were setting tables with long white cloths. The air was fresh, pine-scented. The trees stretched for miles, broken up by pleasing meadows and lakes. Wildlife flourished, tended by hordes of foresters and huntsmen. The lodge was in the process of being transformed into a palace, and its grounds into a truly colossal estate. The sound of sawing and hammering filled the air. Göring was extending the lodge everywhere. A small zoo appeared to be going up at one end.

We were further off, where the day's hunting had been organised. Our host, Göring, was in fine form, wearing a white shirt like a tent, stout hunting breeches of green cloth and knee boots. He looked like a mobile cask.

Kurt and I were dressed in *Lederhosen*, with knee socks and white shirts. Despite our casual country clothes, we both wore our armbands. I had stressed the importance of being like the others, were we to succeed in finding Hilde and having her released, and Kurt was old enough to understand.

Göring was discussing the arrangements with his head huntsman. He saw us coming up and gestured for me to come over. I could see Himmler not far away. Dressed like myself in *lederhosen*, he looked like a filing clerk on vacation. He seemed quite pleased to be there, looking about and making remarks to his small entourage, all the while inflating his puny chest with the fresh air. I noticed with surprise that Huber was there. The former Freikorps *Frontkämpfer* was uncompromisingly dressed in the jet-black breeches and brown shirt of the SS. His boots gleamed with an old soldier's shine, and he stood comfortably, an *alte Kämpfer* for whom the years of struggle had brought their final reward.

'Come on,' Göring said to me, 'I'll take you over. You can go for a walk with him. He walks in the forest and looks at the birds and bees and flowers while we primitives get on with the real business. Hey, Heinrich, meet an old comrade of mine, Hans Wolff! We flew together with Richtofen.'

Short-sighted, steel-blue eyes peered beadily at me through his pince-nez glasses. He suddenly smiled primly. 'But I know you!' he exclaimed. 'Were you not at the university, Herr Wolff?'

'I fought a duel against a man who had you for a second,' I smiled.

'*Ja, ja!*' He ran a proud finger over faint white lines on his cheeks. 'I, too, fought, not long afterwards.'

'Shall I leave you two *Frontschwein* to exchange war stories?' Göring asked genially. I thought I detected a note of irony – Himmler had never got near the war. 'Heinrich, are you going for a walk? *Ja*? Take care, we are shooting over *there*. I might mistake you for a leaping deer!' He turned to me as he waddled away to collect his rifle. 'Or a bunny rabbit,' he chuckled to me. 'Enjoy your walk, Hans.'

'This is your son?' Himmler asked me.

'Yes. Kurt, this is Reichsführer SS Himmler.'

Kurt bowed formally, and Himmler stood for a moment in admiration. 'You must be proud!' he exclaimed to me. 'A perfect Nordic man in the making – broad-shouldered, narrow-hipped, blond. Such shining skin, flushed with blood, and clear, conquering eyes. I salute you, Hans – shall I call you Hans? – your child is a member of the new royal species among men!'

I beamed. 'Thank you!' I said effusively. 'His mother and I, we are of the same type.' That'll get it started, I thought.

'*Komm, komm!*' Himmler clapped his hands and his acolytes paid attention. 'Let us go into the forest while our host slaughters its inhabitants. Will you come, Hans? Good.'

We set off down a path through the trees, following a charming stream, its edges strewn with flowers. I found myself near Huber.

'Good to see you again, Hauptmann,' he grinned.

'I've been abroad in Russia,' I explained, 'with the aircraft.'

'Ah, *ja*?'

'I thought you were with the SA,' I said.

'This is a good detail,' he replied. He patted a shoulder bar with plaited silver threads. Strange occult devices of stars and wreaths decorated his collar patches. 'Look at that. Sturmbannführer! Me, an old *Frontschwein*. And I can go further than that, Hauptmann. Reichsheini – him there, the boss – is going far. The big boss likes him.'

Himmler had stopped with one of his followers and was picking the leaves off a plant.

'Who are these people?' I muttered.

'That one's his herbalist. He makes medicines from herbs. That one's his astrologer – Hanussen's his name – he divines his future from the stars. That one's a professor, knows all about race.'

He grinned at me. 'And this one's the bodyguard,' he said.

'An *astrologer*?' I said disbelievingly.

'Oh yes,' he looked at me, smiling faintly, and cynically. 'Very good he is, I'm told. He had a vision sometime in February, so he did. He saw into the future, he saw a blood-curdling crime committed by the communists. He saw blazing flames. He saw a firebrand that lit up the world.'

'And?'

'Reichstag burned down the following evening,' Huber said, poker-faced. 'And we rounded up all the commies what did it, didn't we?'

'That's seeing into the future all right,' I agreed.

'Hans!' Himmler called to me. 'Smell this.' He held out some crushed leaves and a faintly bitter aroma floated up. 'Marrob!' he cried triumphantly. 'At the first signs of a cold, infuse the leaves in hot water and drink. It will cure you.'

'I shall remember that,' I said politely.

'This is the place to find a cure for all ills. The pure, clean countryside.'

We began to meander along the path again.

'All ills,' he repeated. 'Out here, in the heartland of the *Volk*. Out here in the country, life is pure, people are pure. It is the city that has made people corrupt and poisoned the race.'

'That's where the Jews are, Reichsführer!' the herbalist interjected.

'And homosexuals!' Himmler agreed. 'Did you know that in the old days there were virtually no homosexuals? It is one of the reasons those days were less poisoned. Homosexuality leads inevitably to mental irresponsibility and madness. Our forefathers who lived here in the heartland knew, because they were so few, what to do with homosexuals – they were called *Urning* – and they were simply taken out and sunk in a bog. Herr professors who find these bodies today in swamps are certainly not aware that in every case they have a homosexual before them, who, with his clothes and all, was plunged into the bog.'

Himmler paused to inhale some more air and all about him did likewise.

'Herr Sturmbannführer! How many cases of this disease do we get in the SS?'

'Very few, Reichsführer!' Huber bellowed.

'Very few indeed,' Himmler said, pleased. 'I have issued instructions as to the method of dealing with them. They will obviously be publicly degraded and dismissed and handed over to the court. After the expiration of their sentence they will by my regulations be taken into a concentration camp – I have set up a model establishment at Dachau – and in the camp they will be shot while escaping. This is not as punishment, one should note; it is simply the extinguishing of an abnormal, undeserving, *wurdig* life in order that the blood of Germany shall become pure. We of the Reich are charged with the task of gathering and preserving the valuable stock of original Germanic racial elements and allowing only the hereditarily sound to propagate.'

I glanced behind me. Kurt had paused by the pool and was skimming flat stones. A waddling creature I took to be the race doctor chimed in to Himmler's monologue.

'We have our new sterilisation laws, Reichsführer, which eliminate the hereditarily diseased, the mentally deficient – schizophrenics, epileptics and so forth – from the genetic stock. Should we not now be thinking about a greater category of *lebensunwertes Leben*?'

'Life-unworthy life? Of course.'

'To be done under strict medical supervision, naturally. I happen to have been doing research into this area. I am thinking of those people who do not possess German blood, the *Mischlinge* – the cross-breeds – the Jews, the negroes, the gypsies . . .'

'Ah!' Himmler stopped, and held up a hand. 'We must not venture too far at once.' He raised himself up, and stood as though to attention. 'But I may tell you that I have been privileged to discuss these matters with the Führer. The genetic and racial purity of the *Volk* is integral and inseparable from the Reich itself.'

He dropped his voice, and all bent nearer to hear.

'But is it not all bound up together? Our necessity to purify the world of Bolshevism? Our *gottlichen* God-ordained task to eliminate the race poison? Our right for *lebensraum*? Yes, let us admit that we the *Volk* are joined in battle with the many-headed hydra. Jews, freemasons, Jesuits, Bolsheviks. The *Minderrassigen*, the racially inferior, and the *Untermenschen*. This struggle is, by historical law, no new thing. It has been the natural order of life on our planet. Did not in ancient times the Hebrew Bolsheviks slaughter the king of Persia, that great Aryan kingdom and his nobility? Thus were the Aryan peoples enslaved by the Jews and their racial purity destroyed by interbreeding so that nothing was left of the high Aryan culture except the words 'once here there was a *Volk*.' This struggle between men and *Untermenschen* has been the rule. This battle of life and death is quite as much a law of nature as man's struggle against some epidemic, as the struggle of the plague bacillus against the healthy, *völkische* body. Let me assure you, these are matters the Führer has in his mind every day, and which he will, before long, put into effect. So, now, let us enjoy our walk in the heart of the *Volk*!'

As we meandered round back towards Göring's hunting, the steady crack of rifles could be heard again. Himmler frowned with disapproval.

'It's disgusting, you know. What possible pleasure can the fat one get from blowing these poor creatures to bits? Is not nature so wonderfully beautiful? Does not every animal have a right to live? I have had to shoot some poor defenceless creature in my time, some gentle deer browsing, and I tell you, it is simply murder. I plan as Reichsführer to issue regulations that will protect animals. Fox-hunting is to be banned! Yes! *Schweinereien*! Obscenities! Children must be taught to love animals. We shall have societies for the protection of animals that will have special police powers of arrest and imprisonment. Animals must have legal rights.' He sucked his teeth and bared them at the thought of proscription.

Huber nudged me. 'There something you want from the boss?' he enquired.

'Yes.'

'Thought so,' he said phlegmatically. 'Now's not a bad time.'

'Not lunch?'

'Doesn't drink more'n a glass – and Göring baits him,' he said with the servant's knowledge. 'Now.'

I moved up in the swirl of acolytes until I was close by Himmler. Huber was right. He beamed affably at me; the prospect of new rules had pleased him. 'It is good to see you again. You are still flying? But not the gliders, I think.' He had a very good memory, like his ultimate boss.

'Developing the new *Jägers* and *Stukas*,' I said.

'Great work! We must be strong again.'

'We shall be,' I assured him.

Kurt had run on ahead a little. He had floated some small branches downstream and was watching them cope with a swift riffle of rapids in the stream. The sun was on his face; he was laughing.

'Such a specimen, your son!' Himmler said admiringly. 'Such perfection of limb and body. A privilege to see. There is a universal psychic energy in the cosmos and it manifests itself on earth in its most perfect form as the blond-haired, blue-eyed Aryan. Truly, you and your wife must be pure Nordic stock.'

'We are,' I assured him.

'What reincarnation of great medieval Teutons can you be?' he mused aloud. 'I am myself the reborn king, Heinrich, you know. It is a thousand years since he walked the earth. Your wife, she is here with you? Or tending to the home?'

There it was. I felt a sudden rush of adrenaline, like spotting the tiny chocolate crosses of the enemy below, in that heart-beat before the screaming dive.

'She is neither, I regret to say. I understand that – I was in Russia with the aircraft – once the Führer came to power a God-sent cleansing of society took place, that all the foul elements within it were purged.'

Himmler looked at me, his blue eyes suddenly very intent behind his thick glasses. You had never to forget with him that although he was mad, on a second plane he was simultaneously completely sane, a fearsome predator in the world which Hitler made. Many were those who regretted making fun of the Reichsführer for his crazy beliefs. But that was something I learned much later, along with much of the rest of Germany.

'That is so,' he agreed.

'Occasionally, with the bad there must sometimes be a little good removed in error,' I suggested. 'My wife, Hilde, the mother of our son Kurt, was taken away by some auxiliary police.'

'Oh yes?' he said softly. 'And where did they take her?'

'To a place of detention in Dachau, I am told. I believe that you have jurisdiction over it, which is why I thought I would bring the matter to your attention, as it is clear that some oversight has occurred.'

'What did your wife do, before the *Machtergreifung*, the seizure of power?' he asked carefully. 'She was a housewife, perhaps?'

'Of course. She looked after our son. She had some friends who were in the theatre – possibly this is why she was picked up in error...'

Friends in the theatre. Only Brecht and Dix and Weill, the kind the man next to me would happily shoot.

'She was in politics?'

I laughed. 'Do women have the capacity for such thought?' I asked.

'Some fancy they do.' he replied darkly, 'which is why we have them locked up while they have their thoughts re-educated.'

He paused on the sun-dappled path, looking at Kurt. Then he turned to look at me, like a farmer examining a likely horse. He had once bred chickens, if unsuccessfully, which is why he was, apparently, at least according to the crowd of astrologers, herbalists and homoeopathic doctors about me, an expert of genetics.

'Truly fine...' he murmured. He suddenly appeared to make up his mind. 'My dear Hans, I see you are a party member.'

'Naturally.'

'But are you of the SS?'

'I have just come back from Russia,' I said apologetically.

'Huber!'

'*Ja, mein Reichsführer!*' Huber bellowed, deafening the sycophants and causing small animals to scuttle in the bushes.

'Hans wishes to join us. See to it.'

'*Ja mein Reichsführer.*'

'And your son. He must be –?'

'Twelve.'

'Ideal! Ready for his next phase of schooling. I am starting special schools for the élite of our future, on the instructions of the Führer himself. What do you say? Shall your Kurt, as fine a Nordic young man as I have seen, join us?'

Kurt was standing quite close by, listening. He looked

Himmler square in the eye. 'Can Mama come back?' he asked.

'Why, yes! She was taken off by mistake. Your father is going off to get her tomorrow. But, now: will you join us at our new school?' He turned to me. 'It is at Wallenburg Castle!' he beamed. 'Our new Teutonic knights shall be trained at the home of the old. Well?'

'Thank you, sir,' said Kurt. 'It is a great privilege.'

'There! It is done. Huber, come and see me later. I want you to take Hans down there tomorrow. And make sure he gets his uniform.'

'*Ja, mein Reichsführer!*'

We came out on to the meadow. There was a sudden smell of blood and guts. Göring's huntsmen were gralloching a deer before carrying it off.

'Bestial,' Himmler said.

Berlin

'I won't stay here,' she said, standing back from the window, but looking out over the trees of the park. Her head had been shaved, and there was a fine, dark fur covering her skull. She had changed out of the grimy, dirt-sheened rags, and she had bathed. She had stayed a long time in the bath. She had put on a blouse and skirt, but they hung on her as though drying on a clothes-horse.

'All this will blow over,' I said. 'The SA are a rabble – they're just settling old scores.'

She turned and held up bruised, cut hands, swollen and scarred. '*Arbeit macht frei,*' she said savagely. 'It says so over the main gates. Work makes you free. The camp is not run by the SA any more, it is run by Himmler. He's the one who had the sign put up, in wrought iron.' She turned away from me again. 'He wants it to last.'

'Himmler's a crackpot,' I protested. 'I tell you, I spent a morning with him while I was getting you released.'

'Yes, thank you, Hans,' she said quietly.

'He's a crank. He rants on about racial purity while surrounded by frauds of all kinds – herbalists, astrologers, so-called geneticists, homoeopaths, you name it. Göring's just a fat gangster. Goebbels is as nutty as Himmler, and Hitler is worse than the lot. Do you seriously imagine a crew of lunatics like that can stay in power? What about the rest of the government – von Schleicher, von Papen, Hugenberg, von Blomberg, von Neumann and the rest? *They* aren't Nazis.'

'Back there,' she said softly, 'what you said would get you hanged. Just forgetting to salute a guard got you flogged, followed by bread and water in a freezing cell. Don't you see, Hans, the lunatics are in charge of the asylum. *Inside* that ... that *place* were all the people who should be running things. Everything from the government to the theatre to business, the newspapers, the Church – you name it, they were there. Social democrats and communists, conservatives and monarchists, Jewish businessmen and journalists, priests and authors, artists and musicians – all brought down to a common level of slobbering fear ... by *them*. The guards. *Dreck*! Just filth, trash, semi-illiterate swine. And they hated us! They hated anyone who was cultured, better than them, had delicate hands. They could do what they wanted with you. The one thing you must never do was beg for mercy ...'

I had seen them. The worst of the SA: thick-necked, bloated; boots like pipes growing out of brown breeches; small, unintelligent eyes filled with the certainty of their own superiority and hatred.

With her back to me, she said again: 'I won't stay here. I won't come back until the battle's won.'

'What battle?'

'Everybody has to choose sides, now. It's us or them. You're either a communist or a Nazi.' She turned back. 'You won't choose, will you, Hans. You think you can go along, keeping your head down, saying the right thing, making a Heil Hitler every now and again. You think you can do that. But I tell you, you can't. *You have to believe*. One side or the other.'

'I don't believe in either.'

'Then you will be squashed like a bug between the two!' she shouted suddenly. She stood by the window, trembling all over. 'Hans, Hans ... You lost the war. Somehow, you've been looking for what you had as a scout pilot, a leader ... You haven't noticed what's been happening. Us, we – you know who I mean, all my kind – we lost a battle just afterwards, when the Freikorps beat us. That was just a battle. We won *afterwards*. The culture, the buildings, the art, the music – that was all ours, not theirs. *Zivilisation*, not *Volk*. We trampled them into the dirt and it was marvellous. Now, somehow, *they've* won – I don't know how – and we are scattered, defeated troops.'

She wrapped her arms about herself as though she were cold.

'I am a combat soldier,' she said. 'I have been a bad wife to you, a bad mother to Kurt. I am sorry. We should never have got married, I know that now. I am not the kind who should get married. All those years ago, I told you I wanted to be a part of making a new world. And I did – me, a woman. That was what was more important to me than anything else. I'm sorry. A bad wife, a bad mother. You will have to put it on my gravestone. But that is how I am. I cannot stop now. I shall go into exile with the others and continue the war from there.'

'With the communists?'

'Of course. Who else is there? Only the communists are fighting against the fascists.'

'In Russia,' I said carefully, 'they are taking people away and putting them in camps or shooting them.'

'You cannot create a new world except by breaking the old,' she replied, as though explaining something to a child.

'I know,' I said. 'Isn't that what Hitler is doing as well?'

She shook her head tormentedly. 'Hitler and the Nazis are just the final excrescence of the capitalist order. Of *course* they want to destroy people like us, who represent what is to come. What the Russians are doing is cleansing their society of all the old reactionary elements who are clinging on to power, who oppress the people in the people's state.'

She turned and walked towards her room. It was hers – we had not been together for some time.

'Thank you for getting me out. I'm surprised you didn't leave me there after all I've done. Look after Kurt. God, I'm a rotten mother.' She glanced back as she went into her room. 'Who's next, Hans? If the lunatics have got rid of all the sane people, who will they turn on next?'

When I woke up in the morning she was gone. The SS uniform, black and sinister, that Himmler had made sure I had, was hanging in the wardrobe. She had pinned a note on it, some little lines of poetry from an Englishman. The book was still on the shelf. Like a seasoned *Frontkämpfer*, she had taken nothing but a few possessions with her. I took out the pin and read it.

> 'There was a young lady of Riga,
> Who went for a ride on a tiger...'

Berlin, June 1934

I worked for Göring. In the swirl of hyenas that marked the beginning of Hitler's Third Reich, Göring had proclaimed himself *der Eiserne*, the Iron One. He was boss of Prussia and the secret police, and the Gestapo was his. He knew, though, that in the snapping over the corpse of Weimar, it was not enough simply to tear off a limb: it wasn't yours until it was digested, and even getting to swallow was difficult when men such as Röhm with his three million SA men, Goebbels with his Ministry of Propaganda, Bormann with the ear of Hitler, and Himmler with the demoniacal Heydrich – they were barely thirty years old, the pair of them – were circling about you. He must have known Himmler much better than I, for although the bespectacled herbalist was undoubtedly insane on one level, on the other – the level of power – he was a lean, formidable competitor. He took the Gestapo from the Iron One, anyhow, in the end, and Göring was a killer in his own right.

It was probably because he knew this that Göring was setting up something else (though Hitler gave him the economy, and what a mess that was) that nobody could take away from him. An airforce. When it came to that, after all, he was the real thing. A genuine, highly decorated ace who commanded the respect of other pilots. Himmler, Goebbels, Röhm, Bormann, Heydrich or any of the others, we would have laughed in their faces if they had been head of the Luftwaffe. But Göring, well, we knew he had been up there too, in the cold killing place in the sky, as we had.

He gave me an office in his palace in the Leipzigerstrasse. One evening when I looked out of the window, hearing sounds of activity below, Reichswehr troops were flinging a cordon round the building. Peering up towards the rooftops I could see machine-gunners setting up their positions. When I opened my door and went out down the corridors, I found that the place – usually quiet at that time – was suddenly alive with activity. Groups of men – adjutants in uniform, Gestapo officers with faces sheened with the heat, bureaucrats with papers in their hands, SS men with guns – stood about, while others came through from distant parts of the building bearing intent looks and pieces of paper that required signatures. Servants in Göring's own livery hurried about with trays of sandwiches.

The centre of activity appeared to be Göring's study, a vast room which had formerly been a ballroom. Two huge swastika flags hung from bronze staffs on the walls faced with marble. The great doors were half open and through them I could see the Iron One in a white tunic and matching high boots. There was a secretary, Koerner, I think it was, and the two *Diaskuren*, devil's twins, in jet-black: Himmler and Heydrich. The three bosses seemed in savagely high spirits – I could hear Göring's occasional bellow and Himmler's high-pitched laugh. A few moments later the two *Diaskuren* swept out, an SS guard attaching itself to them as they hurried away down the corridor. At his desk Göring saw me looking in.

'Hans!' he yelled. 'Here, *komm*, I was going to send for you.'

Inside the great room some desks with telephones had been set up, they were manned, with people waiting for them to ring.

'I need someone I can trust to go down to Munich.'

'What's going on?'

'We're fixing that bastard Röhm,' he said grinning at me, his eyes shining, slamming a huge fist into his palm. 'There's a spare seat on the Führer's Junkers tonight, I want you on it. Keep me informed. Take a revolver.'

The three engines droned, slightly out of synch, sending a slow harmonic through the large cabin. We climbed through the clouds, and the black of the sky was suffused with moonlight. I could see Hitler sitting right at the front, quite silent in a leather coat, staring ahead of him. In the seats behind were the huge forms of his personal guards in their black Leibstandarte uniforms. Somewhere amongst them was SA Obergruppenführer Lutze, Röhm's subordinate. A ghoulish expression of expectancy illuminated his face. Opposite me was Goebbels, who had arrived separately, carrying a thick sheaf of papers. By the light of a small lamp by his seat, he was going through the papers, writing something down at the back from time to time. Finally he shuffled them together, and glanced across at me; a small, emaciated man with very sharp eyes.

'You're Göring's man, the *Richtofensflieger*,' he said.

'Hans Wolff.'

A rodent smile flashed across his face. He glanced up at the front, where Hitler was still staring ahead, and held out the sheaf of paper. 'Here,' he said, 'feel free. Everybody else has.'

I took the papers. The top one was headed 'Reichsliste of Unwanted Persons'. There was name after name. The entire SA leadership was there, with the exception of Lutze, licking his lips in the seat in front of me. There were many others, including most of the national government that were not Nazi. Von Schleicher, the former Chancellor; Brüning, likewise; von Bredow, Schleicher's second-in-command; von Kahr, who had opposed Hitler in the 1923 failed *Putsch*; the Catholic Erich Klausener; vice-chancellor von Papen and his ideas man, Edgar Jung; Gregor Strasser . . .

The list degenerated into a scrawl of hand-written names appended by signatures. Heydrich had put in the head of the Gestapo, Rudolf Diels. Göring had crossed him out. Himmler, Heydrich, Göring and now Goebbels had added names in their own handwriting. The name of Strasser, Goebbels' old enemy, was written in Goebbels' own hand, duly signed.

Wir misten aus! An old Nazi election slogan. We'll clear the shit from the stables. Here it was, cleaning day.

I made myself go through the list. Somewhere near the middle, I found Hoeppner and his Munich address. I had a pen. The altitude had made it leak and I got ink all over my fingers. Goebbels was looking out of the window at his future. I drew a line through Hoeppner's name. Göring's signature was above, confirming a man to be shot, and I forged his initials.

Wiping my hands on a handkerchief I gave the sheaf back to

Goebbels. 'Anybody you want?' he enquired pleasantly.

'He was already there,' I said with a smile. 'Somebody else wanted him too.'

He laughed.

I awoke with a sudden start in my chair by the fire. It was not out, the logs still glowed. My heart was pounding. What was it?

A man screaming. I was sure I had heard a man screaming.

With my stiff legs, I got up and lobbed another log on to the fire. Then I hobbled over to the window. It takes some time for my joints to work properly. They do not care for screaming men to wake them up in the night. They prefer eight hours of doing nothing.

It was dark, with only faint starlight through the icy clear air showing the mountain slope. I waited, but it was silent. There was just the crackle of the log beginning to burn in the hearth. In the yellow-white light of the flames I could see my waiting desk, my notebook, lying ready for the morning.

What was I thinking of? My memories were filling up my dreams. A man screaming? Not just one, but many. Many men screaming. Gunshots and oaths, the crunching thud of the bludgeon, the howl of orders and acknowledgement, the screams of disbelief of the dying. *Heil Hitler. Heil Hitler. Sieg heil. Sieg heil*... men dying with their murderer's name on their lips.

I stood in the chill glow of the fire, an icy sweat breaking over me. I poured a tot of schnapps into a tumbler and took it with me back to the chair.

Screaming... the superchargers of the huge open Mercedes limousines had screamed...

The big cars raced us through the dawn light as we left the airfield behind. At the Interior Ministry, SS men dragged out two of the local SA leaders, Schneidhuber and Schmid, grinning broadly at their terror and shock as Hitler cursed and struck them, ripping their insignia from their shoulders, his spittle flying in their faces.

I slipped into a room. It was big, a reception room. An SS

man was manning a desk. The room was dim, the heavy velvet curtains still drawn.

'I have come with the Führer,' I snapped. 'I have to talk with Göring on the telephone.'

The man – young, like all the SS – jumped to his feet, pushing his phone to me. I seized the receiver and dialled.

There was a smell in the room. Musty and acrid, unpleasant. They needed to throw open the windows.

The number was local. I heard Hoeppner's bleary voice, awakened from sleep.

'We have arrived in Munich!' I shouted. 'The Führer is taking care of the traitors here at the Ministry before we go on to clean out the others.'

There was silence at the other end. Outside, Hitler was still screaming and the SA men bleating pitifully.

'Is that you, Hans?' Hoeppner said, his voice suddenly fearful.

'All the traitors will die!' I yelled.

'Thanks, Hans. I'm running.'

I heard the clatter of the receiver going down, and I put my phone down.

The lights suddenly flashed all about me. A huge chandelier glowed iridescent. I whirled round and saw Hitler standing at the entrance to the room, some local SS men clustered proud at his shoulders.

The chandelier blazed down on a rough pile of corpses, all flung together in a great bloody heap on the polished parquet. They were SA – I could see it from their uniforms. Hitler had summoned the SA to a grand reunion. They were all in their best to greet their Führer.

His face was working, twitching and blinking as he surveyed his dead. 'Good work!' he suddenly shouted. 'Let us complete the job!' He turned on his heel and was gone. The blood was congealing in pools.

Bile rose in my throat. I swallowed hard, forcing it back down, and went after Hitler. In the corridor the SS, shouting and laughing, were giving Schneidhuber and Schmid a kicking. Blood was spattering the cream walls as the two men yelled for mercy amidst the laughter. Hitler was going for the doors, and I went after him in a scrum of Gestapo and SS.

The superchargers howled inside the long shining bonnets of the open-topped Mercedes as we tore down the great open road to the resort town of Bad Wiesee. Labourers and farm-carts were trudging and trotting along and they jumped back and pulled over in alarm at the approach of the mighty, speeding limousines.

When we pulled up in a scrunch of huge hard tyres outside a fine high hotel, there was a squad of SS waiting, all in black, fully armed with revolvers and automatic weapons. At their head was Huber, as savage and ready as a Doberman hound. They swirled about their Führer as he hurried into the great building, his hippo-hide whip in his hand, Goebbels scurrying like a dog at his heels.

Röhm was still in bed, a young catamite sleeping at his side. His *Stabschef* dress uniform stood hung ready nearby, ready for the second-most powerful man in Germany to dress in style to welcome the first.

'Heil, mein Führer!' he said sleepily, and then they dragged him away. His bugger boy they threw down the stairs on the way to kicking in the bedroom door of Heines, the Silesian SA boss. He was in bed with his blond chauffeur. They had pistols under their pillows, but Huber and his boys blew them apart as they screamed under the sheets.

Out in the courtyard, where the tables were set for breakfast, the SS were driving the SA men out in their underpants, in britches and bare feet, bleeding and incoherent. They shot them down as they raised their arms in the Nazi salute, seeing Hitler staring down at them from the balcony above. 'Heil Hitler! Heil Hitler!' they yelled as Huber's men blasted bullets into them. Blood spattered the white tablecloths; the raked and brushed Bavarian lawn was disfigured with brains and gore.

Hitler looked down on his enemies.

Röhm lasted a couple of days. Up in Berlin, Heydrich shot Strasser, Hitler's old party comrade, through the barred window of his cell, and laughed like a maniac as he lay bleeding to death inside. They blew General von Schleicher away in his study. His wife came running and they did her in, too, just for the hell of it.

Röhm had to die. He was supposed to have been plotting a

coup against Hitler, after all. Perhaps he was going to poison the vegetarian meal he had specially ordered for his boss at the great shindig that had been planned. Who cared? He had to go, though. There was no point in slaughtering the others and leaving the leader alive. Göring told me to be there.

Huber did it. They gave Röhm a Browning with one bullet in his cell and told him to act like a gentleman. Röhm had never been a gentleman in his life – he despised them. Huber kicked the door open and he was still sitting there, bare-chested.

'Shoot straight, you bastard,' he said, and Huber shot him in the throat. 'Mein Führer!' he screamed, blood spraying everywhere, and Huber did it to him again, blowing him backwards. He fell to the floor of the cell and Huber fired into his head.

He came out, putting his pistol away. 'Being queer isn't good for you,' he said, to nobody in particular.

Röhm's being queer was good for Huber – he was promoted to Standartenführer SS by order of Hitler, three days later. And he was there at the *Sekt* champagne bash Göring threw in his palace for everybody when Hitler ordered a finish to the executions after three days of spilling blood and brains throughout the country.

The grand reception room was filled with liveried servants passing trays of the best French champagne and tasty nibbles, with many, many men in the jet-black uniforms of the SS. Göring was in his element. Having proved himself *der Eiserne*, he was in full jovial mood, mein jolly host.

I caught a glimpse of General von Fritsch in his Reichswehr uniform. His face was ashen, his hand trembled, spilling champagne as he stared about him at all the black uniforms.

The generals – hereditary nobility all – had kept their exalted status, their landed estates and offices. They had supported Hitler against the coarse upstart Röhm and his swaggering bully boys. Von Fritsch had been one such. As he stared about him at the terrifying sharks that had somehow emerged from the dark waters that he now swam in, I could see he had realised, much too late, the cost of it all. Much too late it was. He was said to share Röhm's taste for young boys, and Himmler gutted him politically some years later. Unlike Röhm, he was a gentleman; when war came he went out into it and got himself killed. They picked up his body and they sent it home, and gave him a grand funeral with all the pomp of state appropriate for a man of his rank.

They sent Gregor Strasser back to his wife in a small jar on which somebody had scrawled *born 30.5.92, died 30.6.34, Gestapo, Berlin*. The other Party comrades went home as ashes in small pasteboard cartons, in the post.

I slept badly for the rest of the night, and it was only the schnapps that enabled me to to doze off at all. I was up early and I decided to put in a full morning on the diary. When I had been to the outhouse at the back – it is a *völkische* house, peasants do not have mains drainage – and was dressed, I poked my nose out of the front door. It was cold, with the smell of snow on the way. There was high cirrus like herringbone in the sky.

Down by the outbuildings there was a white vehicle. Him. Cabbage-Gas. Maybe he heard the creak of Speer's carved oak door opening, for he looked up and waved at me. He went to the back of his car and opened the rear door, taking out a box and carrying it up to me.

'I passed through the village,' he said. 'I brought your supplies. The meat has not come in yet, the man says; he will bring it later. Or I will, if I am passing.' He put the box down on the porch.

'Have you no police duties to attend to?' I asked testily.

'Indeed I have,' he said, quite calmly, 'for the agents of Mother Nature have struck again.'

'What now? More unfortunate restaurateurs?'

'They have widened their scope. They have captured the French Minister of Agriculture, a supporter of modern farming methods and a keen huntsman. He hunts deer and boar.'

'French? Why French?'

He shrugged. 'Presumably the struggle against the tyrannies of modern man knows no borders.'

'Then you had better catch these *Schweinehund*. Who knows what they will do next.'

'Who knows indeed?' he said. 'We believe that they are about to make their first attack on the masses within a city. First individuals, next the people.'

'What kind of attack?'

'Gas. Nerve gas. To be released into the underground railway system. Many will die.'

I looked out over the lovely valley. '*Grüss Gott*. Has there not been enough of this in the past? Why should people going about their everyday business be gassed?'

'One assumes that most of them are meat-eaters, that they support the ongoing holocaust,' he said without expression.

'Hitler called them *Untermenschen*, undesirables, sub-humans. And gassed them.'

'So I believe,' he said. 'I was not, of course, alive in those days.'

'You had better find them then, if you do not want those days to return,' I said shortly.

'To be sure,' he said. He turned and loped away down the slope to his car. It started with the smoky rattle of a cold diesel. The wiper blades swept the windscreen clear of dew, and he drove away down the lane, towards the bridge which crosses the ravine.

I stood staring after him. I am an engineer – I know what a cold diesel engine sounds like. I saw the thick coat of dew on the car, wiped clear by the blades.

On the porch was the box of groceries he had brought. I picked it up and took it inside. The cans and packages, the vegetables and packets were icy cold. I looked out down the mountainside. The river wriggled grey down on the valley floor, hundreds upon hundreds of metres below the little village.

It was quiet, high on the mountain. There was not a sound. Above me, riding on the standing wave, some kites flew, hanging in the air, looking for food.

Berlin, June 1936

We sat in two of the best seats, appropriate for officers such as us. Hoeppner wore the grey uniform of the Wehrmacht, I my blue one of the Luftwaffe. We both wore our medal ribbons from the First World War, which shone on their bars in a multicoloured array across our chests.

'*Brustschmerzen*,' Hoeppner said affably. 'That's what we

suffer from. Chest trouble.'

People were coming into the cinema in a steady stream, passing under the huge banner proclaiming the film we were about to see. *Triumph des Willens*. An enormous picture of Hitler on the Nuremberg podium designed by Speer covered the side of the building.

The lights dimmed and the screen lit up. *Triumph of the Will*, directed by Leni Riefenstahl.

A Junkers descending from the clouds. Marching stormtroopers. Crowds of people, ecstatic, their faces looking up at the coming Messiah, their hands raised high. The cruciform shadow of the aircraft sweeping over the streets, the rhythmic crashing of the boots, the swastikas, the cross. The Messiah.

Hitler, making his way through the ranks. Standard-bearers, children, *völkische* peasant women bearing the nature of the people in their traditional costumes, their wise, kindly faces looking to the Führer. Strong blond people, smiling with grateful joy. Young people, Hitler jugend. Massed ranks of musicians, their drums decorated with flames, their trumpeters holding runic banners. The stadium filled with people standing shoulder to shoulder. Banners, flags, swastikas. Ecstatic, worshipping faces. Hitler. Small shadows behind him, Göring, Himmler, Goebbels, Hess . . . just shadows . . .

Hitler.

The young people. A promise. Loyalty. They will be loyal to Hitler, for ever and ever.

A temple. A temple of light. A cathedral of dazzling light in the night sky. Gigantic, icy-white searchlights, one hundred and fifty of them, building a pinnacle of belief, a temple for the souls of the hundreds of thousands in their serried ranks, a temple for the soul of Germany, of all Germans.

Hitler.

Last of all, Hess, stepping forward from the darkness: 'The Party is Hitler. But Hitler is Germany, just as Germany is Hitler. Hitler! Sieg heil!'

We came out into the June sunshine. All about us the audience buzzed with pleasure and approval. Only Hoeppner and I, it seemed, were silent. Our uniforms protected us, visual symbols of our support for the régime. Others put out flags for every celebration day of the Nazi calendar, and there were many.

Hoeppner cleared his throat. It was too easy to stand out, in public. 'A beer?' he suggested.

We walked down Unter den Linden. The vast boulevard was a sea of swastika banners. Occasionally the white of the Olympic flag peeped through. Garlands and enormous gold ribbons hung from government buildings. The Olympic Games were in full swing, and the signs saying 'Jews not welcome' and 'Jews enter at their own risk' had been discreetly taken away. The excursion steamers on the Havel had been stripped of their banners that proclaimed 'Buying from the Jews robs the *Volk*'.

Six miles away, on the Reich Sports Field, Hitler, who hated sport, was watching the Olympics and Leni Riefenstahl was filming him watching.

'How's your boy?' Hoeppner asked.

'Kurt? I don't see him as much as I'd like. He spends a lot of time at this school – he seems to like it there. I suppose he's at the age when boys like to be with their peers. It's a sort of *wandervogel* place. They do a lot of outdoor things – mountain-climbing, parachuting, sharpshooting – as far as I can gather. He likes all that.'

'He can read?' Hoppner asked jocularly.

'Oh, yes. Junk, of course. Karl May, you know? Westerns. American Wild West stories, and the cowboys and Indians speak German!'

'*Drang nach Osten*,' Hoeppner said succinctly. 'The drive to the east, in our case, also known as *Lebensraum*. How's Hilde?'

'I don't know where Hilde is. I heard that she was in Paris, with the Anti-Fascist Front, but somebody said she was going to Moscow.'

We sat down at a table under the limes, and a waiter brought us beer.

'*Gott mit uns*,' Hoeppner remarked cynically, but quietly. He raised his glass. '*Prost*.'

'He seems to be here already,' I agreed.

'Riefenstahl is a clever young woman,' said Hoeppner. 'She makes Goebbels very cross because she won't sleep with him.'

'Very sensible, but how does she get away with that?' I asked. The requirements for any pretty woman wanting to be somebody in the Reich's film industry were well known and unattractive.

'She won't take any creative advice from him either. She doesn't have to. She's answerable only to Hitler. She gives him what he wants, this – this – *myth* that's being created about him.'

'Hilde would weep,' I said. 'They've stolen all the clothes of the *neue Sachlichkeit* and put them to work to make that.'

'The Messiah,' said Hoeppner softly, almost in disbelief. 'Don't we officers have to swear a personal oath – before God – to Adolf Hitler, the Führer of the German Reich and the German people? It makes him king, a monarch, no – more than a monarch. I was right, he is the Chosen One, the Messiah? Who would believe you can turn Korporal Hitler into the Messiah?'

'Isn't that what propaganda is all about?' I asked. 'The big lie, Goebbels calls it. I talked to him, you know, in the Junkers when we were flying down to Munich.'

'Aren't you flying down somewhere else soon?' he asked. Hoeppner was safe now, the killing time had passed. He was back in the army and as far as I knew he kept his real identity a secret from everyone except a tiny few like me.

'Spain,' I said succinctly. 'Göring feels the war starting up there is an ideal opportunity to test the new aircraft under battle conditions.'

'What do we have?'

'All the elements of the new fighting philosophy. The Stukas, the Junkers dive-bombers, the Heinkel bombers, the Junkers transports, the Messerschmitt fighters. Göring's right, we need to test them.'

'War's coming,' Hoeppner said absently, staring across the boulevard at nothing.

'Not here,' I countered. 'Spain, yes. A limited involvement. Who are we going to fight?'

'Everybody, before we're through. Hitler said so.'

'When?'

'In his nasty little book. *Mein Kampf*. I have a copy. I read it from time to time. I can quote passages by heart, just like any good Nazi. "He who wants to live must fight, and he who does not want to fight ... has no right to exist." I notice that Hitler has, so far, done everything he *said* he would. He has destroyed democracy in this country. He persecutes the Jews. He has made himself into the heroic, longed-for great leader. He *is* the Führer! Nobody can accuse him of hiding his intentions, if he sticks to them this well. Shall I quote you another passage? "We National Socialists consciously draw a line beneath the foreign policy of our pre-war period. We take up where we left off six hundred years ago. We stop the endless German movement to the south and west and turn our gaze to the land in the east. At long last we break off the colonial and commercial policy of the pre-war period and shift to the territorial policy of the future. And if we speak of territory in Europe, we can have in mind only Russia and her vassal states." I read it last night.'

'Nobody in their right mind is going to attack Russia,' I protested. 'Do you know how *big* it is?'

'I didn't say he *was* in his right mind,' observed Hoeppner quietly. 'I simply said he was going to do what he said he would do. He's free from constraint, you see. The public worship him, and he gives them what they want. He slaughtered the SA leadership, people like Röhm who terrified everybody, and they were *grateful*. In March, didn't he prove himself the Iron leader when he walked back into the Rhineland? The French and the British just backed down. What's next? Confiscation of all Jewish assets? People wouldn't mind that a bit, and it'd help pay for all the new arms. After that? Reunification of all the German peoples in Austria, Poland and Czechoslovakia? He said he would, and I believe him. People won't mind that either. You see, if you think that way, it makes sense. *Lebensraum*, killing, destruction, the annihilation of international Jewry, the purification of the blood of the *Volk*, the strangulation of the international Bolshevik Jewish Marxist conspiracy, killing, destruction . . .'

Hoeppner tipped back his beer and signalled the waiter for more.

'He liked the killing and destruction in the war, did Korporal Hitler. I could never get him to leave it. He liked it there in the mud and horror. I know my little Korporal, I do . . .'

The beer arrived. Above the steady rumble of the traffic we began to hear bawling voices raised in song. Some drunken SA men were making their way down the boulevard. As they came closer, we could hear their song. It was simple, with a repeated chorus: '*When the Olympics are past, the Jews will be gassed* . . .'

'Judaism is the plague of the world,' Hoeppner said, and I realised he was still quoting. He drank some more, as if to wash away the sight and sound of the SA.

The drunks changed tune in unison and began to bawl out the Horst Wessel song. German Song Week was just past.

'You know what we need to do?' he said, leaning forward, his voice so low I could only just hear him. 'We need to kill the little bastard,' he whispered.

Berlin, November 1938

'Do they do it?' he demanded. 'Will they do what I want?'

Very carefully, Hitler pinned the gold medal to my uniform, the *Spanienkreuz* with diamonds. He was wearing simple army dress with an armband and his Iron Cross, First Class. He adjusted the Spanish Cross to his satisfaction. His breath was faintly sweet, like a rotting plum, the smell of countless cream cakes.

His eyes snapped up, held mine. 'Well? Does it work?'

Six thousand metres high in a clear, icy sky. The wrinkled brown and green land of Guadalajara flung out like a map beneath us. Four Messerschmitt Me 109s in a *Vierfingerschwarm*, each about two hundred metres apart.

There they were, a big formation of Republican I-16s, dark against the ground below, like a hurrying pack of locusts, the SB bombers heavy as beetles in their midst.

The formation began to wheel on to track and I put the nose down. The others came with me. Glancing across, I could see the *Zylinderhut* top-hat emblems clear on their sides as we dived.

They hadn't seen us. An I-16 began to fill the sight. A straggler from the rear. A novice. I recall thinking that somebody should warn him, should tell him what was about to happen to him. I didn't fire until he filled the sight. Pieces blew off him, tumbling past my cockpit. He half-rolled, streaming black smoke and I was over him. A bomber, an SB, a Russian Katiuska, frantically pulling away as the formation broke up. I tightened my turn, firing short bursts into him. I saw the cannon shells stitch up the fuselage towards the cockpit and suddenly the whole aircraft blew up in a ball of flame as the unprotected fuel-tanks exploded.

I shot through the fireball. Aircraft were swirling everywhere. Separate smoke trails stained the sky. Dirty oil smeared my windscreen from the bomber. I shot at an I-16, who put his nose down near vertical and I followed. The Russian fighter was fast in a dive. I twisted about in my seat to see behind the high back of the cockpit. Nothing. Just some gnats high above, peppering the dirty sky. I fired a burst at long range. A novice could always be frightened into turning. By doing that he shortened the distance between himself and my pursuing plane. The next burst was then fatal.

He wasn't having it. The ground was large and detailed as we hurtled down upon it like thunderbolts. Fields, trees, woods and streams. The I-16 went down into the country in a wild, whirling chase, using all the cover there was, every dip and curve and wood and valley. Dust ripped up from the fields from his wake as my shells shattered a stone wall, sending fragments high in the air; trees disintegrated into flying matchwood, the shells set dry hay alight.

A village, a church, a steeple. He saw it late and zoomed over and I saw him clear against the sky. I fired into him and the wing folded at the root. He slammed into the graveyard on the side of the valley, shattering the tombs, coating the graves with fire.

I climbed away into an empty sky.

I looked down at Hitler. He had won two victories in less than six months. Austria was now part of Germany. Czechoslovakia, dismembered and disarmed, had practically ceased to exist. He had done it all by political, not military, warfare. The threat of force, not the reality.

Spain was the only place where the new German armed forces had fought. And Hitler wanted to know if they would do what he wanted.

The generals had been afraid that his actions would lead to all-out war with the imperial powers of France and Great Britain. They dreaded a repeat of 1914. It was whispered that there were those who were planning to take or kill Hitler to stop him before he could go too far.

Who had been right, and who wrong? Deladier and

Chamberlain had given him everything he wanted, hurrying across Europe to sign away other nations' territory, fearful of war, desperate to appease at any price.

Hitler had evolved a new form of political warfare. He had only badges of victory to show. The generals were humbled, the conspirators silenced and powerless. The map was a different shape. Hitler pinned on my chest a small golden badge. His own awards were real countries, real people who now bowed down. He had been right every time.

His protruberant blue eyes looked searchingly into mine. *Did it work?*

Not everybody would give in without fighting. The Poles would not. *We are not Czechs*, they snarled menacingly. The French would not. The descendants of the Sun King and Napoleon would have to fight. The British, secure behind their twenty-five miles of running water, would fight, it was in their blood. They had been ready to fight with anyone for centuries and had the world's greatest empire to show for it.

The new warfare, did it work? That combination of infiltration, shock action and psychological disorientation. Tanks and artillery and ground-support aircraft, shock troops. *Speed.* A single gigantic stroke. Did it work, were the elements of the right quality, did the command and control systems weld them into a single massive blade?

Lightning war. Blitzkrieg.

Klotzen, nicht kleckern. Smash, don't tap.

Adolf Hitler was Führer. Ultimate decisions rested within one man. He had always been right. Versailles was but a discarded piece of paper, 1918 a memory, Weimar a faded irrelevance.

'Will they do what I want?' he demanded. 'Does it work?'

'Yes,' I said.

I sat at my desk in the apartment, working on my report. I actually had two – one full one of some two hundred pages, and one of only three pages long. The shorter of the two was the more important, as it was the one Göring would read. Göring did not care for reading, and refused to look at anything longer than four pages. Three was better. So I sat at my desk that evening attempting to compress what was important into three pages. I had my jacket with its medals hung over the back of the chair. As the Kaiser had known thirty years earlier, it paid to wear military uniform. I thought I might go down to the restaurant a little later and get some supper. I led a lonely life: Hilde was gone, who knew where, and Kurt rarely came home, preferring the company of his comrades. To be fair to him, I had been away a long time.

The window flickered orange. It caught my eye as I concentrated on the paper, and I looked up. The window flared with light. A fire. I got up, pulling back the half-open curtain. In the darkness a building was beginning to blaze. I quickly picked up the telephone, calling for the fire service.

'There is a fire, a bad one,' I told them, and gave my address.

'Thank you,' the voice said, calmly.

'You had better send the appliances, quickly.'

'We are aware of the fire,' she said.

I stood at the window, waiting, but nobody came. Some men came running down the street and I heard the noise of shattering glass, yelling voices. I put on my jacket and greatcoat against the cold, and went down.

I hurried towards the blaze. As I came round the corner I saw what was burning: it was the Jewish synagogue. A crowd of SA men were standing about nearby, laughing and warming their hands at the gigantic fire.

As I watched, part of the roof fell in, sending a Roman candle of red and gold sparks flying high into the dark sky. From a side door a figure came running, and the SA men let out howls of drunken joy. It was the rabbi, his locks swinging. He beat at his smouldering robes – he must have been hiding inside until he was forced out by the heat.

He saw the SA men and tried to run away into the darkness. But they were younger than he was and they ran him down. I heard him shriek as they thrashed him on the pavement. As I hesitated, looking around, I saw a policeman standing in a shop doorway, watching silently.

'Hey!' I called. 'You had better stop them before they kill him.'

The man stared at me without a word.

The SA men picked up the rabbi and hoisted him above their heads. They ran back towards the synagogue with him flailing weakly and calling out in Yiddish. They grabbed a hold of his arms and legs and began to swing him by the still standing wall, flames gushing out of the shattered window above.

'*Eins!*' they yelled, and the watching *sturmers* took up the cry.

'*Zwei!*' they all roared.

They ran towards the furnace and swung him in a huge arc.

'*Drei!*'

He screamed a fearful falsetto death-cry as he hurtled into the flames, and then all was silent but the roar of the burning building, and the triumphant laughter of the killers. They pulled bottles of liquor from their pockets and drank. Then they were off, running along the street.

I looked at the policeman.

'*Befehl*,' he said shortly, uncomfortably. 'I obey my orders. I do what I am told to.'

I thought of Eisenmann. I hurried along through the streets, my boots crunching and tinkling over the shattered glass of the Jewish-owned stores. Bawling, drunken, triumphant SA men could be seen all over the place, carrying off goods they had looted. The air smelled of smoke.

At Eisenmann's apartment block my Luftwaffe uniform was sufficient for the apprehensive porter to let me in, and I took the lift upstairs. I rang at Eisenmann's bell, and called out my name.

'It's me, Hans!'

The door opened briefly, and Eisenmann pulled me inside quickly, shutting it behind us. His apartment was dark and unlit except for the flickering illumination of the city outside.

'The SA are conducting some kind of pogrom!' I told him.

'I know,' he muttered. 'I knew this would happen, it's the ninth of November.'

'What's that –'

Then I realised, of course. The ninth of November, a hallowed date for the *Frontkämpfers* and the SA: the anniversary of the failed 1923 *Putsch*. They had a grand reunion every year in Munich – Hitler never missed it.

'I've been waiting for it,' he said very quietly, peering out at the lurid sky, careful not to show his face. 'That boy killed the diplomat in Paris. He was a Jew. They'd deported his family to Poland, his relatives were killed. I knew something like this would happen.'

'Where are your family?'

He smiled crookedly in the darkness. 'I got them out while I still could. A "holiday" in America. My brother's out there.'

'Why the hell haven't you gone too? They killed a rabbi, Claus. I saw them . . .'

'It's a pogrom . . . some of us always die in pogroms,' he said fatalistically.

'But if you've got your family out, why not you?'

'What with?' he demanded savagely. 'All my capital is tied up in the business. I'll be damned if I've worked all these years for nothing. I'm too old to start anew. I need my capital.'

'You know that Göring's calling for Aryanisation of the economy? That he wants the Jews driven out of business altogether?'

'Of course I know,' snorted Eisenmann contemptuously. 'You think I can't see the Fat One coming? I saw what happened in Austria once the Nazis took over. I'm a businessman, I have ways of hearing things. But *der Dicke* isn't going to let the *alte kampfers* have it all, oh no.'

He waved a hand outside.

'That's the most they'll get – what they can drag off with them. But the *real* wealth, Göring wants that for himself, for his empire, doesn't he? Well, he won't get *my* company, Hans. No, he won't.'

'Are you sure of that?' I asked, slightly nervously. '*Der Dicke*, he's not the buffoon you think, you know. He's very avaricious, and he gets what he wants.'

'He can't have what I haven't got,' Eisenmann said with some satisfaction. 'The company is no longer under the name of Eisenmann. Early this year I made it over to my completely Aryan manager, Peltz. My price to him was very reasonable. He's going to pay me from the profits. In two years I'll have what I need. Then I'll go to America.' He looked grimly out into the night. 'I fought for four years at the front against real soldiers, Hans. I have the Iron Cross, First Class. I'm damned if I'll run away from *Dreck* like them.'

I stayed a while with him, and we drank two bottles of wine in the darkness. When I walked home the streets were completely covered with shattered glass. *Kristallnacht*, the SA joyfully called it.

I looked out of the window. The sky was that strange, yellowy-grey colour, heavy with snow. My pen was stiff in my fingers, the notebook covered with steady lines of writing. I got up and decided to fetch a few trolley-loads of wood from the shed. I put on my padded jacket and went out, across to the big barn overlooking the steep slope down the meadow. The trolley was waiting by the piles of chopped wood. The axe still stood in the block, next to my hammer and wedges. Some people play golf; I chop wood. I am over ninety and still fit, thank you. I began to load up the trolley with logs. It is a special kind of trolley, the central load-bearing compartment rides on caterpillar tracks, which are powered by a battery-driven electric motor.

While I was doing this, a shadow fell across the opening. *Gott im Himmel*, I thought, is there no peace?

It was him, of course. Who else would it be? I am rather deaf and had not heard his car coming.

He held up a hand, smiling apologetically to fend up my spleen. 'I know, I know,' he said. 'Excuse me for coming here yet again, Herr Wolff. It is just that I have had confirmation of something.'

'Yes, yes?' I said irritably. 'What is it that will not wait until next spring?'

'We have reason to believe that members of the terrorist group we are searching for may be in this area.'

'Ah, *ja*? And what might they want out here? We have no restaurants here for them to despoil. No food factories or ministries. Only me, and I cannot be of much interest to them.'

'Your land is situated in a very remote part,' Cabbage-Gas pointed out. 'Were they to require a meeting-place, then somewhere like this might be most suitable, far away from the public gaze.'

'I suppose so.'

'I . . . I have a confession to make. I spent last night out here, keeping watch. But I saw nothing.'

That would explain the dew on his car.

He pulled out a black oblong device from his pocket. 'May I give you this?'

'What is it?'

'A telephone,' he said, smiling in surprise. 'A mobile telephone. As your own is not connected . . . '

I took it, peering at the lightweight machine. 'Very clever,' I commented.

'All you have to do is press the buttons here. Look, I have put my number under this piece of sticky tape. If you see *anything* suspicious, I want you to call me.'

'Very well,' I said. I put it away in the pocket of my jacket. 'These maniacs, they are not yet caught. And what of the French Minister they kidnapped?'

'Oh, he has been found.'

I realised from his voice that the unfortunate politician had not simply been discovered recovering from excesses in his mistress's bed.

'Where?'

'There is, you may know, a great office in Brussels, the centre of the European Community, which deals with the common agricultural policy of all these nations.'

'If you say so.'

'There is. He was discovered there. On the wall.'

'The wall?'

'*Ja*. That is . . . you know the boar you shot, whose head you have mounted on a shield, on your wall? Like that. His head was mounted on a wooden shield and hung upon this wall. It was discovered early in the morning by a secretary.'

'How dull we must seem to these mad people!' I said, after a while. 'For when they are caught, all we shall do to them is lock them up for the rest of their lives. So little imagination! Should they not at least be finely minced and spread upon the ground as fertiliser?'

'But we have to catch them first,' he said softly.

'I am sure the resources of the German police are adequate for the task. Though the terrorists appear to be spreading their wings.'

'Yes. We believe the movement to be international. We believe that massive attacks of terror are to be synchronised for many different countries . . . '

He was looking at my trolley in a puzzled fashion.

'*Was ist* – a small tank, perhaps?'

'In a manner.' I picked up the small hand-control. 'I designed something like this for house-fighting. The original was equipped with television cameras behind armoured glass and a variety of weaponry. The tracks make it capable of climbing stairs, and it is strong enough to break through thin walls and doors. I considered it a better use of resources than having élite troops killed. The armed forces, which have never objected to having troops killed, disagreed with me, which is why I now use it to carry my wood.'

His eyes had become accustomed to the gloom, and he was peering with even greater incredulity at what lay inside the rest of the barn. 'It is an aircraft of some sort?' he said in amazement.

I am used to seeing it, I suppose. It has lost its power to shock me, but I recall my feelings when I first saw it. You have to understand that when it was made, the very best fighters around had propellers and tail wheels; they were large and muscular. The Messerschmitt Me 163, on the other hand, is like a beautiful swept-winged egg. It is a rocket. The pilot puts it on like a fine suit of clothes.

It is also the most dangerous aircraft ever made – for everybody concerned. If you could get it within the killing space of a heavy bomber, a Flying Fortress, then all in it were dead. But the pilot had to get back down to earth and land it, and it was a most deadly killer. Rocket-fuel swilled in the depths of its tanks, volatile fumes turned into explosive gas just ready to go off. It was justly an egg – a bad landing spread all over the scenery.

'It is a fighter,' I admitted. 'Mine.'

'How did it *get* here?'

'I flew it in.' I stepped outside to show him. 'I came over the trees there, and put it down on the path that runs along the top of the meadow.'

'When?'

'Fifth of April, 1945. It was a clear spring day, and the flowers were out here. I got out and sat among them for some time, I remember.'

'It has been here for fifty years?'

'Yes. It sits on its take-off dolly, you will see. Two wheels on an axle there, which fall away as the aircraft flies. I found those after the war was over, and brought them up here. I suppose it should be in a museum.'

He stood by it, shaking his head in wonder. The Teutonic crosses were flat on the wings, the black and white *hakenkreuz* still stood out on the high rudder. It was dusty; I made a note that I should wash it sometime.

'Can it fly?'

'It could, I suppose, were you to find *C-stoff* and *T-stoff*, and someone willing to get in it.'

'Amazing . . . how would you take off?'

'With difficulty. I have pondered that thought myself.' I pointed down the meadow. 'I think, were you to do it, straight down towards the ravine. You would certainly have to hope nothing went wrong! But after that, if you were airborne, you would be safe. It is a glider, you see. The rocket engine blasted it high in the sky, and then you could glide. Fast. Very, very fast.'

I was standing by the fighter, that we had called 'Komet'. Near the wall lay some lengths of heavy iron. I looked at them, puzzled. My memory can be recalcitrant, arbitrary. I can recall the very shade of Hilde's eyes, but not the real name of Cabbage-Gas. What lay on the floor were the parts of a barbecue spit, a very big one, one that could roast a pig. I did not recall leaving them there. They should have been propped against the wall, for it had been over twenty years since I had used them.

I frowned and went forward, bending to pick them up. I put them back where they belonged, and then stood staring at my hand.

'What is it?' Cabbage-Gas asked.

'There is grease on my hand,' I said, 'from the spit. Somebody has used it.'

'The chef . . . he was barbecued,' he said softly.

'It seems you may be right. As to the terrorists.'

'Yes . . . I shall arrange a watch, surveillance . . . You are not afraid to stay?'

'I am an old man,' I said. 'I may die tomorrow.'

I thumbed the switches and the powerful electric-motor hummed. There was a high-pitched, rapid clatter as the on-board generator cut in, and the trolley swung smoothly out and up the hill to the house.

'I must get on,' I said. 'Thank you for the telephone. Should I see your mad people, I will use it to tell you of their presence.'

I walked up the path behind the wood-laden trolley. Small flakes of snow were beginning to fall from the yellow lead sky. It would soon be Christmas.

The trolley climbed the steps effortlessly. I stopped it in the porch and unloaded the wood into the great basket I keep inside the hall. I decided to walk down again after I had done some work, and fetch more. When the snow lay thick it was not easy to get about.

I put logs on to the fire. Cabbage-Gas was gone. I sat down at my desk. It was yesterday, once again...

It was snowing outside. The streets of Berlin were marked with the black lines of vehicles which had cut through the white. The room smelled of the small pine tree I had bought and placed in a corner by the window. Kurt was singing in the bath. He was getting ready to go back to the castle, the *Ordensburg*. I had hoped he would stay for Christmas but he had determined to go. They were celebrating the rebirth of the Sun God, and he could not be apart from his comrades. He had grown, my son, he was eighteen. He had a fine baritone voice, raised in song.

'Who'er against us stands
Shall fall beneath our hands.
Our lives our loyalty,
Our Führer, are pledged to thee.

We have no need of Christian truth;
For Adolf Hitler is our Leader
And our Interceder.

No evil old priest these ties can sever;
We're Hitler's children now and ever.'

He was going back to celebrate the rebirth of the Sun God, about to rise from his own ashes at the winter solstice. They held the ceremony around a glittering pine tree erected in the armoury of the castle and surrounded by weaponry. They felt the souls of the ancient Teutonic knights, conquerors of lesser races, arise from Valhalla to be reborn within them. I knew, he had told me so. Since I did not believe in a God, it was hard for me to refute him. I did not believe in Adolf Hitler as a deity either, and it was difficult for me to come to terms with the fact that my son did.

Far too late in the day, I realised that I had made a mess of my life. A rucksack lay on the table, a *wandervogel* affair of canvas, stained with grass and earth. A small pile of books stood nearby, ready to be stuffed away. Some new, some old. Junger's *The Storm of Steel*, much thumbed. I understood Junger. Like me, he had not got over the war, was still trying to come to terms with the incandescent emotion produced by battle.

What else? Herman Hesse's *Demian*. Some weapons manuals, stained and still smelling of gun oil. The Kar 98k carbine, the MP181 machine-pistol, looking like some kind of blowlamp. Who was this? Knut Hamsun? I had never heard of him. *Pan, The Road to the Open, Growth of the Soil* ... I peered at the blurb. It appeared to be some kind of semi-mystical work, a hymn to the rhythms of the earth and the cycle of the seasons. Unless we humans placed ourselves in harmony with these, the author threatened, we were all doomed. I tossed it back on the pile. The end of the world is always nigh. And always, somehow, postponed.

Kurt was out of the bath and I could hear him moving about in his room. A little later he came out. I got a shock. He was clothed in black. Gone was his Junker's grey and brown of the *Ordensburg*; he was fully dressed as an SS man. Only his collar patches were missing.

'What do you think?' he demanded proudly.

'I didn't know you wanted to join the SS,' I said. 'Are you sure –'

'Sure? What else have I been training for? I am now a candidate, and next April the thirtieth, on the Führer's birthday, I shall receive my passbook and collar patches. Aren't you proud of me?'

'I could arrange for the Luftwaffe –'

'*Nein nein*' he said impatiently. 'I respect you, of course, but you do not understand. We of the SS have an appointment with destiny. We are to do the work of the gods.'

'God?' I said, startled.

'No, not the Jewish God the churches preach of. The old gods, the German gods of *blut und boden*, blood and soil.'

He packed away his books and a parcel of food.

'The time is coming,' he remarked.

I thought it best not to pursue the subject. 'I wish you could stay.'

'I have to go back. It is an important time for us. What will you do?'

'Oh, probably end up with Eisenmann. He's on his own.'

His forehead crinkled. 'Eisenmann?'

'He's someone I knew from the war.'

'Jews can be called Eisenmann.'

'He is a Jew,' I said quietly. 'He is also a German who fought in the war. He has the Iron Cross, First Class.'

'See? They are everywhere.'

'Of course Jews are everywhere. They are a scattered race.'

He nodded his head vehemently. 'That is so! They are everywhere in the world, that is how they are able to conspire against all other races.'

'Eisenmann is a businessman,' I protested.

'How do you know he is just that? If he is a businessman, he is a member of the tribe of Judah, dedicated to the destruction of craftsmen by the Jewish methods of mass production.'

'What is this?'

'You don't know?' he demanded angrily. 'Don't you know that the tribes of Israel are conspiring to enslave the world? Are they not everywhere you look? The Bolsheviks are Jews. The Freemasons are a Jewish front. The Christian Church is but a Jewish organisation. It is our German mission in the twentieth century to free the world from the Jewish conspiracy.'

'Who told you this?'

'The Führer,' he whispered intensely. 'Adolf Hitler himself came to *Vogelsang* and spoke to us. He told us how the Jews practise stealth, how ubiquitous they are. That is why we of the

SS must copy them – become stealthy ourselves, be everywhere ourselves. We have been chosen by the old gods to free the world from the devil's agents, who are the Jews.

'Has not a start been made? Before the *machtergreifung*, did you not see Jews everywhere? The tribes of Issachar and Zebulon were at their most successful. They mocked the old military class, they poured scorn on our patriotism. Their filthy magazines were everywhere, their shows were on every stage. Did they not preach free thought and radicalism? And have they not been swept away by Adolf Hitler? Did they not preach revolution in Russia and win? Did the tribe of Menassah not capture the press here in Germany? Now it has been won back, thanks to Adolf Hitler.'

He did up the straps of his rucksack and slung it over his back.

'Jesus Christ was a Jew,' he said scornfully. 'It is Adolf Hitler our Führer who has come to lead us to the promised land.'

I stood at the window and watched him stride away down the street.

I hardly saw my son again. Our apartment block took a direct hit from a Lancaster bomber one night in 1943, thus giving everybody in it the right to call Göring Meier. The Thick One had boasted that not a bomb would fall on Germany, but by then they came out of the sky like rain.

I was not in the apartment – I did not use it much anyhow, for by then I was far away developing the Messerschmitt Me 163 – and long before that I spent much of my time occupying other people's countries. War came, as Hitler had intended it would. First Poland, then Norway, Holland, Belgium and France. Lightning war, lightning victories. Göring gave me a squadron of Me 109s in the *Schlageter* fighter group. I held the rank of Lieutenant-Colonel.

The Luftwaffe did what it was meant to. We acted as aerial artillery for the army, we provided fighter cover for the battlefield, we harried the enemy forces, we bombed their supplies, formations and communications. We had good internal communications ourselves, we were well trained in our roles and we had numerical superiority. Our enemies failed to mass their air forces together or to co-operate effectively in deciding upon primary targets and battlefield tactics. Thus we were able to destroy one air force at a time.

So I was away from Berlin for some time. I did not see Kurt, who had taken up a commission in the Waffen SS. I had, of course, lost him far earlier than that.

With our troops in Paris and the smoke from the burning supplies and oil dumps around Dunkirk only slowly clearing to reveal empty beaches and sea – for the British soldiers had managed to go home – I was granted some leave. I went back to Berlin.

The first night in the apartment, once it was dark, there came a furtive knocking at the door. I opened it, and there was Eisenmann. He was thin and looked frightened. Despite the warm weather he was wearing a raincoat.

'Hans, thank God you're back,' he said, hurrying inside from the hallway. He pulled off the coat and I saw that a yellow star was sewn to his jacket. 'Please get me out.'

'I'm hiding out along with some communists,' he said, talking quickly. 'The SS, they came to the factory to arrest me, but I wasn't there. They took Peltz away, my manager.'

'The one you sold the business to?'

'Yes, yes . . . oh, *Scheisse*, how could I have been so stupid? I thought, you know, all the hateful things they did to us – the Jews Enter At Their Own Risk, even the burning of the synagogues – I thought it was all just to scare us. I even welcomed the Nuremberg laws! I thought they'd leave us alone then, if we agreed to be second-class citizens! I should have gone, Hans . . .'

He looked at me fearfully, his eyes hollow in their sockets.

'They're killing us, Hans. In the war against Poland, they had SS men behind the troops to kill the Jews. They chased them through the streets, they threw grenades at them for sport, they shut them up in synagogues and burned them. They said all we Jews must be *ausgebrannt und vernichtet*, burned out and destroyed – *abgeschlachtet*, slaughtered . . .'

'What do you want me to do?'

'I have ways of hearing things,' he whispered, as though he had not heard me. 'I am head of a big business, I get to hear things . . . They are gassing all the Jews in the mental asylums, they have card indexes and Jews, gypsies and negroes are given separate status. It is all official and on file, Hans, they know who we are –'

'Claus!' I said sharply. 'I am back to the front in a day or two. Then I cannot help you. What is it you want of me?'

'The SS have taken Peltz away, for having dealings with a Jew. I am wanted. I just need to get out of the country.'

'I cannot drop you from my fighter like a bomb,' I said. 'Let me think. I know: give your factory to Göring. Give him your apartment and your country house in return for a passport with an exit stamp. I have to see him tomorrow about the air war with Britain. I'll see to it for you.'

'But will he want my small possessions?' Eisenmann asked, hope and fear equally balanced.

'Göring wants everything,' I assured him. 'He is a great fat shark, he swims in water with other sharks, he takes anything that comes his way.'

And so it proved. I mentioned it to Göring the next day, as we discussed the coming aerial battle with the RAF. Göring had promised the Führer that the Luftwaffe would inflict such damage upon Britain that they would sue for peace, and it was people like me who were to carry out the fighting. Göring had swelled with joy at the thought of being able to deliver such a prize to Hitler – the only man he feared. To my offer of some more possessions in return for a passport stamp – which I made almost casually, for an old *Frontkämpfer*, Eisenmann – Göring agreed just as absent-mindedly, telephone in hand at his desk, he told one of his juniors, a Leutnant Schmitt, to get on with it.

I had told Eisenmann to stay at the apartment. He and Schmitt bustled about sorting out the details the next day and his factory slipped out of the grasp of the SS and into that vast, amorphous industrial empire that took its name from the man who owned it, Hermann Göring. Eisenmann's homes slid into Göring's gift, useful currency for bribes.

I packed my bag. I was back to the front, the air war against Britain about to start. The bell rang and young Schmitt came in, smiling, holding a passport stamped with its exit visa. '*Komm*, Herr Eisenmann,' he said. 'I shall take you to the station for your train.'

Eisenmann shook me by the hand, tears standing out in his

sunken eyes. 'Thank you, thank you,' he choked. 'Thank you a thousand times.'

All he had as he went out to the lift with Schmitt was a small bag. And his life.

I locked up the apartment, and went back to the war.

September 1940

At two thousand metres the Channel was as wrinkled as the bags under an old man's eyes, and as bluish-grey as a corpse. The oxygen in my mask tasted of rubber. My 109 fighters were at altitude, and we went around in a circle as we watched the bombers clambering up to us. Come on, come on. I was impatient. We had so little time over the target area as it was. We needed drop tanks, but Göring had turned some of the fighters into bombers instead, lumbering along with a 500 lb bomb underneath.

The bombers were here. A mixed formation of twin-engined Heinkels and Stuka dive-bombers. The Calais coastline merged into the haze behind us, and soon we could see the famous white cliffs.

There it was. London. The great River Thames winding its way through. A tremendous pyramid of flak rising up above the barrage balloons below. The bombers twitching nervously.

Where were the fighters?

They would find us, that was certain. The British had eyes, they had radar, they knew precisely where we were, altitude and heading, their ground controllers directing them at us like men throwing spears.

The 109s jinked left and right, like hounds on a leash. We were not allowed to leave the bombers. It was a very unpleasant feeling, for it gave the initiative to the enemy. Since the war that they called the Battle of Britain had started, I had lost over half my pilots. We too had shot down RAF pilots, but I knew that when they floated down on their parachutes they could be back attacking me tomorrow, or even later the same day.

My head rotated up, down, to the side, behind, in constant

movement. There. A flash above us. A wing catching the sun.

'Here they come, boys. Three o'clock above.'

With my thumb I released the safety catch of the guns and switched on the sight. Through it, London shone in its glow. My boys were waggling their wings restlessly, swinging to the left and the right, as though animated by some electric current.

'Yellow leader, six aircraft nine o'clock above!'

'Yellow leader, blue one, ten Spitfires at eight o'clock above!'

The radio was getting nervous. A shout in my eardrums. 'Yellow leader break starboard!'

I glanced quickly to the right and saw an avalanche of Hurricanes falling on us out of the sun. There were twenty or thirty of them. Four or five no more than six hundred metres away, on my tail.

'Yellow squadron 180 starboard, quick, go!'

Tight in the turn, tracer blasting metres from my wingtip. Throttle wide open. Heinkels and Stukas scattering like chickens with the fox in the run. A Stuka exploding, falling into a Heinkel beneath, the smoke trails of dying aircraft beginning to fill the sky.

Spitfires! I hauled back on the stick, the engine screaming at full power, climbing in an almost vertical turn. The Spitfires flashed through between our sections like thunderbolts, sleek, green and brown, ignoring us, going in to kill the bombers. I fired with a 40-degree deflection, and missed.

There was one! I pulled the stick into my stomach and the world went black. My oxygen mask dragged down over my face with the g-forces, scraping the skin from my nose. Blood spat over my chin.

There, I had him: 5-degrees deflection, firing in short bursts. *Bam bam bam*, the machine-guns and cannon. Explosions, one after the other, on the wing root.

He suddenly put his nose down and I followed him, the airspeed indicator going up and up: 550 kilometres, 600 kilometres. The Spitfire was keeping ahead of me. I fired, and the recoil slowed me up. I was to one side and could see the pilot looking back at me, see his face, like some strange insect with goggle-eyes.

The air was clear. Black vertical trails of smoke marked the funeral pyres of shot aircraft. In the meadows below, debris blazed.

Roads and villages passed below our wings. Suddenly we were at ground level. A church steeple went whistling by. I had caught him. I fired again and there was a sudden explosion of smoke. His cockpit cover blew off, tumbling and glittering towards me in the sun. He yanked back the stick as his aircraft died and I saw him jump. There was the white blossom of a parachute, and he went sailing away towards the ground.

The Spitfire rolled on to its back. It hit the ground at enormous speed, sliding, spraying incandescent fragments everywhere, leaving a trail of blazing fuel across a meadow, smashing through a hedge to burst upon a bank in a shower of sparks.

Bam bam bam.

Jesus! Something slammed into my instrument panel. Pieces of glass and boiling liquid sprayed across my face and I screamed in pain. I slammed the stick left and right, my feet dancing on the pedals as tracer sliced through the air. Full throttle!

Desperately peering behind me, I could see another Spitfire. He had followed his comrade down as I attacked him. His wings flickered with light as he fired at me, the biter bit.

Water. The Thames estuary. A ship, some sailors waving their arms with excitement as we blasted by, ripping up spray in our wake.

Bang bang *bang*.

Smoke, shuddering blows as shells hit my fighter. Some giant lashed out at my arm with his boot. Blood sprayed the inside of the windshield. At full throttle, I pulled back the stick, climbing high. If I had to jump I would need altitude.

Where was he?

Behind me.

I was dead.

Why did he not shoot?

I climbed and climbed. The Spitfire suddenly dropped away, turning for home.

Out of ammunition.

I was alive, I could live.

My left arm was bent at a strange angle. I opened my flying

jacket and managed to put it inside, zipping it up. Gauges hung out of the panel by their wires and tubing. Smoke was seeping through their eyeless sockets. Outside, dirty oil was seeping across my windshield like sticky drizzle.

I pulled the throttle back as much as I dared. The gyro-driven heading was turning round and round and I set a course with the whisky compass like some fisherman going for home with a hold full of cod.

There was something below me. Please God, not an enemy fighter. The 109 was trembling like an old man and behind me I could hear something torn loose banging in the fuselage.

It was a Stuka, trailing black smoke. I edged over towards it in a gesture of mutual protection. As I got closer, I could see the holes blown in it, see the trailing fabric, the shattered canopy. The single gun stuck forlornly upwards. The glass was covered in blood, the gunner slumped dead and mangled in his seat. The pilot looked up fearfully as I came close, and then gave me a short wave.

As I flew alongside I saw a flicker of flame underneath. The thin trail of black smoke suddenly thickened into a great rope. The inside of the cockpit was lit up in a roaring bonfire and I saw the pilot thrashing to open the canopy.

The Stuka rolled on to its back and hit the sea in a bloom of white foam. As it cleared, there was nothing visible at all, except the truncated trail of smoke.

A red light glowed in the ruin of my panel. I was running out of fuel. Pas de Calais. Land. The engine stuttered at a hundred metres. The prop flickered and stopped. A field. Where was the wind coming from? Oh, *scheisse*, I was downwind. Trees swept under the wings. A small orchard. I heaved on the straps. A wall shot underneath me.

Some sort of crop ... I put the nose in and the earth grabbed me in a terrific grip. A first, huge shock. The Messerschmitt bounced up under me like a boat hitting the rapids, the wings folding like tissue paper. Something screeching like the devil in my ear. My good arm across my face ...

Sudden, stunning silence ... sitting dazed in the seat, a whiff of hot air, scrabbling at the catches of the cockpit. The smell of hot oil, a blast of flame about me as it caught. Struggling with the heavy cover, pushing it back, falling heavily on to the torn remains of the wing. Picking myself up, staggering away from the wreck. Explosions, smoke, the rattle of ammunition going off, the scent of burning hay, the taste of blood in my mouth.

Schmitt. That was his name. Leutnant Schmitt. Our group of fighter commanders stood about by the cars, waiting for *der Dicke* to emerge from his train. The Thick One was keeping us waiting, to indicate the low esteem in which he held us. Schmitt had emerged from the long line of coaches, with their blue-and-gold paintwork, as elaborate as a Romanov's dining-room, and was standing to one side, waiting like the rest of us. I gave up trying to scratch the itchy spot under the plaster that encased my arm and sidled over to him.

'Ah, hello, Colonel,' he said. 'The Marschall will be out soon, I am certain.'

'He will if he doesn't want to miss the bombers take off,' I assured him.

'The Reichsmarschall is not happy,' he warned me. 'He promised the Führer personally that the Luftwaffe would bring Britain to her knees. Now the attacks must take place at night – so many losses –'

'I do not think we pilots ever thought it possible to reduce Britain by air,' I said shortly. 'Whatever the Reichsmarschall may have promised.'

I glanced round. The other fighter boys were mooching about on the platform, fur collars turned up against the gathering chill.

'Say, you remember the old *frontkampfer* you helped with? The one who gave his factory and houses?'

'Oh, *ja*. The Jew.'

'That's him. Didn't you take him to the train? I thought so. I heard from his wife, she lives in America – she was expecting him. She sent me a letter. He hasn't turned up.'

Schmitt peered at his nails. 'Perhaps he will arrive soon,' he suggested.

'She's heard *nothing*.'

'Colonel, *die Juden sind unser Unglück, nicht wahr?*' he said, sounding bored. 'The Jews are our misfortune. Who cares where this Jew is?'

'I would like to know,' I said stubbornly.

'Very well! I put him on the train as the Marschall told me to.'

'*Which* train?'

Schmitt grinned suddenly. 'The one I was *told* to! The one that went to Poland.' He turned to face me. 'The Marschall and Reichsführer Himmler understand the new situation. They are not interested in Jews leaving any more. All Jews are to be put to work, to repay the damage they have done to Germany. The Jew Eisenmann is in Poland, working for the *Vaterland*. Ah, here we are!'

The door of the carriage swung back, and Göring pushed through the gap. He was resplendent in his new Marschall's uniform, several square metres of sky-blue decorated with ropes of golden braid. He scowled at us through his make-up and waddled to the car and we followed to ours. The cavalcade headed to the airfield, where the Heinkels and Ju 88s were bombing up. The sight of them seemed to revive Göring's spirits.

'Now at last!' he cried. 'Now we shall smash the British. The cloak of the night will accomplish what the fighters could not do by day – keep the bombers safe.'

You could see the fighter-pilots all about tense with resentment. I saw some of the younger boys glance at me; they knew I had flown with Göring in the Richtofen circus.

'That is a little unfair, Marschall,' I called.

He turned to look at me in a swirl of blue cloth. 'Ah, Wolff!' he grunted. He peered dismissively at my arm and scabbed face. 'What happened to you? Fall downstairs drunk? If it is unfair, then why am I having to order the bombers to go out at night, eh? Answer me that!'

'For a start, the Stukas are like sitting ducks when you put them up against good fighters. We *cannot* guard them in the dive, and the Hurricanes and Spitfires eat them alive.'

'We have withdrawn the Stukas. You still did not defend the other bombers.'

'Wrong tactics,' I said shortly. 'We are *Jägers*, hunters; unless we are allowed to roam freely we cannot defend properly. Do you not remember what our old leader Freiherr von Richtofen said? "The fighter pilots have to rove in the area allotted to them in any way they like, and when they spot an enemy they attack and shoot him down; anything else is rubbish." We were made to use different tactics.'

'*My* tactics,' he growled dangerously, 'which would have worked if I had pilots with some guts! Let's see what the bombers can do!'

I had lost a lot of my boys, as had all the other commanders there. We had done everything we were meant to. Rage suddenly flared within me.

'They are brave men, as we fighter-pilots are. Yet I predict they will do little to break the will of the British except anger them.'

'Oh, and why is that, may I ask?' Göring said softly. Some of the other pilots were easing away from me. They knew the danger signs.

'These are medium bombers. They carry a light load, and there are not enough of them. Furthermore, all our aircraft are in the front line. We do not build adequate reserves, and attrition will wear away this spearpoint to a stump. All we are doing here is providing the British with practice to come back and do it to us.'

'Next year the Heinkel four-engined bomber will be available and we will finish the British off!'

'It is a bad design. Four engines driving two propellers is unsound. It won't work.'

'Bah! Personal heroism counts more than technical novelties.'

'Unless the technical aspects of design and production are kept in unity with the requirements of air fighting, you might as well send brave men up in Fokkers from 1918 for all the good they will do,' I snapped.

The bombers were firing up their engines, blue-edged flames flickering in the gathering gloom. One after the other, they lumbered along the grass and into the air, heading for the coast. Gradually the sound of the massed engines died away in the darkness and we were left in the empty airfield. Göring stared after them, the grin on his face slowly dying away.

He turned, and began to walk towards his car. Then he stopped, and wheeled on me. 'You want to know why the fighters failed?' he yelled suddenly. 'They failed because they were led by gutless old farts like you! I need young men in command who haven't lost their nerve. Look at you! You're fat and bald – you look like an old cockatoo! You're past it. You know so much about technical things, Wolff? Very well, go and hide among the cowards in the rear, those blasted civilians who make the aircraft. You're through here! We only want heroes at the front.'

'Very good, Reichsmarschall,' I said coldly. I was beyond caring. 'And as one fatter, older and dressed up exactly like a parrot, you will be leaving too?'

I stood at the window, looking out. A mountain fox was loping across the meadow, already dusted with snow. Down near the trees he vanished. Some black kites suddenly appeared, cawing hoarsely, circling about, settling in the branches in an irritable fashion. I assumed that something had died down there, that the fox had disturbed them in the pleasurable task – to them – of stripping its bones. The winters are hard and they needed to feed up when they could.

Göring recovered sufficent of his good humour to arrange a posting for me. I wasn't simply dumped as a paper-pusher, as happened to some of the other *alte Fliegers*. He was never as affable again, however, for the air war did not go as well for his Luftwaffe as it had before, once the Battle of Britain started; and as its fortunes fell, so did his own, in the eyes of Hitler, the only man he feared. The bombers failed to break the British, as I had predicted. The attrition was such that the attacks simply fizzled out in the end. And then the direction of the war turned a different way, to the east. We attacked Russia . . .

Me, I took up a post as an engineer and test-pilot with Messerschmitt. In a final venting of spleen on his part, Göring instructed that as I knew so much about technical matters and had such a high opinion of my own courage, I was to be given the most dangerous project on their books. Thus it was that I became involved with the Messerschmitt Me 163 rocket-fighter development programme. In June, as the vast forces of Operation Barbarossa crashed over the border with Russia on a three-thousand-kilometre front, I was far away in Peenemünde, where the development team for the radical new fighter was based. For me, the war was suddenly another land. I was a test-pilot, a development engineer; nobody shot at me. I returned to the 1920s. I flew gliders.

There was a certain symmetry about it all. In the 1920s I had flown a very unusual glider called a *Storch*, or Stork, designed by a young man called Alexander Lippisch. It had no tail, but was an all-wing aircraft. Lippisch was a great advocate of such designs and soon came up with a swept-wing tail-less aircraft, the shape of the Greek letter *delta*. The Air Ministry of the day showed the bureaucrat's usual intelligence by declaring it unsafe, as it had no tail.

Time passed, and by 1940 Lippisch had designed a small, swept-wing, tail-less interceptor that would be able to use the very compact and light rocket-engine then being designed by Hellmuth Walter, which was to run on a combination of hydrogen peroxide and various hydrocarbons known as *T-stoff*, and hydrazine hydrate in methyl alcohol, known as *C-stoff*. Once mixed together, a decomposing reaction took place which, if contained in a chamber, produced enormous thrust.

This it did under very carefully controlled conditions. To illustrate this, if – as happened – some mechanic dumped a litre or two of *C-stoff* into a bucket containing dregs of *T-stoff*, the entire thing, mechanic and all, vanished in a blinding flash of violet smoke.

The 163 was designed to carry two tons of *C-stoff* and *T-stoff*. It was given the name Komet. Furthermore, *T-stoff* caught fire at the simplest contact with organic material, and *C-stoff* would corrode and dissolve anything other than glass or enamel, including the pilot.

However, what the engine would *do* was this: a propeller-driven fighter might take half an hour to climb to altitude. The 163 took a minute. A propeller fighter could do six hundred kilometres an hour. The 163 knocked on the door of the sound barrier at over one thousand.

Getting it to work was something else, however. While they were sorting out the development, some of the rest of us were getting to grips with the airframe. When the fuel ran out, the 163 was a high-speed glider, so we began with gliders. The *Versuch*,

Experimental Model 163A, was so fast that it landed at some 160 km, and it was calculated that the fully-equipped 163B fighter would put down on its retractable skid – no wheels – at 260. The 163 took off on a jettisonable steel dolly, but it landed on a skid.

Because it was a glider, it had no power to help the pilot set up his landing approach. The landing either was, or was not, right first time. If it was, you climbed out and went to the mess for a drink. If it was not, then a variety of options presented themselves on a scale of rising awfulness from being blown to bits or dissolved like an aspirin in a tide of volatile chemicals. It was no accident that the 163 quickly became known as the 'devil's sledge'.

So it was very necessary to get the landing approach right. To train the pilots, we used gliders. We began with regular types such as the Grünau Baby and then graduated to the Habicht series. As the pilots got better, we made the wings shorter. We soon had them screaming in like bullets.

The flying side moved to Bad Zwischenahn, out in the beautiful, peaceful Friesian countryside. Lippisch found he could not stand Professor Messerschmitt, whose company was building the fighter, and in 1943 he moved over to Vienna to head his own aeronautical research institute. He designed supersonic delta-winged jet-fighters and bombers. I never met him again, although I read about him after the war was over. The American company of Convair became impressed with his thinking. They took it up and made supersonic jets such as the Delta Dagger, the Delta Dart and the B-58 Hustler which, like the 163, was ten years ahead of its time.

In the beautiful farmland around the Zwischenahn Lake, we set about developing the experimental aircraft into an armed fighter, a devastating weapon of war. Over Germany, the British four-engined bomber fleets were beginning to set alight entire towns, even by night, and the Americans in their Flying Fortresses were destroying our industry by day. The 163, if we could develop it and produce it in sufficient quantities, was a weapon capable of inflicting such losses on the Americans as to make them cease their attacks.

In Bad Zwischenahn we were far, far away from the war. And so the war came to me. I received a letter from Hoeppner. He was on leave from the Eastern Front. We arranged to have dinner in Bad Zwischenahn, in a little restaurant I had come to know.

'I hear I'm not supposed to ask what it is you do here,' Hoeppner said jovially.

'It has some super-secret rating,' I agreed. He looked much older than when I had last seen him, and was walking with a stick while he recovered from leg wounds. But he was still the same Hoeppner. Like me, he had the rank of colonel.

'That doesn't bother me,' he said. 'I'm used to having to keep some things secret myself. Now, what have we here? You have good food out in these parts!'

'The owner has some agreement with the local farmers,' I said. 'And he goes fishing on the lake. Try the smoked eel to start with, it's excellent. What's more, he has a pre-war cellar!'

'It's certainly good,' Hoeppner agreed reverently, when he had taken his first sip of the Tokay.

'Better than you get at the front,' I suggested quietly.

'Ah . . . the front. There we eat bullets and bombs and hate as we retreat through the ruins of places where we rode in triumph. Yet, you know, we could have won.'

'You think so?'

'I know it is so.' He glanced around, but I had chosen a little booth where I knew we could not be overheard. 'They hated Stalin for what he did to them,' he said quietly but clearly. 'Stalin massacred and starved and oppressed millions and millions of people. When we first came through the Ukraine we were treated as liberators. They would have fought with us all the way to Moscow, and put Stalin's head on a pole! I tell you, it would have taken nothing to get them fighting on our side. We had men and officers defect to us by the thousand. But that was before the SS started killing people . . .'

'Who?'

'Liquidation squads, *Einsatzkommandos*. They are supposedly to kill Bolshevik commissars. I have seen massed graves of women, children and old men . . . the word came down from Hitler himself. He thinks Slavs are *Untermenschen* like the Jews. He wants them obliterated from the face of the earth. This is a race war, they are simply killing just about anybody – Jews, Slavs, gypsies – the very people who would have helped us win.'

'Eisenmann was sent to Poland,' I blurted out suddenly. 'I tried to get him out, but they sent him to Poland as forced labour.'

'Eisenmann was a Jew, and must be dead by now,' Hoeppner said quietly. 'In Poland, I assure you, Himmler has very big concentration camps dedicated to actual killing of Jews. *En masse.* Many, many at a time . . .'

'You're certain of it?'

'I am . . . on the staff of Army Group Centre, under Von Tresckow. We . . . have ways of finding things out. They arrive by the trainload. They are . . . gassed. Eisenmann will have been gassed, his body burned in a great furnace.'

'This is insane,' I muttered. 'Himmler is a crank, a health-food fool –'

'He is also a bureaucrat and a man who will follow Hitler's will to the end. He has an elaborate organisation solely designed to round up Jews and *Untermenschen* and put them to death.'

Hoeppner was quiet for a few moments, then he picked up his knife and fork again and recommenced eating his ham.

'You are so fortunate!' he said. 'I haven't tasted better, not even when peace was here.'

'The pigs are a long way from the war,' I suggested. 'They are content to find full troughs.'

'I can see it is pleasant round here. How do you like research and development after being in the front line?'

'I was proud to lead my boys,' I said. 'I would be there still, but the Fat One, he blamed all the older men for failing to win the battle over Britain. He called me a coward . . .'

Hoeppner's face wrinkled with distaste. 'I have always considered you on the foolhardy side,' he murmured, 'though that too may have its advantages. But your courage is beyond question. You must still have to deal with him, if at long range. What is it like?'

'He has no understanding of the links – the organic unity – between the waging of air war and production and supply. Air strategy, of which he knows little, depends totally upon the development of new weapons and the large-scale output of aircraft. Once you have that in place then of course you may turn to questions of a purely military nature, but not before.

'We suffer from his preference for the younger fighting officers. He despises engineers and civilians – the very people who must produce the new weapons. He tried to have some of us shot recently because, he claimed, we were not producing fast enough!'

'The *alte Kämpfers* are all much the same,' said Hoeppner. 'They have acquired levels of command that are enormously beyond their capabilities. I was there when General Bittrich attempted to instruct Sepp Dietrich, who had been Hitler's chauffeur and bodyguard, in the elementary principles of strategy, as opposed to tactics. Dietrich, who is, as you know, a Waffen SS general, knows what tactics are. You go straight for the enemy and try to do him in, at whatever cost in your own men's lives. Strategy? He could not come to terms with the idea at all.'

He drank a little of his wine.

'How is your son?' he asked.

'Kurt is dead,' I said steadily. 'His unit was blown into bloody mud somewhere in Stalingrad. He was with Von Paulus. Hitler was about to issue the order for Von Paulus to withdraw when *der Dicke*, the Fat One, Göring himself, boasted he could keep Stalingrad supplied from the air. The fat bastard, anything to get Hitler's favour... So Hitler forbade them to withdraw and now they are all dead, and *der Dicke* has a new uniform.'

'I'm sorry... there are so many dead.'

'I lost him well before that. I let him go to that *ordensburg* school in the castle. I didn't realise it was a place of indoctrination for the young. By the time I knew, it was far too late. I blame myself. Kurt was like Hilde – he had her kind of personality. He wanted to believe in something, he was ready to be soaked in an ideology. Hilde was that way too. She thought that communism was the new world. Kurt, he believed all that stuff about *Rassenschande* and poisoning of the blood...'

'I don't suppose you know where Hilde is these days.'

'Who knows where anybody is?' I said bitterly.

'It's true. Where is Army Group Centre? Our losses exceeded our replacements by over one million soldiers last year. *One million*, Hans. I have calculated a date at which the entire

Wehrmacht will cease to exist. We shall all be bloody mud . . .'

The waiter brought coffee, real coffee. Our test commando was well supplied with both tea and coffee, and I had made an arrangement with the man who owned the restaurant. I passed Hoeppner a cigar, and we puffed for a few moments, enjoying the fine tobacco.

'The killing is set to get worse,' Hoeppner said quietly. 'The British and Americans are advancing up through Italy. They will soon invade the coast of France from Britain and march into Germany, while the Soviets come in from the east. All the time, Himmler will be stoking his ovens, putting Hitler's final solution to the Jewish race into effect. I cannot tell you how many will die, and for those Germans left alive at the finish – what? Domination by the régime of Stalin, which is quite as evil as the one we suffer under now. And disgrace, dishonour for all of us, for letting it happen. They will overrun the concentration camps, they will find Himmler's work, and all we Germans will be dishonoured. Unless . . .'

'Unless what?'

Hoeppner did not reply for a moment. He peered at the glowing tip of his cigar.

'Very fine, this . . .' he murmured. 'Men of the future are purged of dishonour, their shoulders released from the shackles of bondage.' He seemed to be quoting from a poem. He looked up from his cigar with penetrating eyes. 'I need a bomb, Hans.'

'A bomb?' I repeated after him, not very loudly. 'What sort of bomb? A big one?'

'No. Nothing that an aircraft would be needed to carry. A small bomb that a man could pick up in a briefcase. Shall I go on, or would you rather not hear any more about it?'

'No,' I said steadily. 'Tell me what it is you want.'

'A bomb powerful enough to kill anybody within a room. It must have a timer, to allow the person carrying to get away. The timer and the fusing device must be simple enough to be set by a man who has only one hand, and only three fingers on that hand. Perhaps two bombs, of the same design.'

I sat at the little table. I had a small workshop out at the test base. I was a trained engineer, I was able to make modifications to the experimental aircraft myself. I had access to the kind of explosive necessary. Three fingers ... pliers, perhaps. An acid/wire fuse.

I put the cigar to my mouth, and drew in the fine, scented smoke. I let it go in a silver grey stream.

'How long are you staying here?' I asked. 'You must take a boat out on to the lake. It is most enjoyable.'

'I should like that,' he said calmly. 'How long do you think I would need?'

'Oh, three days should do it,' I said. 'No longer than that.'

I stood looking out of the window, as I do. High up in the valley, higher than I was, I could see a kestrel circling. I am somewhat deaf but my eyes are still keen. A fighter pilot must have sharp vision. He has to see tiny speeding specks in the distance, spot wings against the sun, make sense of a brief swirl of chocolate crosses. Those who cannot are cut down by those who can.

There.

The kestrel folded its wings and dropped like a spearhead. Where was its prey?

There it was. A fast-moving pigeon, grey and sleek. Especially in the cold weather, you must eat. If you cannot eat, the cold will kill you. The pigeon had seen the kestrel. It swerved and dodged. The pursuing predator opened its swept wings, swaying and weaving in *Totentanz*, the two birds locked into a dance of death.

From the ground, you could see the Flying Fortresses coming. Great broad phalanxes of them pulling huge contrails across the sky. Our tiny 163 Komet rocket-fighters drew delicate filigrees in the sky about them as we dived and soared through the bombers and the jinking, protective enemy fighters, slashing into the mighty boxes of aircraft. You could see the occasional bomber coming down, glinting and tumbling, pieces of tinfoil scattered across the sky.

They knew where we were by then, the Mustangs of the American fighter-pilots, they followed us down. They knew we were gliders, that we did not have the power of an engine to save us, as they did; they knew that as the ground came up we had to land, that we had to fly, just for a few seconds, straight and level, that the flak guns could not fire for fear of hitting us.

I stood waiting for them to come down as, high above Leipzig, the Forts poured high explosive into the burning hell beneath them. They could aim for the gigantic cloud of choking, acrid smoke that poured without cease from what had once been a city.

I saw Sergeant Kolb coming down. Twisting, turning, almost cavorting, he seemed, but with him was a Mustang, circling and twisting, spiralling down with him.

The pigeon came over the meadow. The kestrel was as close as its shadow. Left, right, left – The kestrel swooped round in a gliding turn, leaving but a cloud of small feathers floating away down the mountainside.

Sergeant Kolb straightened out at the last possible second, side-slipping over the trees. The Mustang opened up with its sextette of 0.5-inch machine-guns. The flail of explosive sliced through the tree-tops, blasting matchwood high into the air, and Sergeant Kolb blazed in fragments all down the runway. As the flak guns opened up, the Mustang was gone, flitting away over the woods, climbing back up to the bomber fleets above.

The kestrel landed on the meadow, looking fiercely around before reaching down with its hooked beak to tear off the flesh of the pigeon in its taloned foot.

We *did* get the 163 Komet operational. It was still plagued with faults that in peacetime would have kept it on a drawing-board, from its habit of filling its cockpit with steam to the rather more serious one of exploding without warning. But as the Russians were steamrollering from one side and the British and Americans pulling themselves ashore on the other, you stood a good chance of getting killed whichever way you sliced it. For we fighter-pilots, it was better to be up in the clear air fighting than cowering on the ground, so we flew.

I joined one of the operational squadrons as their chief instructor and I, too, flew against the massive bomber fleets that filled our skies. We hid our operational 163s in the woods about the field, while those of us on readiness sat in our cockpits, dozing fitfully over the controls as we waited for our take-off orders.

It was a hot July day. Sweltering. I had the cockpit canopy open, and an umbrella up to keep off the hot sun. Insects buzzed and there was the pervading smell of chemicals in the air.

The R/T crackled in my ears, and I jerked awake.

'*Ja?* Gunther?' I asked, over the radio. Gunther was our controller, who guided us to our prey, so high up above.

'It's me, Hans,' he said. 'Not yet. A few more minutes. I thought you might want to hear the news.'

'What?'

'Somebody tried to get the Führer. With a bomb.'

'Did they get him?'

'No. They blew up some others about him, but he lived.'

Truly, I thought, the devil looks after his own. 'When was this?'

'Two days ago.'

I sat quiet in the tiny, cramped cockpit. Now the war would not stop, not until all Germany was smashed into ruins, and most of us dead in them.

'Just tell me when to go,' I said.

There they were. White contrails blossoming in the blue sky, pushing forward towards us. The clatter of cockpit canopies closing, the whine and hum of the turbine-starters. The first diamond-wave pattern blazing from the lead Komet. An ear-splitting roar, deafening even inside the cockpit; the gigantic frenzied hiss of an immense red-hot iron being plunged into water, the breath of Siegfried's dragon; a huge violet-black cloud driving a leaping, skipping winged egg ahead of it. The Komet left the ground, the steel wheels falling free, and shot up into the sky, vanishing into the blue, leaving only a near-vertical violet trail of smoke drifting away in the breeze.

One, two, three . . . my turn . . .

The thump in the small of the back. My eyes dancing between runway and gauges. My foot easing in rudder. The controls beginning to bite, the grass speeding past in a brown-green blur, lifting up . . . about five metres, and I pulled the release of the wheels, the fighter accelerating faster and faster. I trimmed her nose heavy and we stabbed across the field like a bolt of lightning. Over the perimeter and a quick glance at the airspeed, the wings thumping like a cobbled road in the rough air. Eight hundred kilometres. I pulled back the stick and shot into the sky like an arrow released from its bow.

There they were, the massed boxes of heavies spilling their

white trails of condensation across the sky. The escort fighters jinking and swooping protectively about them. Twelve thousand metres, and I climbed higher than them, alone like an eagle in the sky. The rocket-motor stopped and there was only the whistle of the thin air rushing over my smooth polished skin as I put the nose over, diving down on the great shining monsters beneath.

The gunsight glowed, the armaments switch was red. With the sun behind me I came down on the Fortress like a speeding angel. At the killing place I squeezed the trigger and the cannon buried in my wing roots thundered. The wing of the mighty bomber folded where it met the fuselage and the craft tumbled into two, the great engines still spinning their huge propellers, the aircraft about it pulling away from the flying wreckage in alarm. Striped stars tumbling... I sliced across the formation and turrets blazed with orange and yellow light. I fired again, and another gigantic machine spewed smoke. Images like photographs. Tiny men crouched about their guns in round glass pillboxes. Grey smoke and glittering gold shellcases.

A bang, a blow, something shaking. The Komet falling away, the silver bomber fleet pushing inexorably onwards. The ground, greenish-brown through the haze, far below.

Whooomph!

I choked inside my mask as steam belched into the cockpit, my eyes steaming tears. It was boiling hot and then suddenly icy cold.

Ice. The inside of the canopy was covered in thick rime frost. The sun blazed on it, blinding me. It was silent, except for the whistling of the wind over the falling fighter. I scratched desperately at the frost on the canopy, trying to see out. With a single blast of his frozen breath, the iceman had swept all my instruments with white. I could see nothing. The fighter shuddered underneath me. *Stall!* Stall...

I felt the little machine buck like an unwilling horse, and then my head was whipped against the canopy, left and right, round and round...

Frantically, I scraped at the ice with hands that flailed about. A smear of clarity, a tumbling earth. I could see. I put the stick forward and trod on the rudder. My world became steady again, the wings ceased their demonic whirling, and I glided downwards.

There. There it was, the city, there our airfield . . .

I came over the perimeter like an arrow, dropping the skid down. The ground tapped me. I held it straight as I slithered to a halt and the little fighter dropped over on to one wing like a tired butterfly.

I trudged over the dry brown grass to the operations room as the ground crew on their *Schlepper* tractor/trailer pulled the Komet off to the hangar to repair the battle damage. The ice still on the canopy shone like cut-glass in the sunshine.

I pushed open the door of the ops room and tossed my parachute on to a chair. At his control desk Gunther sat silent, looking fearfully at the armed men arrayed about him.

'What in hell –' I cried out.

One of the SS men, thin and young, a face like a ferret lighting up with joy. 'Colonel Wolff!' he shouted. 'We thought you were never coming!' He slashed me across the face with a whip and I reeled across the room. They clubbed me to the floor with hoarse cries of hate. They dragged me out, threw me into the darkness of a van, and locked the door before they drove me away.

I could hear a voice. A gravelly voice of coarse tobacco and alcohol, a voice that shouted easily, that was checking a list, grunting from time to time. It was coming through the ventilation shaft of the cell.

It was not Rasch's voice – Rasch's voice I knew. It had screamed in my ear as I sat strapped to the heavy wooden chair. It had ordered me beaten each time I failed to come up with any useful names. Rasch was the young SS officer with the thin, weasel face who had come to arrest me. He was a product of eleven years of indoctrination, and in his eyes I was one of the devil's cohorts. When the Gestapo men got tired of hitting me he took the rubber club and did it himself. He called it 'sharpened interrogation'.

My ears sang from the beating. Hoeppner was dead. The *coup* had failed. He had been taken along with the man who had planted the bomb, Colonel Claus von Stauffenberg. They had been in the War Office on the Bendlerstrasse. If Hitler had been dead, they would have taken over control. The bomb, left in a briefcase by Von Stauffenberg under a table at which Hitler was sitting, had unwittingly been moved by another. When it went off, its force had only managed to shock Hitler badly, to singe his trousers, stun him and make him madder and more vengeful than he had been before.

Hoeppner was dead, as was Von Stauffenberg. They had taken them out and shot them with some others in the courtyard. Now Hitler wanted revenge on anybody and everybody who might have had anything to do with it.

The voice still came through the ventilation shaft. Names, checking names with somebody. A quota.

I knew that voice.

I sat up on the bare planks that formed a kind of bed along the wall, and almost cried out with pain. 'Huber!' I yelled. 'Huber, it's me, Hans-Joachim, the pilot.'

I heard the voice hesitate, stop.

'Here!' I shouted. 'In this cell here. Wolff, Hans-Joachim Wolff!'

There was the sound of boots clumping on the stone floor. We were in the Ploetzensee prison in Berlin, that was where they had taken us. The door to the cell clanked as somebody unlocked it. Huber walked in. A guard was with him and he motioned for him to wait outside.

He peered at me.

'They've whacked you about a bit, Hauptmann,' he observed. He sat down on the planks next to me.

'Colonel,' I said. 'I got promoted.'

'Me, too,' he replied. He was wearing the uniform of the Waffen SS. He pulled out a pack of dark cigarettes and gave me one. The tobacco washed over me, soothing the pain.

'What are you doing here?'

'They think I had something to do with that attempt on the Führer's life,' I said. 'How could I have? I'm a pilot.'

'They shot Hoeppner,' he observed quietly.

'They will probably shoot me too, then, if I stay here.'

A list – Huber had been wanting names, he had been putting them on a list.

'Why are *you* here?' I asked.

'Obergruppenführer von dem Bach-Zelewski sent me,' he

said laconically. 'I'm to scrape up a couple of hundred criminals who look like they can fight.'

'Why?'

'To go and slaughter the Poles,' he said frankly. 'The bastards have risen in Warsaw and Himmler wants him to sort it out.'

I had heard of Bach-Zelewski. A bespectacled figure who looked more like a schoolteacher than an SS general, he was a counter-insurgency expert, a veteran of killing grounds all over the east.

'Two brigades to do it,' Huber said, sucking in tobacco smoke. 'Dirlewanger's police and Kaminski's Russians. I'd hardly call either crack troops. The idea is to slaughter the Poles with people we don't mind getting wiped out ourselves.'

'Take me,' I said quietly.

'Hauptmann,' he protested, 'I'm recruiting trash, not gentlemen. The dregs. Real slime . . .'

'There is a young SS man here who interrogates me. His name is Rasch. He has promised me that when he thinks I have nothing else to say he will have me shot. I believe him. He is . . . one of *those*. The ones who believe that we are losing the war because of traitors . . .'

Huber looked thoughtfully, and then shrugged his wide shoulders. 'Don't say I didn't warn you, then. Come on. Trucks're down in the yard.'

We got up, and I limped out with Huber. The guard was waiting outside.

'I'm taking this one too.' Huber said.

'He's for interrogation,' the man objected. 'Sturmführer Rasch wants him.'

Huber thrust his battered, scarred face into the other's. 'I don't give a toss what he wants. I'm allowed to have anybody I want, see? The Reichsführer says so.'

'But –'

'Do you want a quick posting to the Russian front?' Huber threatened. He pushed the man aside, and we went out and down into the courtyard. Trucks were there, and men scrambling aboard. Huber gave me a shove. 'Best of luck, Hauptmann,' he said. I joined in the throng and clambered up. I heard Huber shouting orders as the engine started up with a rattle, blue smoke belching from beneath us. We began to move out.

A man ran out of the doorway nearby. It was Rasch. He was yelling angrily, looking about him, but the gates were open and we were driving through. He saw me staring at him and shook his fist, screaming some threat, some promise of death, and then we were in the street, and driving away.

'Well, this is a bit of all right,' my neighbour said happily. 'They were going to damn well shoot me tomorrow.'

The scrapings of the Ploetzensee jail were in fact some kind of upper crust of the vile crew that assembled on the Warsaw outskirts. We could at least speak German. The others were assorted Muslims, Cossacks, Turkomen, Hungarians, Galicians and Ukrainians. The only real common denominator was murder.

Our commanding officer was a former doctor of political science at Frankfurt University. Himmler liked him. He'd got him out of jail, where he had been sent for the buggery of a very young boy. Oskar Dirlewanger had done much more than that since then. Even the SS found the activities of him and his motley band hard to stomach, but in the swirling disorder behind the lines of the eastern front they had enjoyed almost uncontrolled licence.

The Polish Home Army had risen in Warsaw, thinking that the Soviet Union's armies were about to liberate them. Stalin had halted them short of the river, however, offering the Germans freedom to do his work for him.

Not caring whether Dirlewanger and his gang lived or died, the Wehrmacht had sent them in.

It was the fifth of August. I had a squad. Our commander had a list of us and he interviewed me on arrival in his command post, which was a looted bus.

'You were an officer,' he said.

'Colonel.'

He tossed a feldwebel's armband on to the table. 'Your lot's outside,' he said. 'I don't suppose you've done this kind of work before, being a pilot.'

'No.'

'Keep them moving,' he grunted. 'No heavy loot, it weighs them down. Keep them moving forward. They can kill anyone they want. Lots of dead. The order is from on high. Warsaw is to be razed to the ground, and everybody in it. The Poles have been a problem to us for seven hundred years, since the First Battle of Tannenberg. The Führer has ordered that the Polish problem is to vanish for us, for all time. Don't let them get slowed down with too much loot. Keep them killing. All Poles are to be killed out of hand. Shoot one or two so the others understand.'

I realised that I was speaking to someone who was – in his field – an expert.

The rabble I had were mostly Galicians and Ukrainians. None of them spoke German. They reminded me of nothing more than a collection of wild dogs.

We were well equipped. We wore strong Waffen SS camouflage uniforms with Wehrmacht belts of tough hide to carry our ammunition pouches, water bottles, trenching tools, grenades and bayonets. Our belt buckles bore the motto *Gott Mit Uns*.

We had MP40 submachine-guns and MP44 assault-rifles, mortars and flamethrowers. Travelling with us into Warsaw were a number of Panzer tanks of the Hermann Göring Brigade, and behind us howitzer-calibre 60cm assault-guns firing a 4850lb shell. We had radio-controlled miniature tanks packed with explosives. Dirlewanger could call on the services of a Stuka squadron. The Führer had given his men whatever they needed to erase the Poles of Warsaw from the face of the earth.

Dirlewanger's brigade went in through Wolska Street, the city's main road, shortly after dawn. To the north were the police units and to the south Kaminsky's Russians, who were about two hours late having boozed their way in from the suburbs.

The distance from Wolska past the Saxon Gardens to the Vistula bridges was about three miles. An hour's walk. It took us three days.

It was not a military operation, despite the quantities of military hardware available to us. Those fighting us were the AK, the Polish Home Army, whom we outnumbered considerably. What the – what do I call them? They were not troops. Convicts? Murderers? Creatures? What the creatures of Dirlewanger and Kaminsky did most of, was slaughter the unarmed population of the city; men, women, children and babies. All houses on and near the battle line were stormed. All the inhabitants were ordered out and herded into the nearest confined space, whether cemeteries, gardens, backyards, factory forecourts or squares. There they were cut down with machine-gun fire. Hand-grenades were tossed into the heaps of writhing wounded and finished off with petrol set ablaze. The buildings we passed were burned down so that the murders took place in an atmosphere of smoke and flame. It was truly hell upon earth. Nobody was spared, not even nurses or nuns. The hospitals were stormed and the patients and staff raped and murdered in an orgy of pillage and death.

I did as I had been ordered to by Dirlewanger: I attempted to keep my squad moving forward. Rabid for loot and liquor, women and killing, they hated me. I made sure I stayed at their backs. By the middle of the afternoon, however, like all the other junior commanders, I had lost control of them. They disappeared into the dust and smoke near one of the hospitals. Exhausted and parched, I found cover in the corner of two walls.

As the sun was setting blood red, lighting up the sky in flames, one of Dirlewanger's officers came down the street with a squad. 'Get them moving!' he screamed at me. 'We haven't made a kilometre! General Rohr wants our heads. Get them moving or be shot!'

Rohr was the Wehrmacht commander. A Prussian general of the old school, he wanted the Home Army defeated, not the Poles annihilated.

As I heaved myself to my feet and jogged forward into the hospital in the red smoke, I suddenly thought of Himmler, responsible for it all. Was it the birthday of King Heinrich? I had the feeling it was. So while we were murdering Poles, Himmler would be meditating at the tomb of the thousand-years' dead king, the founder of the Holy Roman Empire, in his castle at Wewelsberg, along with the twelve SS Knights. Himmler believed himself the reincarnation of the king.

I kicked open a door and went into a corridor strewn with bodies. Patients with trailing bandages, doctors in bloody white coats, half-naked nurses, all shot, bludgeoned and stabbed to death. The floor was sticky with congealing blood.

Himmler would be drinking herbal tea, down at the castle.

KILLING PLACE

There was a smell of burning in the corridors of the dead. From a smashed window I could hear the whine and grind of a tank coming up. People were still screaming inside the building, in a drained, exhausted manner, overlain with yelling, and the occasional shot.

I found four of my squad in a small ward. They were drunk, their eyeballs red with alcohol and propellant. A patient, an old woman, lay like a broken doll on the floor, her throat cut. A doctor in a coat was in the corner, holes blown in the palms of his hands, where he had held them out against the bullets. Two of the men sat slumped in a corner, almost incapable, empty bottles about them. One sat on a seat, pouring a stream of gold rings, watches and jewellery from each hand into his lap. One was on the bed, raping a nurse.

I shot the two in the corner first with one brief burst of the submachine-gun, and then the one in the chair. They were so full of liquor they splattered all over the wall. Jewellery flew everywhere. The Ukrainian raping the girl stared at me in bewilderment, his jaw wide open. I put the muzzle of the gun up close to his head and blew him off the bed. The girl did not scream, she only rolled to one side, huddling herself into a ball.

Smoke was drifting into the room, the corridor suddenly flickered with yellow light. I yanked her off.

'The place is burning,' I shouted. She scrambled to her feet, and was suddenly off down the corridor, tripping and stumbling over the dead, slipping on the blood, bouncing off the walls. She ran through the door and out into the street. I followed her, the smoke gushing down the corridor.

Himmler, it was said, suffered from gastric pains, he took special capsules made of bacteria cultures cultured from the excrement of a Bulgarian peasant. Hitler had provided them, dosing himself with them every day.

There was a burst of fire and the girl tumbled over the pavement like a shot duck. More of Dirlewanger's men were pushing up the street, the sun painting them as red as blood.

The Poles fought to the end. Short of ammunition, short of weapons, short of food, short of medicine, short of soldiers, they simply fought to the last man or woman. We were heavily supplied, and once Rohr had got the slaughter stopped, the military aspects of the operation were able to resume. He provided us with Stukas whose thousand-pound bombs blew apart barricades and tore vast holes in their pillbox lines. Their communications were destroyed and they became reduced to fighting in groups.

Fight they did. Their favourite method was the ambush. Snipers shot down the officers and a hail of Molotov cocktails rained down on the advancing soldiers. Dirlewanger countered with the capture of Polish hostages, whom he had lashed to ladders. The hostages were then made to advance up the street with his troops behind.

The Poles at first had humanitarian scruples about killing their own. But when it was seen that Poles died whatever happened, that the wounded were just wrapped up in bundles by barbed wire, doused in petrol and set alight, then they killed as many of the enemy, hostages or no hostages, as they could before they too died.

It took a month to reach the Old Town. By now Dirlewanger was using the 600mm mortars to flatten the houses, which collapsed on top of their occupants.

Still they fought. They were using the sewers of the city as a transport and communications system, wading sometimes chest-deep through the fast-flowing ordure. The battle went underground and men fought hand-to-hand in the darkness. Men and women died as Dirlewanger set up booby-traps in the tunnels: hand-grenades dangling from the roof, a tide of petrol set ablaze, explosive gas that plastered men and women, rats and cats against the walls like postage stamps.

In the Old Town the Poles fought house by house, floor by floor. In the street, fire blazed in smoky patches where they had thrown petrol bombs. The road was thickly coated with rubble and dust. I crouched behind a smashed truck with some others. An officer lay nearby, painting the white dirt red with his blood. The window sockets of the house glowed as bright as cherries, as fire belched out as a flamethrower erupted inside.

Somebody screamed up there; the sniper. A blazing, shrieking thing tumbled out of a window, hitting the ground with the sound of a sack of wet sand. It lay there, burning fitfully, dirty black smoke drifting past us.

Inside the building there was the crump of a grenade, the rattle of machine-gun fire. Then the squad came out, the flamethrower operator in their midst, a blue flame seeping from the short, evil muzzle of his weapon, and we all began moving forward to the crossroads. The man with the flamethrower tanks on his back paused by the still-burning body of the sniper and kicked it in the face. 'Bitch,' he said malevolently.

As I passed I looked down at her, and then I stood still. It was Hilde.

I knew her. She was as laminated with blood and dirt as I was. Her face was much older, far more lined; it bore scars. Her eyes were open; blue-grey, they looked into a new world. I bent and closed them. How had she got there? By what long road had she travelled to fight with Poles to the death, in a dying city?

A burst of fire ripped past me. Dirlewanger's armed police were coming up behind us. They killed stragglers. I left Hilde dead on a burning street, with nobody to bury her.

Three days later the battle was over and the winners razed the city to the ground as Hitler had demanded. They retreated then, and the waiting Russians resumed their march, driving over the rubble and the dead into Germany.

Dirlewanger held an actual parade, before the *Raumungs* clearance Kommandos moved in and the survivors were moved out. The remnants of the Home Army were saved by Wehrmacht out of some mutual military respect. Himmler took the civilians to the slave camps and the gas-chambers.

We had a parade. Dirlewanger went off to get his Knight's Cross. Himmler – ever one to abandon a friend in need – gave Kaminski, his equally revolting co-commander, to Rohr, the Wehrmacht general, who had him shot.

When I came from the parade-ground – a flattened part of the Old Town – a car was waiting for me. Three SS men were standing by it. One was Rasch.

'Colonel Wolff,' he said very politely. 'I am so glad you have survived.'

I would have shot him on reflex but we had had to turn in our weapons. Nobody trusted us with them outside the killing place we had made.

'I have your uniform, Colonel. And there is a bath waiting. You would like a bath, no doubt?'

A bath. I had not had a bath in six weeks, nor changed my filthy, bloody uniform. The parade-ground stank like an abattoir.

'The Führer wants to see you, Colonel.'

Wolfsschanze, Rastenberg, September 1944

A man was dying in a stench of old cream-cakes and half-digested vegetable spaghetti.

He stood on a chair, an old man in a collarless shirt and a pair of coarse trousers too large for him. They had no belt and he had to hold them up with his hands. His face was expressionless.

By my side Hitler belched, and the stink of fermenting cabbage wafted about me. 'Prussian *Schwein!*' he snarled.

The executioner took a swig of schnapps from the bottle on the table, grinning demonically. The old man ignored him. The executioner, a fat-bellied man in a singlet, wobbled the chair. As the old man swayed desperately, the people sitting watching nearby roared with laughter, and beside me Hitler guffawed, recovering his good humour. There was a thin, shiny wire running around the victim's neck in a cutting noose.

'Go on, go on!' Hitler urged, leaning forward expectantly, his pale-blue eyes fixed on the scene in front of him.

On cue, the executioner tipped the chair forward, very deliberately, still grinning. The old man's feet clawed for grip, and then he slipped and swung with a jerk from the butcher's hook above his head. The noose whipped into his neck; his hands scratched frantically at his throat, ripping the skin as he tried to pull the choking noose free. Blood streamed down his neck and his eyes bulged as he began to die. The executioner watched him, slapping his thighs and roaring with laughter at his efforts.

'Watch this bit,' Hitler urged me, 'this bit's very funny.'

The old man's trousers fell down about his ankles as he

thrashed in the air like a fish. Hitler laughed hoarsely, and all laughed with him.

The old man's tongue was protruding through his teeth, his eyes were rolling back in his head.

'Yes, yes,' Hitler urged. 'Go on . . .'

The executioner stood up on the chair, moving nimbly for a big man. He had a pair of wire-cutters in his hand. Deftly, he snipped the piano wire, and his victim fell to the floor like a sack, crumpling up like a rag doll into a heap.

The camera followed him down. A thin arm moved, a bloody claw pulled at the noose. Eyes in a face like a skull opened.

'*Guten Morgen, Feldmarschall*!' Hitler called hoarsely, mockingly.

The old officer's chest heaved as he pulled air into his lungs, and the executioner bent down to pull him to his feet. He stood there swaying, his pants down about his ankles, blood streaming from the lacerations about his throat.

'That's more like it,' Hitler said viciously. He turned to me, the sagging skin about his mouth twitching uncontrollably, eyes like old poached eggs in his ashen face. 'Let's see a bit more, shall we?' he said. 'Yes, there's plenty more.'

They hauled the general up on to the chair again, and a fresh noose coiled down from the ceiling. The executioner took his gulp of schnapps, and made a joke that had the ghouls sitting about the killing place rocking with laughter. On the chair, Field Marshal von Witzleben closed his eyes.

They hanged him five times, and in the end he no longer breathed when they cut him down.

The lights went up as the film projector whirled a few scattered frames on to the screen before going blank.

'That's how to treat those bastards,' Hitler said to me, his head nodding rhythmically, his hands clutching at each other in a tremor. 'We had that done in Berlin,' he confided. 'But Bormann's fixed up a room here in case we have to make a few more dance in the air.'

Rasch, standing behind him, pulled back his chair for him and he got up.

'Care to see?' he asked me.

The effort of rising to his feet sent more gases erupting in his stomach and he belched wetly at me. It was like opening a festering dustbin.

He led the way out. One foot dragged, he shuffled like an old man. Rasch and his goons were at my back. We came out into autumnal sunshine. Behind us was the bunker itself, a vast block of concrete like an ancient Egyptian tomb, its walls five metres thick, unpainted, windowless. The mouldy stench of the grim, stygian pine forest about us pervaded all.

Hitler led the way to a long, half-ruined hut. The windows were blown out and there were black blast marks on the walls. 'This is it,' he said intensely. 'This is where those vile traitors did their worst.' He went inside. Rasch gave me a push and I followed.

The room smelled of damp and, still, of an explosion. The debris had been taken out and the floor had been filled in with concrete. From one of the roof beams a row of new butcher's hooks shone, and thin wire nooses snaked down from them. A wooden kitchen chair stood under one. Hitler stood still, looking at them, washing his hands together.

'Get up,' he said quietly.

'What?' I said. You do. You have understood perfectly, you just wish to put it off as long as is possible.

'The chair,' Hitler said, quite affably. 'Get up on it. Try it for size.'

I felt Rasch's hand at my elbow, I turned to him, taking off my officer's cap. 'Hold this for me,' I ordered. I climbed up on to the chair and stood looking down at Hitler. 'Shall I try on the noose?' I suggested. It is no good snivelling.

He smiled – surprised, I think. 'Yes, yes. Go ahead,' he agreed.

I slipped it over my head and gave it a little tug to fasten it.

'The Field Marschal would not beg for mercy,' he said discontentedly. 'I would have liked that.'

I said nothing. The chair suddenly wobbled as Rasch gave it a push.

'Hoops . . .' I heard myself say. The blood was rushing in my head, a pounding in my ears.

The second push was far firmer. My boots scrabbled for a second, then I slipped. The wire bit into my throat. I thrashed about, the room slowly twirling, my hands clawing, breath gargling and rasping, cutting off little by little.

They stood watching me, their only expression one of a kind of benign interest. I could not hear. I saw Hitler remark to Rasch, saw him say something respectfully in return, their mouths flapping silently. I could feel nothing below the white-hot band about my neck. My hands had fallen away, the light coming through the window sockets was dim. It was dark.

I was on the floor. A noose of bloody wire was in my hand, breath rattled in my chest. I coughed up blood, pushed myself to my hands and knees. Rasch's goons pulled me to my feet. I saw Hitler's face before me, peering interestedly at me. The excitement had made his intestines move and the air stank of rotten vegetables. He belched, his throat working as he gulped back down the acid stew of cake and spaghetti.

'I am a *frontkampfer*, I fought with you in the trench,' I managed to rasp. Bloody phlegm filled my mouth and I spat it out. 'I wish to die in battle, defending Germany and my Führer. Send me up into the skies and let me fight.'

He stood staring at me, the tic about his mouth very evident. Finally, he nodded. 'I didn't believe you were one of them,' he said. He fumbled in his jacket pocket and brought out a small box. With shaking fingers he managed to open it and extract a silver-and-black Maltese Cross, a *Ritterkreuz*, a Knight's Cross. Breathing heavily he reached up to put it about my neck. The false teeth in the bridge across his mouth were edged in black from decaying sugar and cream-cake, which breathed over me as the cross dropped about my neck. My blood stained his fingers but he did not seem to notice.

He turned his back, shuffling away towards the hideous blank slab of the bunker.

'Send him back,' he said.

The snow lay fresh and white like a pure wool blanket over the mountainside. I picked up the heavy medal bar, peering at the Knight's Cross that hung there next to the Blue Max. I didn't get any more, although the Führer sent me one last present before the war ended.

Absently, I ran my fingers about my neck. The scar was still there, as it always would be, a corded ridge where the piano wire had opened my throat like an exhibit on a slab. I had bled into my Luftwaffe uniform all the way to Rastenberg, where a silent doctor sewed me up.

I got up, putting the bar away in the drawer. I went to peer out at the snow. The kites were circling and landing over by the slope going down into the wood, very black against the shimmering white of the snow.

I felt a sudden stab of interest. There was obviously something dead over there which had caught their attention. I would not be able to get out much once the snow was thick and I felt the desire to get some fresh air and take a little walk – I would have little enough of it once winter set in properly.

My thick jacket was hanging on the peg, and I pulled on my strong boots with their ribbed soles. I took my shepherd's crook for support, and went outside. The air was crisp and fresh and the layer of snow crunched pleasingly under my boots. I did not so much hear it as feel it, and left a trail of outlines like washboards behind me.

I shouted harshly as I came up and the kites lifted into the air, circling about resentfully.

The land goes down into a deep ditch along there, taking the meltwater away in the spring, when the river turns into a roaring grey torrent. It was dry now, just lined with snow-covered brambles. Moving cautiously, and supporting myself with my crook, I peered down there.

There was a dead man hung up in the brambles.

He was naked, and the kites had been eating him. He had no head.

I stood there for a while. There was no doubt. A man, a dead man. A man whose head had been cleanly sliced off. What was it Cabbage-Gas had told me? A man, a government minister, whose head had been mounted and hung upon his office wall . . .

I stood looking out over the valley as I thought, trying to come to terms with this.

Something flew past me.

Silent, its wings wobbling gently in the updraught, a white paper aeroplane glided past.

A dart, the kind every schoolboy makes behind the cover of

his desk and sends gliding across the classroom when he thinks the maths master is not looking, hoping to strike a comrade on the ear. A white paper dart, gliding down the hillside and out over the valley.

I turned, trying to see where it had come from, who it was that was throwing white paper darts at me. There was nobody on the hillside. There was only my outbuildings, the old stone byre higher up.

My eyes are still keen. I am, it is true, somewhat deaf, but my eyes still see, if not as sharply as when I was a warrior in the sky, then still better than most.

Something white moved to and fro in the small high window in the byre. There was somebody in there.

There was also a dead man lying tangled up in my brambles, without his head.

I reasoned that whoever was in the byre waving a small white flag at me had also propelled the paper dart past me, in an attempt to attract my attention. If they had intended to make me shorter by a head and chuck me in the brambles as well, they could have done it without the bother of having me climb up the hill to the byre.

So I climbed up the hill, leaving a trail of footprints behind me in the sunshine, and a dotted line of holes from my crook.

I had not been to the byre for some while. There was a time when I walked my property every day, but with age one gets about less. I was breathing quite hard as I came up the slope and round to the door.

Somebody had been doing things to my byre. A steel-barred grille filled the doorway, securely held fast with a heavy padlock. Through it, I saw a man standing by the far wall, huddled up inside a ski anorak and padded boots.

'You are very deaf,' he said. 'You do not hear me when I shout at you.'

'I am on the outside of this door and you on the inside,' I said. 'I would not insult me too much if I were you.'

'I was only observing,' he said. 'It is frustrating.'

'Well, I am here now. Why are you caged up inside my byre?'

'To keep me prisoner.'

'Who are you?'

'My name is Fischer and I am a police officer working undercover.'

'You are not much undercover if you are locked up here,' I pointed out.

He sighed, and shifted from one foot to the other. There was a sound of chain clanking, and I saw that he was securely fastened to the wall by a length of it. 'I would not cut the head off the Minister,' he explained. 'Pan ordered me to. When I would not, he realised who I was.'

'Perhaps you should have overcome your scruples. The Minister, for I assume it is he, lies down in the ditch there without his head. That, they found mounted to a plaque and secured to a wall in his office.'

'How do you know this?'

'The policeman told me.'

'Which policeman?'

'There is a policeman who has been visiting me for some time, ever since he brought me the news that my accountant, who used to visit me with supplies, was dead – murdered with his wife and children. He is a great bore, a tiresome eater of cabbages and lentils and such things. I have forgotten his name. He warned me that some terrorists called –'

'Mother Nature,' Fischer said quietly.

'Yes, yes. That these terrorists were thought to be somewhere about here. I see that he was correct.'

'I had infiltrated the group,' Fischer said. 'Before Pan tested me ... Each Guardian has to commit a suitable atrocity against a human being before he is accepted.'

'Guardian?'

'That is what Pan calls them. The Guardians of Mother Nature. Pan is their leader – there are many, all over the world.' He gestured to the corner of the room. There a table had been set up, with what I took to be a computer on it, a screen like a television. 'They communicate through the Net,' he said. I did not understand him at all. 'They seek the destruction of human society as we know it. This policeman, what does he look like?'

'Tall, thin. A complexion like ploughed porridge. Short hair.'

'Pan,' Fischer said quietly. 'You have been dealing with Pan. He chose your estate here because it is so remote and far away from anybody. Do you have a phone?'

'No, I had it cut off years – no, wait, wait. Yes I have.' I remembered the portable one that he had given me.

'Call the police,' he urged. 'Do it quickly. Tell them that Sergeant Fischer is here. Tell them to send the squad out here, as fast as they can.'

'Very well,' I said. 'I will do it as swiftly as I am able, then I shall rejoin you.'

I retraced my steps down the slope, and went back to the house. I found the telephone, and moved the small power switch. A red light glowed. I pressed the buttons of the emergency code. A voice spoke in my ear.

'*Ja?*'

'My name is Wolff, Hans-Joachim Wolff. I wish the police to come out to my house, for I have a police officer here, a Sergeant Fischer who has been made prisoner by the terrorists of Mother Nature.'

There was silence on the line for a few moments.

'Do you hear me?' I demanded.

'I am taking down your information. Where do you live?' I told him.

'Police will be with you very shortly,' he promised.

It was very cold outside. I switched off the telephone. I knew how far away I was from anywhere; it would be a while before anybody could get to us. I put a kettle on, and found my old thermos flask. I made hot coffee, and took some biscuits. Then I climbed back up the slope.

'The police are on their way,' I said to Fischer. 'Here, I have brought some coffee to warm you. We may have to wait a little while as I am quite far from any town.'

I poured coffee into the cup and slipped it through the bars, together with the biscuits. He sipped on it gratefully, and munched at the biscuits.

'Why do you live out here, so far from anywhere?'

'I have always liked the mountains. When I was in favour with Göring, he provided the materials from his hunting palace. After the war I kept it on. In the end I decided to live here.'

'No family?'

'I had a family once, but Naziism killed them, one way or the other. When the war was over, I found that it was too late for me to try again. I turned to my business of inventing.'

'And in the end, came here.'

'That was my decision,' I said. 'I found that I myself felt that although they were gone, the monsters, what they made was still there. I do not much like people, Sergeant Fischer. I am what you call a recluse. I decided to live up here for the rest of my life.'

'You are writing your memoirs,' he observed. 'Pan said so. Why now?'

'I am not sure . . .' I said slowly. 'Somehow, when he came, when he came here in the guise of a policeman, and told me that my accountant and his family had been murdered . . . somehow it brought it all back to me. How it began. What happened. For I was in there, I knew many of them. It brought back memories . . .'

He held out his mug for another cup, and I filled it for him.

'When I was first put in, to find out about Mother Nature, I thought that they were just – if I can say "just" – a bunch of eco-freaks, some species of extreme animal-rights veggies. They are, of course, but they're much more than that. I am not surprised that meeting Pan made you think of the old Nazis again. That's what Mother Nature is. A new Nazi movement, fit for the twenty-first century.'

'The Nazis believed in thinking with the blood. That is what they called it. They were proud that they were not rational. They despised rationality; they *knew*.'

'Pan knows. He *knows* that the human race is going to destroy the world. He is in a hurry; he knows he has been sent by the earth to save her.'

'Hitler was in a hurry too,' I told him. 'He was the only man who could save Germany from *Rassenschande*, race defilement.'

I stood by the cold steel grille, remembering.

'I am sorry I cannot get you out,' I apologised, 'but I can see that we require an oxy-acetylene torch. Once the police are here we can have them call for one.

'You know, everybody forgot that, when the war was over. The Allies, they were too busy concentrating on all the terrible things the Nazis did – the camps, the killing of the Jews, the murder squads – that they forgot to ask themselves *why*. Göring told them, at Nuremberg. He admitted he was responsible for killing the opposition. He said it was justified. Monarchy and democracy had failed, he said. Only the Nazis could save the German race, by a new race nationalism. If they'd won, there was to be a new world order. The Germans – Himmler's Aryans – were to be the only human race. All other races were to become *untermenschen*, subhuman species, mere slaves incapable of creating civilisations or culture of their own.'

'I think Pan wants something like that,' Fischer said quietly. 'He's completely mad. Thank God we've got him before he can murder any more people. Mother Nature were getting ready to commit really huge acts of destruction in major cities. Bombing buildings, nerve gas in the subway, poisoning water supplies, incendiary devices ...'

'To what end?'

'Pan believes that cities are the embodiment of human evil. He wants them destroyed. He wants human society destroyed, since its whole history is one of extermination and exploitation of the earth. His beliefs are those of Cambodian Pol Pot on a very large scale. Humans are to become savages in a world returned to wilderness.'

'Him too?' I asked.

Fischer smiled faintly. 'Somebody has to guard the concentration camp,' he observed. 'Somebody has to be the commandant.'

It was getting dark. Through the tiny high window a flicker of blue appeared. Soon it brightened into a regular flashing. Fischer sighed with relief.

'I shan't be sorry to get out of here,' he said. He cupped his hands. 'Here! Up here!'

There was a tramping of feet on the snow. A group of men came up the hill. Their leader turned in towards the byre and the flashing blue light lit up his face. It was Pan. A huge, thickly-furred hound was at his side, glaring with fierce yellow eyes.

He held up a small black object in his hand. 'Thank you for calling me,' he said softly, and then laughed triumphantly, his cohorts laughing with him. 'You can only call me,' he said. 'All the numbers get through to me.'

It was dark, the snow outside lit only by the moonlight. Pan reached into a pocket of his padded jacket and I heard something clink.

'We are Mother Nature's Guardians,' he said. He was looking straight through the bars at Fischer. 'You are the technological human. There you stand, the epitome of polluted, devastated evil. You are a toxin, an artificial chemical, an interference with the purity of the world. You are drenched in the blood of the animals you have murdered. In the name of the earth, you must die.'

'Save the claptrap for your loony friends, Pan,' Fischer said contemptuously. 'I have become sick to my stomach listening to it. I need no more.'

'You shall die as Mother Nature demands,' Pan said, ignoring him. 'How does she construct her pure world? It is the survival of those supremely fit. The fittest live, the weak die.'

'That's why we humans run things, Pan,' Fischer jeered. 'We *are* the supreme creation.'

Pan's eyes suddenly flashed with emotion. 'Let us see about that,' he said, dangerous now. 'We shall do it as Mother Nature intends, for we are but her servants.'

His hand jingled metal in his pocket. He took something out and tossed it at my feet. I bent down and fumbled about on the ground, and my hands came across two keys. When I looked up, Pan, the great dog and the others were gone.

A large key fitted the heavy padlock of the steel grille. I turned it, and the door swung open. Fischer was secured by a second about his ankle, and I turned this key too, releasing him.

'I need a weapon,' he said quietly. 'Have you got anything?'

'Where have they gone?'

'They are waiting to hunt me,' he said. 'When humans are once again reduced to savagery, Pan says that the Guardians will hunt them for sport, the way humans have hunted animals. They are out there waiting to hunt me down. Now, do you have any weapons?'

'I gave my hunting rifles away,' I said regretfully. 'But in the house I have knives.'

'They will be expecting that. Two or three will be about the house, in the shadows, waiting for me.'

'Wait – down below us, in the barns, where I chop my wood

for the fire. On the chopping block is my axe.'

'Right. Now tell me, how can I escape from here? I am a fast runner, if I can get free. What about the river one passes on the way in along your little road?'

'No. Not there,' I told him. 'The river runs through the ravine, but it leads to a cliff-face, and it spills down in a waterfall to a pool below before continuing on its way. The drop would kill you. No, if you are strong enough, you should go up the slope behind us. You will see a line of trees to your left as you climb. Head for them. That will take you over the hill, and you will find a road on the other side. It is a gruelling journey, however.'

'I have little choice,' he said grimly. 'I will have that axe, though, if I can.'

He came out, and stood for a few seconds in the shadow of the byre, looking about him. The land seemed bare. The moon had risen over the side of the mountain and all about the slope was white, except where the shadows lay, black as pitch.

'Here goes, then,' he said, taking a deep breath. 'I should have enjoyed talking to you some more about the old times, Herr Wolff, but I feel that time is pressing me.'

'The axe you will find in the barn nearest the steep meadow,' I told him. 'It's buried in a chopping-block by the door, which is open.'

'Thank you,' he said.

Then he was gone, loping down the slope, the only moving creature in the moonscape.

Going as quickly as I could while taking care not to slip, I too went down towards the long lane that runs along the top of the meadow.

There. Out of deep shadow, something flitting across the snow like a wolf. 'Behind you!' I shouted. 'Eight o'clock.'

The dark creatures merged, tumbled down the slope. Somebody screamed, hoarsely. One got up and continued to run. I reached the lane, the breath panting in my throat. It had been many years since I had moved at this kind of pace.

The moonlit land was still again. From the barns, there came an animal howl, a human curse, a short, cut-off shriek. I panted along the lane, my boots kicking up puffs of snow. Glancing over my shoulder I saw Fischer running from the barns. Somebody came at him. The axe suddenly swung in his hand, flashing in the moonlight, and a body tumbled through the air.

I was at the trees. Ahead I could hear the steady rushing of the river falling down the mountain in the little gorge. I looked back one last time. Creatures like wolves were on the slope. Cut off, Fischer was swinging his axe. I thought I heard him yell defiance. I went down the lane. I knew these parts. Once across the narrow stone bridge I could leave the road and push round the side of the mountain. There was a rocky path I knew well that way – years ago when I was more active I used to go out all day, traversing the mountains. Pan and his cohorts would not know the route. I should soon be away, and, by dawn, down in the village.

Through the trees, my dim ears caught the sounds of animals snarling.

I pressed on. The trees on either side had caught most of the snow and it hung above me like icing. The path was passable. I could hear the rushing of the river. I came round the bend in the road, and there was the bridge.

Something had been thrown across it. In the gloom it shone a faint silver, like a great spider's web. I stood on the bridge, as the river tumbled beneath me, trying to see a way through. A steel gate, barring the peak of the bridge, sharp curving fingers ready to claw at anyone so bold as to climb it. Spike-topped steel webs over the parapets. The breath heaved in my chest. There was no way past.

'Care to try?' a voice called mockingly behind me.

I turned. It was Pan. He had my axe casually over one shoulder. The great hound sat silently on its haunches by his side, staring malevolently at me with eyes that were yellow even in the pale moonlight.

'Wolf,' he said to it, 'this is Herr Wolff. *Ja*! A wolf for a Wolff!' He laughed, insanely, and the huge dog looked at him, drawing back its own lips over its shining white teeth. 'You can eat Herr Wolff if he tries to escape,' he said, reaching down into the thick fur about the beast's neck. It turned its attention from him to me, and I knew that it had understood every word. 'Well, shall we get back?' he said, and I trudged along the road the way I had come.

The barns were lit by an orange glow. As we walked along

the lane I saw people tending a long fire in the ground, tipping sacks of charcoal into a blazing bed of heat. When we came close, I could see that the roasting trestles were in place.

Some dead bodies lay in a pile, three, perhaps four, in the darkness. The man who had killed them was still, unmoving, near the blazing coals. It was Fischer. He was naked, and they had gutted him like a boar. His insides lay in a heap on the snow and they were fixing the spit through his body.

Pan reached down. He found a kidney in the offal and chopped it free with the axe. It steamed in the icy air. He tossed it to the dog, Wolf, who ate it, his jaws snapping with pleasure.

'Wolf likes human meat,' Pan said to me. 'He ate your accountant.'

They hoisted Fischer on to the forks, and began to barbecue him.

The dead clustered about me in the night. Those I knew, those who were strangers to me. Some gibing and mocking, some pleading, many screaming. Göring, in his make-up and red nail-polish, grinning ghoulishly. Himmler, peering at me through his thick glasses as I sat in my chair, as though at a bug he might wish to squash. Goebbels, with his sly smile, passing me the list. It was huge, a great roll, and on it were inscribed the names of everybody I ever knew. Go on, go on, he urged me. Who else do you want killed? It's all right, we may put anybody on we want.

There they were, all the dead. They hid in the shadows so that the executioners could not see them, and yet still I heard them scream in fear and agony as they died. There was Hilde, and there was Kurt. They were burning, on fire. Eisenmann, naked and in fear, choking in the frightful darkness.

The Führer watched them all without expression. The stench of rotting vegetables and cakes seeped out from between his teeth, exuded from his pores. It washed over me as I sat in the darkness in my chair, and however I turned my head I could not escape it. Each time I moved the huge dog opened his eyes, yellow in the dim firelight, and stared intently at me.

The living were in the room, too; they slept all about the ruins of the ghastly meal they had made. Fischer's terrible roasted body lay along my *volkische* wooden dining-table. Pan had carved him; ribs and long bones gleamed in the firelight, his teeth shining in his last fighting grimace. His killers slept all about, his flesh inside them. For them, he was the first of many.

The dawn came, and the dead finally retreated to whatever hell they inhabited.

Pan and his men awoke seemingly at the same time, like dogs. I sat where I was. They went out and I could hear them talking, though not what they said, for I am deaf. There was the noise of car engines, the cold of a draught.

Pan stood looking at me. 'I shall be away for a little while,' he said. 'Though not long, and I am not going far. If Wolf gets hungry he's going to eat you. If you try to escape he *will* eat you.'

The giant hound stared at me as Pan talked, and I knew that what I was told was true.

'I am too old to try to climb over the mountain in the ice and snow,' I said. 'And that is the only way out, since the bridge is barred.'

'I know,' said Pan. 'Then you had better hope I am not too long, for Wolf likes to eat a good meal before sundown.'

He turned on his heel and was gone. I heard the sound of his car starting up, and then it was quiet, and I was alone with the dog.

Once I was sure that Pan was gone, I got up, and the dog rose with me. I went slowly over to the hall to put on my boots and padded jacket and he came too, his claws clicking on the boards.

'Come on,' I ordered gruffly, and he stared coldly at me. It was not that I expected him to obey me – he would only do that for the man who had trained him – but I was intent of presenting myself as a being at least equal to him. Once he felt I was a lesser creature he would savage me without compunction. I stared back at him with my old scout pilot's eyes, and after a while he turned away, as if indifferent.

'Come on,' I repeated. 'It's breakfast time.'

We went out over the snow, the dog's fur rising to make him even larger than he was. The snow was covered in the ruts and wedges of tyre marks. Down by the outbuildings the charcoal was grey with ash, and cold. The forks stood at the ends of the trench, the spit lay discarded on the ground.

They had put their dead in my barn, by the woodpile, had thrown them in a heap. Pan had said that Mother Nature judged, and only the fit survived. They were dead, killed by Fischer, and therefore unworthy. Those still living had eaten their dead friends' conqueror.

My axe was back in the chopping-block. I eased it from the wood, and hefted it. A deep rumble came from the dog's chest.

'I am not going to hurt you, you stupid beast,' I told him. I would not have cared to try, even back when I was a young man. Fighting and killing with his own natural weapons was what Wolf did, and I had little doubt that he could defeat me in open combat, if he so chose.

The bodies were naked. With the axe I hacked some limbs into joints. I picked up a leg and tossed it to the dog. He sniffed it, liked the smell of the blood, and settled down to eat. When I was certain he was happy, I went over to the Messerschmitt 163, my own Komet fighter that I had flown in so many years before. It sat on its take-off dolly, its nose pointing to the open door, to the steep mountainside below.

The clear canopy was dusty. I took a handkerchief from my jacket pocket and cleaned it until it shone. I have always feared a smeared canopy: you cannot see where you are going, or who is coming after you.

I sat on the chopping-block while Wolf ate. I let him eat as much as he desired, and the floor was littered with lengths and fragments of bloody bone, scraps of skin, strips of sinew. Finally he rose, his long pink tongue washing his chops, and I got up too. 'Let's get inside where it's warm,' I suggested.

There was a bucket in the corner, which I picked up. Outside, near the barbecue pit, was the pile of offal that had been Fischer's guts. I scooped it all up into the bucket and carried it inside, where I put some fresh logs on the fire and began work.

The intestines, congealed blood, fat and massacred organs I made up into a parcel, containing them in thin plastic. Pan had slept in my old bed, a fine, large affair carved from solid oak, which sat immovable four-square on the floor. I suspended the sack of offal above the bed, high up in the ceiling, standing on my step ladder while the dog stared suspiciously up at me from below. His stomach, however, was full, and provided I did not actually attempt to leave the vicinity of the house, I knew that he would not attack me.

What I had to do after that took me much of the morning. When all was done, I gathered what I needed and put it in a sack. I spent some time setting the clock above Pan's bed. I took my prime mover, that could draw a tank across country, and checked that it had fuel. Then I went back out, the dog at my heels.

Moving carefully on the steep slope, I buried the blade into the ground below the barn, then walked up, paying out the clear line. The prime mover itself I hid out of sight under the dolly. Then I worked some more in the barn, climbing up from time to time on the ladder, pulling up logs, making my arrangements.

I was certainly tired by then. I went back up into the house, very weary, and kicked the snow off my boots. I ate some biscuits and drank some coffee with a shot of schnapps in it. I put logs on the fire, sat down in my chair and went to sleep with the dog staring at me from his great yellow eyes.

It was dark. Pan stood in front of me. Wolf had got up to sit on his haunches by his master.

'You're still alive,' Pan said. 'I had thought that Wolf would have eaten you by now.'

'He knows I am one like you,' I said.

'Like me?' Pan put his head back and laughed. 'You are a technological fool! What do you know of the needs and commands of Mother Earth?'

'You're quite wrong.' I said, looking up at him. 'Don't you know I was in the SS?'

'The SS? So what?'

'*We* – the SS – were like *you*: the Guardians of Mother Nature. We hated those that were not as we were, we slaughtered them by the million. We loved the forests. There the true spirit of our nation resided! We too loved herbs and the ancient rites. We consulted the stars, we read the runes to know our past and our future. We were like you! It was *them*, the evil ones with their machines, who conquered us.'

Pan stared at me through slitted eyes, suspicious.

'Let me join you!' I cried. 'Why didn't you tell me? I would have been one of you. Why do you think I have lived up here in the fastnesses of nature for so long, if not to stay away from their pollution, their foulness?'

'Join us . . .' he said thoughtfully.

'I know you are about to strike at them!' I said. 'The dead one there, the policeman, he told me so. Let me join you. Would not a seemingly harmless old man be useful?'

'Perhaps . . . there are fewer of us now that he has killed those who failed . . .'

He moved quickly, going over to the table where Fischer lay massacred. He took a knife, and carved a piece of flesh from him.

'But you must become as we are,' he said.

'He told me that to prove oneself, it was necessary to kill one of *them*. The evil ones who are destroying the earth.'

He tossed the knife down. 'Very well,' he said. 'Tomorrow. We will go out and you shall cut the throat of one. Then you shall be as we are.'

'What is it that you have planned?'

He smiled. From a pack he took out a bottle of perfume in its patterned card wrapping. 'Sweet scent,' he crooned. 'No security system will object to it – you can take it on board any aircraft at all. Then, on the flight, as the plane flies to its destination, you go into the toilet. You open the vent of the air-conditioning and undo the first, outer, cap of the perfume bottle. You will like this – you are an engineer. Inside is a second cap, which still keeps it sealed. You place the perfume inside and secure it. You replace the vent, you wash your hands and return to your seat. The aircraft lands safely, and you leave with all the other passengers.

'Here is the clever part. The return to normal air pressure cocks the inner cap. When the plane takes off on its next flight, as it climbs into the sky, although the cabin is pressurised, the air pressure inside it is less than it is on the ground. At about two thousand metres the inner cap pops open. Inside the perfume bottle is instant-acting nerve gas! The air-conditioning whisks it through the aircraft. The pilots are among the first to die! There! All over the world, flying bombs! Flying until their fuel runs out, falling to burst into flames upon the evil ones beneath!'

He stood in the firelight, his chest heaving, his face gleaming with a sheen of sweat.

'Is that not wonderful?' he demanded. 'And it is only the start. We have much, much more to do before we are finished, before the city foulnesses are dark and empty and abandoned, until the evil ones run naked and afraid in the forests of Mother Nature . . .'

His voice faded away.

'Yes, yes . . .' he whispered. 'Soon, it will be soon . . .'

My throat hurt. I rubbed the old scar, ribbed and gristly, like a length of cord about my neck, and the dog woke, raising his head to look at me by the fire. Pan slept. I could hear him snore.

The dead had come back. I could feel them pressing against me. Million upon million. Adolf Hitler killed them. Or I did.

If we had blown up the Führer on 20 July 1944 the war would have stopped. Rommel, or some other general the Allies respected, would have negotiated a halt to the fighting. But it was bungled: the creature was left alive, and even madder than he had been before. His appetite for destruction was a thing that could not be appeased; it eventually consumed him too, but not before millions more had been taken as well. Most of the killing in the camps. The slaughter on the west and on the east as the war contracted in upon Berlin. Millions dead . . .

It would not have happened if we had got him with the bomb. But there is a problem you run into, when you want to kill somebody as well guarded as he was. It is very difficult to do, unless you do not mind dying yourself. Then it is fairly easy, if you have access to the person you want to kill. Something as simple as a ceremonial dagger through the throat will do it. The dead man's guards may take a while longer to kill you, of course.

I could have killed Hitler. I was one of those who could have got to him. But I gave Hoeppner the bombs instead, and it was bungled. So millions died. The killing went on to the end. Not just with machine-guns and artillery. With men, sent out to settle the score before the twilight of the gods.

Rasch came for me.

The gods were dying all about us. The bombers poured their fire and brimstone into the hell they had made out of the city. At the airfield the white finger of death reached out towards us, the markers of the daylight raiders, we ran for our foxholes, scrapings of earth to protect us against the carpet of bombs flying down towards us. The Komet fighters were stuck out in the open, noses up at readiness.

The bombs hit. Nausea rising up in our throats, the whistle, the explosion, the blast, the tremor of the very ground, and then the silence, just the singing in the ears, the thud of falling debris.

The hangar was on fire. Somehow, the Komets were unharmed, still packed tight with *C-stoff* and *T-stoff*. We set to, clearing up the damage, and it was then I saw Rasch. He was getting out of a truck in his full SS dress uniform. He had a submachine-gun and he was completely insane.

'The Führer sends you justice!' he screamed, and glass shattered as he loosed off a burst of fire at me. I ran, jinking here and there between bomb-trolleys and empty fuel bowsers, shattered store huts and ruined fighter-planes. People scattered, running for their lives – at the end of the war, all anyone wanted was to live.

I threw myself flat and crawled under a truck. I could hear bursts of submachine-gun fire, and Rasch's voice, shouting my name.

The Komet sat plump and deadly on the hard standing, its nose pointed straight ahead. I pushed myself out on my hands and knees, and I scuttled for it like a rabbit.

The canopy swung open and shut. I keyed the switches, the red light glowed. As the little turbine whined, I heard a man scream in fury.

Rasch ran out on to the tarmac as the Komet bumped off its stop. Out of the corner of my eye, I saw something streak across the field. The world about us disintegrated into a storm of flying debris. Flashes of light, bombs and rockets, screeching metal, American Thunderbolts howling across the field.

Rasch vanished and the world engulfed him in its fury. The rocket engine kicked me in the back and I shot across the exploding airfield, Thunderbolt fighters with their huge noses passing to the left and right like sharks. I pulled the stick back and shot almost vertically into the air. Below there was a maelstrom of smoke and flame.

The air was clear and smooth. In front of me I could see the mountains. High, high in the sky, kilometres up, as the rocket motor cut out, I put the nose down and levelled out. I glided towards them.

I found my valley, I knew where it was. There was my *völkisches* house, nestled on the slope. I lost height with the little village far below, and came in over the little bridge that brought the lane over the river, rushing down the mountainside in its ravine.

The sun was up, the meadow covered in a carpet of spring flowers. I dropped over the trees, silent as a hawk, the overgrown lane rushing up at me. I dropped the skid and hit the ground with a rushing rumble. The long grass and the flowers gripped me; we slowed, and stopped. The little fighter leaned over on one wing. I pushed up the canopy and the smell of crushed grass and flowers burst in. A bee buzzed curiously, a butterfly fluttered past uncaring. I clambered out, and walked up to my house.

Dawn seeped through the window, painting the thick fur of the beast by my feet in its true colours. The old clock on the mantel said it was time. Pan was still asleep.

I got up, and the great yellow eyes snapped open. I shuffled out the back way, pulling my jacket about me, as though to visit the outhouse, and the hound loped at my side.

It was very cold, my breath froze in drifting puffs of white. The mountain peaks were beginning to glow in the lightening gloom. My boots crunched on the crisp snow and I walked carefully down towards the barns, the ground as a slippery as a skating-rink.

Inside, the corpses were still piled roughly in their heap. I picked up a haunch that I had chopped up the day before, and tossed it to the dog, Wolf. He settled down to gnawing at the hard flesh with a great deal of chomping and slobbering.

I stood by the Komet. The alloy skin was icy to the touch as my fingers fumbled with the cockpit catch. It came out of its housing with a well-machined movement of metal and raised the canopy up on its hinges. The little cockpit was exposed, simple and small, the hard seat surrounded by the tanks for the *T-stoff*, the flat panel of gauges in front, the stumpy stick between the knees, the rudder pedals with their waiting thongs like huge sandshoes.

I shuffled round to the front of the Komet, and pulled out my prime mover from under the wheeled dolly. I held the electromagnet to the steel of the axle, and flicked the radial engine. With a blare of power from the exhaust, the little engine caught. The winch whirled and the strong line began to come in on its reel.

The dog looked up at me from his hideous meal, a man's thigh between his teeth. He snarled in alarm as I climbed into the cockpit of the Komet.

Dogs are stupid. If a canopy can open it can also close, but they do not realise that. I reached up and pulled the canopy down over me with one smooth movement. The latch shut firmly, and the dog went wild, trying to get at me.

I am deaf, I am very deaf, but I could hear Pan scream. It was the scream of a man who is going to kill. He could hear the frenzied barking of the dog, trying to get through the canopy to tear me into bloody chunks.

He ran round the corner of the barn. He was an appalling sight, completely drenched in blood, ordure and offal. It was in his hair, over his face, and he spat it out of his mouth. Demented, he beat on the canopy with his bare hands, and the dog redoubled its fury, but the canopy was strong, it availed them nothing.

The Komet jerked forward as the prime mover drew in its wire. Pan seemed to realise what was about to happen. He looked wildly about him and saw the axe, its head buried in the chopping-block. He leapt over to it, and jerked it free with a single heave.

I heard him scream again, this time in sudden terror. I twisted round in my seat, and there he was, suspended from the roof of the barn, swinging upside-down. The great bag of logs had crashed to the floor, the noose hidden in the dirt had whipped up about his legs and jerked him up like a fish, and there he flapped, screaming like a banshee.

I turned back to my task. The Komet jerked as it went over the stop. In front of me the steep meadow shone in the new light, as smooth and slippery as a ski-jump. At its end I could just see the ravine and the tumbling waters of the river below.

There was a tremble, the wings shivering as we moved out of

the barn. The second cord I had attached to the dolly grew tight. There was a snap, and the knife blade cut the fishing-line that held Pan from the roof. He fell like a sack of coal to the ground. He was still held to the dolly. We began to roll. I heard him shriek as the line dragged him out with us, and on to the slope.

Now! The ground was icy, as hard as rock, smooth and slippery. We slithered forward, the wheels rumbling and bouncing.

A maniacal barking at my ear, the huge dog leaping at me as I escaped it, terrible snapping jaws that left a white scar on the perspex. A great howl of fury, a thud, a jerk, a snapping of bones, a howl cut suddenly, wonderfully short as the beast vanished under the furiously whirling wheels.

We were going like an insane toboggan, the slope a white blur, the stick in my hand beginning to stir as it took life, the airspeed indicator moving around its dial. A thumping, a rumbling, a whistle of the air over the cockpit, the slope falling away to the ravine and . . .

As we hurtled out into the void I heaved the lever that dropped the steel take-off dolly. The Komet lurched as it fell away. The stick was alive in my hand, I put the nose down, and I was flying.

The walls were grey and silver and brown on each side. The icy river hurtled below me, blue and grey, rushing over the rocks, swirling about its path, and I banked above it, first this way and then that, following the ravine.

The wings shuddered gently. I put the nose down. I was settling fast, my journey a race between the rushing slope beneath me and the desire of the little gliding fighter to fly at a steeper angle.

The Komet shuddered again as the wings came near to the stall. We sank; I put the nose down. The water was so close, spray whipped over the canopy, the mountainside towering above.

With a bang we hit the water, caroming back up into the air like a skimming stone. Again. Bang, bang, and from somewhere icy spray coated my feet. Just ahead, a boiling maelstrom; as the fighter lifted, I pulled back the stick and leapt a metre or two into the air. Then it stalled, and the nose fell forward of its own volition. We dived like a plunging dolphin.

And flew. The rushing waterfall of water vanished under

the wings, the air whistling as it whipped over the canopy. The airspeed showed four hundred kilometres as the pine-covered slope grew large through the armoured glass and the gunsight. I eased back on the stick and we soared out over the valley like an eagle.

Outside the village the road ran straight alongside the river. I circled round as I dropped down and at two hundred metres I held the Komet straight. I put the road between my feet and dropped the landing skid. There was no traffic, the road was empty.

With a rushing, rumbling roar, the little fighter touched down, skidding along the tarmac. It slowed and I held it straight with stick and rudder. It stopped and gently dropped one wing to the ground like a tired butterfly.

I undid the catch and pushed up the canopy. High on the side of the valley, the rising sun was painting the mountainside with gold. I clambered out carefully and sat on the wing. I patted my pockets and found my pipe and pouch. Beside me the river tumbled, gurgling to itself after its wild ride down the mountain. Golden strands of tobacco filled the pipe bowl and I stuffed in a few ends before lighting it. The smoke was fragrant and drifted away on the breeze.

From the village a small blue light appeared, winking steadily. A little white car appeared under it, carrying it towards me. It stopped in the middle of the road. It could go no further, as the Komet blocked its way. I had landed dead on the centre line, and I felt somewhat pleased with myself. A man in a policeman's uniform got out, and stood goggling.

'Well, what do you think?' I demanded. 'Not bad after fifty years, wouldn't you say? Hmm?'

I looked down the river. About half a kilometre upstream something was rolling and tumbling in the water, coming towards us. I am deaf but my eyesight is still sharp.

'If you move sharply, you will be in time to extract a body from the river,' I told the man.

He moved with some speed – I don't suppose he had many opportunities to deal with cases of that sort, in those parts. As Pan's body rolled towards us, he waded into the icy water and managed to drag it to the thickly pebbled shore.

KILLING PLACE

I stood looking down at him. His journey down the mountain had altered him somewhat. The line that had attached him to the steel dolly had removed his leg below the knee and his passage through the rocks had turned a considerable amount of him into pulp. He lay on the round rocks oozing what was left inside him like some kind of squashed slug.

The policeman was at his car, his soaked trousers clinging to him as he talked rapidly and urgently on his radio.

I could not hear what he said; I am somewhat deaf. My eyes are still keen, and I possess my sense of smell. I moved upwind of the thing on the river-bank, and sat on a rock while I puffed my pipe.